ALICE -
PERDITION

by

SURREAL

CHIMERA

Alice – Shadows of Perdition first published in 2003 by
Chimera Publishing Ltd
PO Box 152
Waterlooville
Hants
PO8 9FS

Printed and bound in Great Britain by
Cox & Wyman Ltd, Reading

ALICE – SHADOWS OF PERDITION

Surreal

This novel is fiction – in real life practice safe sex

Harris picked up the mid-sized cane and bent it between his fists. 'All I saw was you making off with my money, and for that you will suffer the consequences. Take off your skirt.'

Wanting nothing more than to get the ordeal over as quickly as possible, Alice obediently unfastened the button at her trim waist and let the skirt fall to her feet, Harris intent on her every move.

'Now place your legs together and bend forward,' he went on.

Alice reached down for her toes and waited, stomach churning with nerves, breathing difficult.

'So far so good,' drooled the fiend. 'Let's hope you can keep it up. You know the rules. You do not rise. You do not attempt to comfort your bottom. Should you do so I will simply begin again until you show restraint.' He flexed the rod, chest out. 'You will receive twelve with this cane.'

Prologue

Abruptly and tragically orphaned, Alice Hussey surrendered her future to the dubious auspices of her uncle, Richard Barker. The man, pious, scheming and uncompromising, soon found excuse to submit the teenager to the rigours of humiliation and corporal punishment.

School fees expired; her parents' Will having left precious little, Alice reluctantly left the cherished *Carters Academy*, to take up residence with her uncle, who made a proposal she couldn't refuse. A private backer would pay all expenses involved in attaining her finals, provided she attend *Heptonstall Moor* and worked for two years thereafter unsalaried. Being thrown onto the streets the only alternative, Alice accepted, but unbeknown to her, Richard had sold her, and intended to oversee the girl's subjugation to ensure her fitness for the role.

Kate Howell, precocious, eccentric and intimate friend, was caned and sacked from *Carters* for gross misconduct. Missing Alice, she tracked her, and using her feminine guile and father's status, she conned Richard into allowing Alice to stay with her family.

Alice immediately fell for the considerable charms of Kate's father, Jonathan, over twenty years her senior. The man battled his conscience and Alice's clumsy attempts at seduction, only to become enmeshed in a web of immoral deceit.

After stopping Richard from completing a brutal act of discipline, Jonathan bought him off, but agreed to arrangements already made. Jonathan adopted the guardianship.

Seduced by one Giulio Di Stasio, an Italian associate of Jonathan's, Alice surrendered her virginity in a moment of drunken weakness. Jonathan arriving too late failed to save her, but falling victim to a confusing mixture of paternal instinct and jealous rage, he assaulted Giulio and threw him out of the house.

Besotted, the naked Alice accepted a consoling embrace, unsure of Jonathan's intentions, and huddled to one another they pondered uncertain futures.

Chapter One

August 1956

Jaw supported by fists, dark brown eyes penetrating, Kate pressed. 'Are you going to tell me what happened last night?'

'You know what happened. I got drunk again and Jay put me to bed.'

'Don't believe you, Ali.'

Alice stared out of a window, hands absently playing with a bead necklace. 'Don't much care, Kate. And I'm getting a little bit tired of the third degree.'

'You disappeared with the rapacious Giulio. You were gone for an hour. Then next thing I see is father carrying you back in a blanket and Giulio has disappeared off the face of the earth.

'I did try to warn you, Ali. I did tell you what he was like. He was circumcised, wasn't he? And he did have a mole on his left buttock, didn't he? Giulio is a predator. He eats naïve girls. I should know, Ali, I fell for his charms too.'

Alice seemed not to listen.

'So he seduced you, and was in the process of giving you a portion when father walked in. Yes?'

Alice ignored the presumption.

'Giulio is an expert lover. A complete bastard, but an expert lover. Not a bad place to start if you're looking for experience.'

Grimfaced, Alice sighed. 'I have all the makings of a

first class whore, Kate.'

'What makes you think you're first class?'

'You're right. I'm not even good at that. A plain harlot, then.'

'Tell Aunt Kate all about it.'

'I don't know if I can. I can't understand me, so what chance does anyone else have?'

'Who said I wanted to understand you? I just want to know the juicy ins and outs, so I can gossip.'

Alice threw a pillow at her friend, a smile flickering briefly. 'It's so horribly complicated, Katy. Giulio furnished me with champagne. It went straight to my head. I suppose I'm frustrated…'

'If I had a cock, Ali, I'd?'

'It's not that. Sex is only a tiny part of it. I've fallen for Jay. Every time I get near him I go all goose-bumpy. The trouble is…' Alice searched for the words.

'He's happily married with a divine and gorgeous daughter, and doesn't want to upset the apple cart.'

'That's part of it. I don't know about the divine and gorgeous daughter, though. More a fractious libertine, I'd say.'

'No good you trying to bamboozle me, Ali. I've passed English as well. And I shocked everyone with a grade one.'

'You didn't shock me, Kate. I can see right through that urchin camouflage. Inside that dizzy noddle of yours lies a bright mind. If we could only separate your fanny from it, then there would be no holding you.'

'That's me sorted – surgery. Now what about you?'

'I'm an emotional mess. I love a man who can't or won't reciprocate. I'm filled with these sick urges that go completely against my religious doctrine. And I quite happily play dip-the-wick with a complete stranger. What the hell did Jay think?' Tears brimmed. Emerald pools filled. Glistening beads cantered down an ashen complexion.

'What exactly are you sorry about, Ali? Losing your virginity or showing father you're not his personal property?'

'I could kill myself. Letting that Latin shit have me, and placing Jay in the awful position of defending my honour. I bet I've lost him money.'

'He's got plenty. Anyway, he doesn't like Giulio. He's thumped him before. I suspect he took great pleasure in hitting him again.'

'How did you know?'

'Powerful binoculars.' Kate laughed. 'I know my father – violence before diplomacy. Anyway, he was looking for the excuse ever since he caught me and Giulio together in bed.'

'Jay told me about that last night.'

'He had me, Ali. He broke me in. Of course, I never admitted that to father. Two dozen of the cane was bad enough.'

'So why didn't it glow? That confuses me as much as anything. Am I a masochist? Now and again I touch that erotic sensation, but then it is always snatched away. I wish I could control it.'

'There's no hard and fast rules. You have to feel sexy, Ali. If you're frightened or humiliated, it will just hurt. When you whipped me, that was erotic. I really built up to that. When father caned me I was petrified. Consequently it hurt like hell. If you can dream up a sensual stimulant then you might succeed.'

'What does that mean, exactly?'

'You love father. You'll do anything for him. Father cherishes whacking arse. So all you have to do is see sex in that light. Foreplay. Let him lift your skirt. Let him pull your panties down. Think of him ogling your bare bum. Get yourself all aroused by it. Imagine that cane whacking naked buttocks... yours. See yourself as he sees you,

9

and concentrate on what comes after.'

'What about Richard, and *Heptonstall*?'

'Richard would dearly love to fill your pussy, Ali. Don't tell me he wouldn't. He's a frustrated old man who's never going to find a woman, because he is what he is. And he knows it. You're all woman. Gorgeous figure. Beautiful looks. Oh, he wants you all right. The trouble is, he can't have you. So he beats you instead. Frustration, you see. At least that way he can get an eyeful and touch you a bit, without forcing himself on you.

'So, Ali, sex hangs in the air. Electricity buzzes between you both. See yourself for what you are, and tease the bastard. Egg him on. Think how you'll frustrate him further. Feeling sexy, you see; that's the answer.'

'And *Heptonstall*?'

'We don't know for sure, do we? But if it happens, then it will be a strange man, perhaps. If it's on the skirt or knicks, then concentrate on the humbling position. See him as the dominant male. When all's said and done, a man cannot think any other way than sexually. When he canes your arse he's got your clothes off, in his mind's eye, that is.'

'I think I get the idea.'

'It's hard to explain. You've got to really want caning, and when you do, it's something else.

'Incidentally, where are your results? You've been very quiet about them.'

'Richard has them.'

'Why?'

'Because they went to my old house and he'd arranged all post to be sent to his.'

'So why's he still got them?'

'He wants me to collect. I keep putting it off.'

'You never said anything. Harry will take you, and I'll come too.'

'There wasn't much to say, Kate. He wants me to go

10

alone. He says he wants to spend some time with me.'

'I bet the bugger does. No way, Ali; we go mob handed or not at all.'

'I knew you'd say that. That's why I haven't told you.' Alice wrung her hands. 'I've got to face him alone, Kate. I've got to stand up to him for my own sanity. Every time I hear the name Richard my heart pounds…'

'Jay does that to you, too.'

Alice smiled, a sad twist to her pout. 'Not in the same way – Richard terrifies me. When I rang him to ask if he had any post for me, he said come and get it. I nearly wet myself. I don't intend spending the rest of my life cringing in fear.'

'When are you going to see the pig, then?'

'We've got one week left. I want to enjoy that.'

'So you're going to get it out of the way?'

Alice shook her head. 'No, I'm going to forget about him until the day before we start at *Heptonstall*. Jenny's going to Manchester tomorrow, so do me a favour, Kate; go with her.'

'Just like that?'

'I'm relying on you, Katy.'

'Another go with daddy, right?'

'Not as such, no. I'm going to try what you suggested. See if it glows.'

'Oh, father will love that. You should wait for his birthday. Tie yourself up in pretty pink ribbon and lie on his desk, bum stuck up. He couldn't ask for a better pressie.'

'When is his birthday, Kate?'

'I was joking, Ali!'

'I know, but when is it?'

'He's the grand old age of forty-two on the twenty-third of October.'

'Half term.'

'That's put a sparkle in your eyes. What you planning?'

11

'Nothing as such, but it's nice to know.'

Expression hopeful, Kate offered, 'I'll tie you up in pink ribbon if you like, Ali.'

Alice returned her attention to the outside world, and gazing at the rolling lawns, she suggested, 'There is something you can do for me.'

'I thought I already was; leaving you to seduce my father.'

'Can I have some of your old clothes?' Alice asked, ignoring the gibe.

'Have? Not borrow?'

'I want to alter them.'

'Oh, I get it, I'm so fat they'll swamp you.'

'The thought never entered my head.'

'What you after?'

'The black skirt you can't get over your hips any more. The scarlet top. You know, the one where your tits hang out.' She smiled audaciously. 'And a pair of your finest lacy white knickers.'

Kate glowered. 'If that's not saying I'm fat, I don't know what is.'

'Please, Katy, please,' Alice begged.

'Even though they're too small for me, they'll still be too big for you. So how you going to make them fit?'

'You know I did dressmaking. All I need is a sewing machine. Please, please, please, Katy.'

'I hate people who are good at everything.'

'I can't cook.'

'Neither can I, so that's no consolation.'

'I'll give you a double whacking,' Alice enticed.

'What with?' Kate enquired, interested.

'Whatever you like.'

'Tell you what. The dear old fogies are going out the night after tomorrow. You can whop me in the basement. I'll borrow daddy's keys.'

'I can have those clothes, then?'

12

'Course you can. You can have anything of mine, you know that.' Kate grinned mischievously. 'And that includes my body.'

Utilising Jenny's sewing machine, Alice set to altering the skirt and top, and she had just completed work on the former when the lady herself strolled in. She picked up the skirt before Alice could hide it.

'What's this, Alice? Surely you don't intend wearing it?' Jenny eyed the black cloth with distaste. 'It'll barely cover your bottom, let alone your honour.'

'Um, just honing my skills, Jenny,' Alice blustered. 'I couldn't make it longer, but I could shorten it. It's the stitch that's important.'

The woman examined the hem and seam, and then lay the garment back down. 'Very neat, Alice,' she said. 'So, it's simply an exercise, is it?'

Alice nodded.

'And there I was thinking it might be for a man.' She fixed stern blue eyes on the girl. 'Shows you how a wife can so easily get the wrong impression, doesn't it?'

'Sorry, I'm not with you.' Alice tried to hide the guilt and the fear.

Jenny smiled, warmth lacking. 'Oh, take no notice, Alice. I just get a touch jealous sometimes. It's what comes of having such a magnetic husband with a roving eye.'

'You've no need to be jealous of me, Jenny,' Alice said unconvincingly, a shaky hand knocking the sewing pins flying. She bent to pick them up, Jenny engaged by the presentation of shapely hips and slim legs, and as she stretched to retrieve the furthest one Jenny stopped her in her tracks.

'What exactly were you doing with my husband for an hour last night, Alice?' she asked.

The girl's buttocks tightened. She could almost feel the woman's cane biting into those delicate flanks. 'Oh,' she

13

whispered, desperately seeking an excuse, 'um, didn't Jay tell you?'

'Jay? Oh, we are on familiar terms, aren't we?'

Alice rose to face the suspicious wife. Unable to look her in the eye, cheeks burning, she tried to explain. 'Something did happen last night, Jenny.'

'Yes? Go on…'

'Something I am deeply ashamed of.'

'I see. And would this have something to do with my husband bringing you back wrapped only in a blanket?'

Alice nodded.

'What happened in my gazebo, Alice?' the woman demanded sternly. 'What were you doing with Jonathan?'

Bottom lip trembling, eyes again filling with tears, Alice met those fierce blue daggers. 'I… I didn't do anything with Jay,' she insisted. 'I… I had sex with Giulio. Jay caught us. He hit Giulio, and then he comforted me.'

'What are you telling me?'

'I was a virgin until last night. Giulio got me drunk. Oh, Jenny, I'm so confused.'

The woman shook her head, and maternal instincts overriding anger she put her arms around the girl. 'I should have known. I'm sorry. The trouble with Jonathan is he's impulsive. And worse, he never thinks to explain his actions. So I inevitably think the worst.'

The words twisted the blade of conscience in Alice's heart, and she sobbed for her selfishness as much as for those misguided romantic notions.

'You'll come to learn, Alice, that most men cannot be trusted. Most seek the shortest route to your knickers. There are some honourable men, of course, but you have to learn to distinguish those from the unscrupulous ones.'

'You don't think me a slut then?' Alice asked meekly.

The woman held Alice at arms' length, expression affable. 'No, Ali, you just fell into the trap that thousands do. The trouble is, the girl ends up wearing the tag, not

14

the man. So follow the simple rule; don't sleep with a man until you really know him. If he's worth anything, he'll wait.'

Retaking her seat, Alice wiped away the tears. 'You're a very attractive woman, Jenny, so I don't see why you should be concerned. I mean, Jay would... sorry, Jonathan would have to go a long way to find someone better.'

Jennifer laughed.

'What's the joke?'

'Katy is seasoned, battle-scarred, even. Her upbringing, I suppose. She had to grow up fast in this family. But you, Alice; you are so refreshing. So sweetly innocent. I don't think I have ever met a girl of your age with such a modest outlook on life.'

'I know I have a lot to learn,' Alice acknowledged sadly.

Jennifer sat on the table edge, crossing her legs. 'Jonathan was born to conquer,' she went on. 'He is aggressively outgoing. He has succeeded in business and I have no doubt he will continue to do so. Offered a challenge he will rise to it.' Jenny fixed her gaze on Alice. 'Attractive women are a call to arms. Oh, he probably doesn't even see it as infidelity. A victory here, a defeat there, a boost for the ego, maybe a kiss, maybe even a fondle; but of course that is never enough.

'Having got away with that, why not oral sex. After all, it's not exactly intercourse, is it? So it's not really infidelity, is it? Then a quickie. There's no love involved. I adore my wife. There can never be anything between us. Eventually temptation proves too much and the dear betrothed is sleeping regularly with other women.

'That is your average man, Ali. Weak, full of excuses and about as reliable as a three legged racehorse. That is Jonathan.'

Her expression grave, not really wanting to hear the answer, Alice asked, 'Has he ever fooled around?'

'Fooled around?' the woman smiled, a bittersweet smile.

15

'He's fucked around, yes. He hasn't fooled anyone but himself.'

'But you're still here?'

'Reality, Alice. I love the man. Come what may, I adore Jonathan. He's generous, kind and a good father. He'll never leave me. I will always live a comfortable life, so I turn a blind eye to his indiscretions.'

'You were quick enough to warn me off.'

'Not for my sake, Ali. Not for Jonathan's, either. For yours. He would hurt you. Oh, not intentionally, but he would hurt you in the end. It's all one big game to him. And as he never feels the pangs of rejection he can't understand why others do.'

'What would you have done, Jenny, if I had been playing around with him?'

'It doesn't arise. You're not that stupid, are you?'

'No.' Alice shook her head, knowing she was.

Jennifer observed the response. She folded her arms. 'In your case, Ali, I would put it down to gullibility. And that I would redress with a stern lesson in life.' She smiled, austerity withdrawn. 'But that's because I like you.' She leaned forward and ruffled the girl's hair, then bowed and kissed those lustrous locks. Then without another word, she left.

'*A stern lesson in life.*' What did that allude to?

Concerned, unsure, Alice finished the task in hand, then the altered clothing she bagged and hid in her room.

The following day at about noon, Alice saw Katy beseeching her mother. 'Oh please, mother. I've been cooped up for days. I need to get out.'

'I'm seeing Dr Johnson, and I'm sorry, Katy, but there is no way I'm taking you with me.'

'Why are you seeing the quack? Nothing wrong, is there?'

'Nothing that you need worry yourself about.'

'Not up the duff, are you?'

'Like I said, Kate, none of your business.'

'Drop me off in Buxton, then. I can do a bit of shopping.'

'No. Get Harry to take you.'

'Can I?' The girl's eyes lit up.

Jennifer opened her handbag. 'I suppose you want some spending money?' Kate nodded, hand held out. 'Three pounds, Kate, and that's it.'

And within the hour mother and daughter had left Jonathan to the tender mercies of Alice's scheming. Jenny, she understood, would be missing most of the afternoon; Katy promised her at least four hours, probably longer.

As usual Jonathan was ensconced in the study, working, and Alice retired to her room to prepare, hopefully a very pleasant shock. She dwelt on Jenny's warning. The woman admitted she generously ignored his dalliance, and that she didn't see other females as a danger. Alice held no expectancy of Jay running away with her, she didn't want to wreck a family, deprive Kate of a father, and then the oddity struck; she would, in such a fanciful scenario, become her best friend's stepmother.

She applied some make-up. Replacing the usual touch of mascara she layered upper and lower lashes. Lids she coated with mid-green, a compliment to sparkling beryl eyes. The smudge of blush surrendered to an overdose, and the trace of pink lipstick ripened to a waxy crimson.

Alice viewed her reflection and digested the image. Tart.

Wearing only the acquired panties, she drew a suspender belt up her graceful legs and stretched it over supple hips, to nestle on her narrow waist. She smiled wistful as she held up a packet containing fishnet stockings. Hands duly softened with cream, she enticed them over elegant calves and stretched them to within five inches of her lace-covered pubic curls. There she clipped them, the contrast of ebony and alabaster provocative.

The top and skirt adopted, Alice slipped on the stiletto

17

shoes that had brought about her collapse into Jonathan's lap. A dab of perfume to her neck and cleavage completed the transition. She checked her appearance in the full-length mirror, and smiling, she approved.

Kate slipped a hand into the chauffeur's groin, and gripping his cock through grey uniform trousers, asked, 'Is this the gear lever, Harry?'

'Does that translate to "I want a good fucking", Miss Kate?'

'How eloquently put, James.'

'Back seat or the woods?'

'How about over the bonnet?'

'The Jag emblem might cause a bit of discomfort.'

'Unscrew it, Harry.' She winked. 'And then screw me.'

Alice descended the stairs and walked determinedly to Jay's study. She didn't knock, but waltzed straight in. Jonathan sat with his back to her, engrossed in his work, seemingly unaware of her presence.

She approached stealthily, reached out and pulled his castor-wheeled chair back. Jonathan looked up in shock and surprise as the shapely figure of Alice inserted itself between him and his work. He stared, eyes agog, as outstretched fingers ran through his dark thatch of hair, Alice gazing seductively down into his eyes.

'Holy shit!' he gasped. 'What the fuck have you done with yourself?'

She bent gracefully from the waist, lips pouting. 'A tart, Jay,' she whispered. 'I'm giving you the tart.'

'You are…' she snuffed out the words, her kiss explicit, practicing every skill she knew in that attempt to seduce. His hands still gripping armrests, fingers gouging the leather, she released him. 'Full of surprises,' he finished.

'I always will be,' she goaded, settling back, her toned bottom giving to the desktop.

Jonathan raised an eyebrow. 'I take it this is another attempt at seduction?'

'Not necessarily.'

Eyeing the length of stockinged leg he pursed his lips. 'I don't think I have ever seen a skirt quite as short as that. It barely covers your bum.'

'Have you seen what's beneath it?' she asked coyly.

'Whatever it is, I'm sure it will have an effect.'

Alice raised first one leg, settling the ankle on the man's shoulder. She smouldered. The second limb followed, resting on the other. Jonathan whistled softly as he drank of their conclusion. A 'V' of white lace offered scant cover to a shadow of dark curls, smooth inner thighs exaggerating the whiteness of the material.

'Well, Jay, what's going through your mind now?' she teased.

'That top,' he said. 'Isn't it Katy's?'

'Yes,' she admitted, 'I altered it.'

'I think it should be a damned sight longer,' he groaned. A crew neck exhibited a semicircle of pale flesh – the upper slopes of her breasts – the material encasing the enticingly firm orbs, the hem terminating just below their lower curves, leaving her flat tummy bare.

'I'm not wearing a bra either, Jay,' she divulged.

'Is that an invitation?' he enquired.

'I'm yours, Jay. To do with as you please. Anything you want.'

'Anything?'

'The good girl is acting the licentious tart… any ideas?'

'Ideas on what?'

'How to thwart such unacceptable behaviour.'

'I have indeed, Alice, but unfortunately I am extremely busy at the moment.'

Undaunted, she lowered her legs. 'Oh, but Jay,' she protested, placing a knee on either side of his thighs and her hands behind his neck. 'We're all alone.' She lowered her breasts, her pretty bottom thrust out, and temptation screamed at him as he viewed that enticing cleavage, the outline of her nipples unmistakable through the tight, skimpy top. 'Jenny is seeing the doctor,' she whispered, 'and Kate has gone shopping with Harry.'

She sank, sitting on his lap, eyes imploring, the erotic fragrance of perfume almost overwhelming him.

Jonathan laid his head back, and eyes fixed on the ceiling he argued, 'Alice, Alice, Alice, there is a time and a place. You are a delectable creature, but now is not the time.'

'Jay,' she purred, nuzzling his neck. 'I'm all aroused.' She pecked his skin. 'I've really had to psyche myself up for this. You're surely not going to disappoint a scantily dressed slut, are you?'

Unable to resist, his hands wandered, and fondling her buttocks through the short skirt he relented. 'And what is this tasty little tease after, exactly?'

'Sensual handling, that's all,' she said. 'The stimulation of a certain part of my anatomy.'

'Which part?'

'The part where your hands are as we speak.'

Jonathan sighed. 'What chance does a man have against the depraved wiles of a stunning coquette?'

'None, master,' she whispered. 'None at all.'

'So what's it to be, temptress?' he asked. 'My hand? A paddle? A cane or a cricket bat?'

Alice promptly straightened up, aghast. 'A cricket bat?' she squealed.

'To bowl a maiden over, of course.'

She pursed her lips in contemplation.

'All right, we'll discount the bat,' he conceded. 'So what, then?'

'Whatever you have to hand,' she decided.

'You will have an exceedingly sore bum,' he warned her.

Alice leaned close to him, their noses touching. 'A

glowing bum, master,' she corrected, and before he could reply she silenced him with the fresh taste of hot breath and malleable lips.

The Jaguar parked at the edge of a cornfield, Harry remarked, 'Any particular reason for the college uniform, Miss Kate?'

'I just thought you might appreciate it, Harry,' she said, beaming cheekily at him.

'Oh, I do, miss. I do.'

'What about what's inside?'

The chauffeur let his tongue loll appreciatively.

'Chase me, Harry,' she coaxed. 'And when you catch me punish me for running away. And then, Harry,' Kate raised an alluring eyebrow, 'fuck me.'

Jonathan patted Alice's buttocks, their tensed outline unmistakable, the short tight skirt moulding to their curves. He smiled with appreciation at their light tremors, the titillating ripples of a youthful body. With Alice lying over his lap, her bottom prominent, he could appreciate the length of her shapely legs, her cheeks peeping bravely from the taut hem of her skirt.

Those lovely thighs he stroked, the sight and feel taking their toll, the contrast of black stockings and creamy flesh sparking an incorrigible urge. Alice, he accepted, was right; the tart did strike a chord; notes of primeval lust.

Fingers slipped between those two appetisers, and thirst wetted, Jonathan yearned to explore further. A gentle prod parting them he sighed, the hunger too great to be totally gratified. Fingers testing that warm division, the succulent gorge noticeably moist, he paid homage to her intrinsic beauty. 'You, Alice, are all female,' he said. 'To be perfectly honest, you're too much female. You inspire a passion that places me on the edge of insanity. Fucking you will never be enough.'

Waiting on his pleasure, dizzy with a burning desire, she replied in a whisper, 'I'm yours, master. Do what you will with me.'

A hand pushed beneath the skirt, lush satin-coated cheeks meeting the foray. 'I rather like this feeling of absolute power over you, wench. It might prove addictive.'

'I rather hope it does, sir.'

Jonathan slapped a provocative dune, the flesh yielding, trembling, and his penis responding he struck the other, Alice sighing.

Breathless, Harry brought the running Kate down with a flying rugby tackle. Flattening corn they sprawled, Katy giggling hysterically. 'You didn't have to run quite so fast, Miss Kate,' he complained.

'Ah, but aren't I worth it, Harry?' she teased, breathless.

He contemplated the reclining form. A fresh and attractive, if not beautiful countenance, flushed with excess. Soft brown eyes, appealing, sparkled with exuberance. Her torso; unbuttoned green blazer draped at her sides, the crisp starched and freshly pressed white blouse filled by an ample bosom, rising and falling with exaggerated respiration. His eyes fell to the bottle-green skirt, pleated and in disarray, emphasising generous thighs, her knees and calves surprisingly slender.

'Yes,' he eventually replied, 'you are worth it.'

'You've caught me, so what now?' she goaded.

Harry's expression changed dramatically, and he unfastened the buckle of his leather belt. 'I'm going to teach you a lesson, young miss,' he vowed. 'I told you what would happen if you ran off like that.'

Kate reached out, expression pleading, and grabbed Harry's shoulders. 'You're not going to beat me, are you?'

He yanked the belt free, and with a flourish held it up. 'Oh yes, miss, without mercy.'

'On my bum?' Her voice quavered.

He put his mouth to her ear and whispered, 'On your *naked* bum, miss.'

'And what makes you think I'm just going to let you?'

'I wouldn't be so presumptuous.'

Kate frowned.

'But I would point out that I am bigger than you. That I am infinitely stronger, and that you won't stand a dog's chance should you try to fight.'

'And who said I was going to?'

Harry straddled the girl, undid the knot of her tie and pulled it free, snapping it taut. Smirking, he dared her to resist, but she remained motionless and silent, her breathing slow as she looked up at him.

Methodically Harry released the blouse buttons, their eyes not parting. He spread the shirt open, and feasted on the vision of her bra tightly clutching creamy breasts. He shook his head and whistled. 'No matter how many times I see those, Katy, they still manage to take my breath away.'

'Scoundrels,' she said, 'are not supposed to compliment. They simply take what they want.'

He lifted the hem of her skirt a couple of inches. 'Stockings…' he drooled. 'I thought they might be. Not exactly schoolgirl, are they?'

'So spank me for them.'

'Oh, I will, miss, I will… Roll over and put your hands behind your back,' he directed, moving clear of her.

With Kate lying prone he removed the blouse, pulling it from her arms. Then he unfastened the bra and cleared her limbs of that, too. Harry held one of her wrists to her lower back and forced the other alongside it, then bound them with the tie. He searched beneath the skirt, freeing first one stocking and then the other, and deprived her legs of covering.

'Get up,' he growled, collecting her discarded clothing, and with difficulty Kate got to her knees and then rose, the bra falling to the ground, ample breasts swinging with the struggle. Then wearing only the skirt and panties she awaited his next command.

Picking up the bra Harry pointed towards the parked car. 'That way,' he said.

'What about my shoes?' she whined.

'You can walk barefoot. In fact…' Harry wrenched her skirt to her ankles, and then the belt cracked on her backside. 'Now move!' he ordered, and in a blissful state Kate trudged through the waist-high corn.

Jonathan rolled up the skirt, satin panties smoothly covering the cheeks they concealed. He licked dry lips and forcibly groped those entrancing flanks, and Alice drifted in a world of undiluted contentment.

With his erection aching he struck with enthusiasm, deliberately stoking that faultless rear; the clap of enduring hand on receptive bottom music to his ears. His intention to arouse, not to hurt, he slowly induced a rosy hue.

Her obsession consummated, Alice succumbed unequivocally. Jonathan, her idol, spanked her. He tended her needs. He fuelled a fire in her belly as well as her rear. She winced at each slap, but the afterglow proved delectable. Katy was right; it was indeed one's attitude. Alice had so wanted to please Jay, willing to do almost anything. She had felt so keyed, so beside herself with lust. All reason had given to a deranged craving. Sexual madness reigned supreme.

Lying over that lap, the wand of depravity continued to dust her with the taste of excess. She matched Jonathan's tortured state, where whatever they did would never be enough. The continuous slap, slap; an inferno kindled. That feeling of heat in her rump aggravated a desire to perpetuate and strengthen. Alice longed for more severity.

Jonathan wrenched those flimsy semitransparent panties clear, his ardour fired. His forearms supporting, he lifted

24

her to meet that flushed posterior with attentive lips and cooling tongue. Crazed beyond redemption and reason, Alice revelled in the deference, inexperience betraying that prurience.

Jonathan lay her back down. He reached for and opened a desk drawer. From its shelter he withdrew a broad leather paddle. Alice, following the movement, sucked in air, desirous of its impact rather than afraid.

He pressed her shoulders down, forcing her bottom up, and lay into those suffering cheeks, the crack loud and alarming. The smart emphasised, Alice grabbed handfuls of thick pile carpet. Her expression concentrated she transcended the immediate blast of pain to banquet on the aftermath. She squirmed. She thrust up that petite bottom, proffering it for further hostility, leaving Jonathan in no doubt.

The man abused the presentation, hitting it with single-minded tenacity. The leather mauled, stimulated, aroused; carried Alice to the brink of gratification, her mind in turmoil, her body in paradise.

Kate reached the car, her buttocks ablaze. Harry had goaded, urged with the belt, the frequency of contact lost to her. She stumbled, fell to her knees and looked up at him, her face imploring. He grinned sadistically, and decisively placing a hand on her shoulder he forced her down.

Her bottom cheeks presented the perfect target. Whistling happily he dumped her clothes and removed his jacket. Unhurriedly he rolled up his sleeves, and the thick belt he snapped tight between large fists. 'Now, girly,' he hissed, 'you get it.'

'And what makes you think I'm going to lie here and let you?' Kate demanded, knowing how he could.

Harry frowned. Seconds ticked by, and that handsome countenance lit as he reached the same conclusion.

Retrieving the stockings from the pile, the man knelt.
'This,' he announced, untying and rebinding her wrists
to her ankles. Then as an afterthought he pulled down her
knickers. Rising, he familiarised himself with that scarlet
moon, his hand stroking the welted flesh. 'Miss Kate,
I'm going to enjoy this,' he divulged unnecessarily.

'So am I,' whispered the girl.

Harry took up position, his legs astride the angled back.
Grinning lewdly he doubled the belt, and with his arm
perpendicular he braced himself, as did Kate. Then, using
his body and ample muscle he launched the first, cracking
with force on the upturned bottom. Katy howled.

He readied the next strike, promising, 'And after I've
welted your lovely backside, I'm going to fuck your tight
wet pussy.'

'Oh, goody!' she gasped, unheard because of leather
hitting vulnerable buttocks again.

With hot sun blazing, Harry wiped the sweat from his
brow. 'That mate of yours, Alice,' he said. 'Do you think
she'd go for some of this too?'

'You're spoiling the elusion of wicked blackguard,' she
sighed. 'Ask me after you've sampled the delights of my
fanny.'

Harry replied with another forceful cut to her scorched
and welted bottom.

With her buttocks burning, each well-directed explosion
compounding erotic flames, Alice writhed, intoxicated.
Her complete rear blazed, the heat driven deep, venereal
responsiveness accentuated to a frenzy.

Jonathan dropped the paddle, and his hands cool and
soothing fell upon that battered rump. He stroked and
consoled, his own mind consumed by tortured lust. 'This
bottom is ripe for the cane, Ali. Are you?'

'Is it to be that brute you used before?' she asked
anxiously, snatched from the abyss of depravity.

'No,' he said. 'I thought I'd stir with a more flexible and less formidable rod.'

'But you will use that awful thing on me?'

'Does the tart deserve it?'

'The tart will do whatever her master desires. If I have to suffer the ultimate, I will. But only for you.'

Jonathan eased her up. He held her before him, hands about her waist, skirt hugging her middle, her lower body exposed. 'I'm puzzled,' he admitted.

'Why?' Alice asked, frowning, believing something wrong.

'What have I done in life to reap such a reward? The most beautiful young woman lands on my doorstep. If it is not enough to merely regale in that splendour, this siren gives herself to me body and soul. Why, Ali? How come I am so lucky?'

Alice clutched his wrists, then led those attentive hands up and laid them to her covered breasts. 'Why question fate, Jay?' she whispered. 'Beauty is in the eye of the beholder. You find me so, but that doesn't mean others will.'

He shook his head, eyes misting. 'You're so wrong there, Ali. You have the looks and personality to be a princess. And you command an undeniable intelligence. Such a sparkle to those lascivious green eyes. I will lose you only too soon.'

Alice lifted the top, her exquisite breasts exposed, the nipples erect, aroused. 'I'm yours, Jay,' she told him. 'For as long as you want me.'

He fingered those succulent nipples. 'Will you stay with us?' he asked.

'I am, aren't I?'

'No, I mean until you meet the right man.'

'I have.'

'It can't be, Ali,' he insisted wearily. 'I find you irresistible, I admit. I would even accept you tug my heartstrings. But I'm destined for old age, and you? You blossom, your whole life ahead of you. I have a wife, and a daughter the same age as you. I won't turn my back on them. If I could have the best of both worlds I would. But that would be so unfair on you.'

'Why even contemplate the future, Jay?' she said. 'Why not follow the road and see where it takes us?'

'To ruin, eventually.' He fondled those mouth-watering breasts. 'Katy already suspects us, and Jenny is no fool. We'll be found out soon enough. And then what? Jenny would insist you go. I would lose you and you your security.'

'There's something you should know, Jay.'

'What's that?' he asked.

'Uncle Richard has spun a deal,' she informed him. 'A private backer is paying for the completion of my studies, and when I've finished at *Heptonstall* I'll be going to work for him.'

Jonathan's eyes narrowed. 'Who is this backer?'

Alice shrugged. 'Some businessman – I don't really know who. There is a name. He's an Arab, I think. But he requires a competent and qualified woman.'

'I bet he does,' Jonathan snorted derisively. 'Have you ever met this man?'

Alice shook her head.

'I'll pay your fees, Alice,' he said decisively. 'Tell this Arab to go fuck himself.'

'The deal's done, Jay. I have a future. I will have a job when I qualify. What more could I want?'

'So, apart from holidays in the meantime, I will lose you?'

She leant forward and kissed him on the forehead. 'It's only for two years. I'll visit as often as possible. There won't be anyone else. I promise, Jay.'

'There's a contract with a man you don't even know?' he pressed. 'Something set up by that weasel Barker?

What is this job?'

Alice shrugged again. 'Personal assistant or something, I think.' She made the title up.

'Let me pay your fees, Ali,' he offered again. 'You can work for me after that.'

'What doing, Jay?' She regarded him with suspicion. 'Modelling? You said yourself you can only use a girl now and again. I'm no photographer or writer. So what, Jay?'

'How about personal assistant?'

'If I was that type of girl, I'd leap at the chance. But I'm not. I will pay my way, Jay. I'd sooner be on the streets than permanently in debt to someone. This way I pay my obligation off in a couple of years.'

'You make it sound like you're working for nothing.'

'I am, as it happens.'

'What?' Jonathan leapt up. 'You can't be serious. How the hell are you going to live?'

'I don't suppose he'll let me starve, Jay. I'd be no good to him that way, would I? No, it's merely unsalaried, but board and lodgings are included.'

'I'll have him checked out,' he insisted.

She idly ran a finger down his chest. 'So jealous, Jay. But I'm not concerned, so why should you be?'

'Quite frankly, because it stinks, Ali,' he stated angrily. 'Because whatever that creep Barker does is bound to be suspect?'

'Jay,' she said, halting his little tirade.

'Yes?'

'Cane me. Whip my backside before Jenny comes home. I want to see if I can reach an orgasm. But be loving, be masterful, and don't keep your hands to yourself.'

Harry trounced those beleaguered cheeks. The belt rose and fell in a brisk fusillade of withering blows. With broad hips a deep carmine, the glow had long since overwhelmed the masochistic Katy. Bound so, she could only toss her head in sublime reaction, galvanised by the icy coating induced by sexual belligerence.

The constant crack of hard leather on fragile buttock stimulated. That humble position, bottom thrust up, enkindled. Harry, man by any description, stood over her, dominant and overbearing, transfixed. The constant smart in her behind and the flare of beaten flesh bore her toward climax.

Harry paused. He reached out and felt her rear, the hide hot, mauled. He grinned, disbelieving that any girl could want that. But it did gratify a dark hunger, an undeniable desire to inflict torment. Oh yes, he had watched the girls being whipped with a lecherous yearning, wishing he had been the one to deal misery. Katy relished it, but that Alice…

Oh yes, Alice, the one with the cock-twisting body. She seemed to hurt beneath the flurry of blows, and that did something for Harry. It touched, ignited a spot that perplexed. He had experienced a feeling that besieged, a sensation he longed to reawaken.

But how…?

'Harry,' Katy roused.

'Yes, miss.'

'Do you know what a birch tree looks like?'

'Silver trunk, miss.'

'Is there one nearby?'

'About a hundred yards away, miss.'

'Go and cut a dozen sticks and whip me with them.'

'Bored with the belt, are you, miss?'

'I can barely feel it, Harry. I need something more aggressive. Alice got birched. It seemed quite a brute of a thing.'

'Do you want me to release you?'

'No, leave me like this. I like the feeling. I feel so vulnerable.'

30

'Tell you what, miss.'

'What, Harry?'

He picked up her socks and used one as a blindfold and the other as a gag. 'Now you really *are* vulnerable. You won't know who is taking advantage, will you? Oh sorry, you can't answer, can you?'

Harry mooched off towards the trees, leaving Katy unsure. They were in the middle of nowhere, camouflaged by a barrier of three-foot corn, and Harry surely wouldn't be far away. With the hot sun on her back she dwelt on that predicament. What if a stranger came by? Walking his dog, say. What would he do? Release her? Call the police? Or take advantage of her inviting position? What would that feel like, to have mister unknown plant his cock in her, to be fucked, not knowing who the perpetrator was? The wicked scenario aroused rather than frightened her.

Harry cut his bundle, and with his penknife he trimmed the twelve straight twigs, bound the thick end with his tie and headed back to Katy. He had already decided on a deceit, that being the reason for the use of her socks.

Circling the girl he approached through the field of corn, then unannounced he stood over her, blocking the sun. She turned her face in his direction, but of course she couldn't see him. The noise of his footfalls and the blocking of direct heat informed her someone had arrived.

He heard her muffled enquiry. ''Awwy?'

Harry answered not. He knelt and stroked that flushed arse. Again she sought clarification, but the chauffeur ignored her. His hand descended, delved between parted legs and pawed her vagina.

Almost certain who toyed with her, Katy refrained from an attempted scream. She knew her man and the stunts he would likely pull. Would anyone risk sexual interference with help only a hundred yards away? But that was if Harry *was* only a hundred yards away. Perhaps he had to

31

travel further to find the right birch.

The hand withdrew and silence reigned. What was occurring? She heard a rasp of breath and felt the hands return. Fingers parted her. A stiffness pressed to her vagina. God! Was it Harry? Or was she about to be taken by a dirty stranger?

The erection slid in, her sex well lubricated. Hands gripped her hips. Fingers delved the flesh. The intrusion withdrew and thrust back with energy, the only sound her assailant's heavy breathing.

Well versed with Harry's cock, Katy adjudged the stretch of her slit to be about him. Even so she could not be sure. The bugger had blindfolded and gagged her. He must have pre-planned the whole exercise.

Katy settled to the steady rhythm, indulging in the favour. A fuck between whippings, that was different. Then the realisation dawned; if he brought her off, then the magic would be lost. That birch would hurt like hell. Still, she could stop him. Harry did what he was told. That was, if he removed the gag!

She tried to switch off, to not let the homing missile bring her to a climax. But the illicitness of it all refused that, an unknown fucking her accentuated the fervour. She noted the growing electricity within.

The cock rode her faster, the man's groin colliding with her buttocks. Every thrust seemed to take her breath away, and her assailant sought air in a rasping fashion too. Or was it more of a wheeze? Harry didn't wheeze. He was fit.

He carried her to a climax, Katy unable to do anything about it. She shuddered with its enormity, possibly the best orgasm she had ever experienced. The man continued, not having reached his. He rutted. He constantly changed the angle of entry, the erection continuing to arouse, Katy sensing the imminent signs of a second crest.

Harry pulled free. He gripped his erection, squeezing

the shaft. He wasn't ready for coming. He wanted Katy to do that at least one more time. And then he would thrash her with the birch, see how she liked it cold.

Imminence retreating he sank his cock back in, Katy squealing either in delight or shock. Harry knew how to please. While he played with Katy he also had three others on the go. Not so young, he would admit, but promiscuous women all the same.

Katy couldn't deny the second coming, that cock thrusting. Harry then let his seed flow, filling the girl with exudation.

He rose, did up his flies and walked away, Katy frowning. Harry left it for some ten minutes, walking a circle and then duly arrived. 'Sorry it took so long, Miss Kate,' he apologised. 'But I had to walk right into the woods to get what you wanted. Now I reckon, young miss, that as you're denied sight and sound I ought to leave you like that. Different, ain't it? Might be more exciting.'

Katy frantically shook her head and mumbled into the gag.

'Sorry, can't understand you, miss.'

'Oh!' she near screamed into the sock as Harry took the bundle of sticks, scrutinised the scarlet sphere and aimed a particularly violent stroke at it. Fine twigs cut the air, hit and decimated the flesh beneath. Katy squealed. Harry smirked.

Chapter Two

Alice felt the glow. Fingers delved the hot flesh. Orgasm had neared and veered, always eluding. Jonathan perched, bum on the desk, a whippy rattan in hand. 'No tears, Ali?' he asked. 'I assume it glows.'

'It does, Jay,' she admitted. 'It's a wonderful feeling, though, and it's all down to you. You're so expert, you're so manly.' She grinned. 'You're so handsome, so horny.'

'At this moment in time I am your headmaster, and I'm not very happy with you,' he said.

'Oh, sir,' she whined.

'Not happy at all. You are lazy, inattentive, slovenly, and a disgrace to this school.'

'I do my best, sir,' Alice protested, playing the game.

'No, I don't think you do, Hussey. Just look at your dishevelled state. And you're wearing make-up, forbidden as you well know.' He ran an eye over her body. 'You have the temerity to present yourself with your skirt around your middle, and I might add with no underwear in sight. What do you think this is? A bordello?'

She couldn't detect even a glimmer of a smile. 'I'm sorry sir, I left the dorm in such a rush I forgot my knickers.'

'You forgot your uniform, you mean.'

'Yes sir.'

'And what do you expect for such licentious behaviour?'

'The cane, sir. A damned good whacking, sir.'

'Then I shall not disappoint you, young lady. Bend over and touch your toes.' He observed the compliance with satisfaction. 'Feet together, legs perfectly straight. No, fingertips on toes and legs straight. That's more like it.'

Jonathan pressed the cane to those tormented flanks. He tapped. '*Heptonstall*, Alice,' he said. 'There, I'm afraid to say, contact between implement and bottom is a regular occurrence.'

'You seem well acquainted,' Alice remarked curiously.

'I wouldn't send my daughter to a school without first investigating.'

'Private detective?'

'He interviewed pupils past and present.'

'And you don't mind Katy being subjected to such?'

'I think she will fair well, don't you?'

Alice giggled nervously. 'I think she will do far better than me.'

The cane ceased to intimidate, a slice of air heralding abrupt discomfort. The rod struck, indented lower buttock, warped then sprung. Alice winced, the immediate smart arresting.

'That was hard, sir,' she complained, taken aback.

'You question the stroke, Hussey? You dress like a floozy, if dress be the right description. You attempt to seduce your educational principal and moral guide, although in both I seem to be losing the war. You also have a definite discoloration to your buttocks which implies I am not the only one to be aggrieved today.'

'It was a wager, sir. I was bet I could not charm you. It would seem I have lost. And as for the warming of my bottom, Miss Wilson dealt me the paddle for smoking behind the bike sheds.'

'I see. A wager, you say?'

'Yes, sir.'

'You know that betting is frowned upon, in any shape or form? And that smoking is a caning offence, not a paddling one?'

'I suppose so, sir,' she played along.

'Very well,' he decided, 'six for your improper dress, six for the wager, six for the smoking, and six for your impertinence.'

'Twenty-two stripes, sir?' she gasped.

'And a further six for your obvious inability to add up,' he decreed. 'How many is that, Hussey?'

'Too many, sir,' she said, with some disquiet.

'It is twenty-nine, girl, as you have already received the first.'

Jonathan caught her off guard, the stroke dealt swift and severe. Alice leapt up, and her face contorted she gripped her bottom with both hands, body jostled by the impact.

'Did I say rise, Hussey?' he demanded, and the smart having stolen her voice, she shook her head. 'So bend back over. Touch those toes. I want that bottom taut.'

'I think it's already been taught, sir,' she said cheekily. 'Taught a cruel lesson, if you ask me.'

Jonathan smiled, and turned away so Alice couldn't witness the surrender of austerity. Control regained, he rebuked her. 'Mind your disrespectful mouth lest I add another six!'

'I'm only following your example, sir,' she appealed. 'That's what you want, isn't it?'

'You are already receiving six for impertinence, Hussey,' he pointed out, 'do you want another half dozen?'

'Not if you're going to whip me that hard, sir.'

Jonathan pressed the cane to those heated cheeks again. He tapped the flesh, intrigued by the smooth quiver. Alice braced herself for another brutal stroke. The rod tapped again, the girl certain it would withdraw at any second and return with cruel vigour. Katy had warned her. Her Jay seemed unable to resist the temptation of striking with power.

36

The rod continued its tap-tapping, the strength increasing, a dozen minor slaps and then it did indeed hit with a sharp reminder of his thirst for severity. It stung, the stripe smarting for some minutes after, but the man returned to his superficial patter.

Confused, Alice anticipated a deception. That flexible wand ranged over her quivering flanks, the assault instigating a curious sensation. A dozen or so taps and the rod cut again, the fire instilled refreshing the embers of the last.

Her bottom began to glow and Alice closed her eyes, settling to the unusual flagellation.

Jonathan persevered. The speed of raps swift, her bottom seemed to simmer, whilst that bubble of energy below gathered momentum. The occasional stroke applied with gusto only served to accentuate the fervour.

Jonathan observed the consequence, transfixed. That perfect bottom constantly trembled, the flesh jostled and in perpetual motion. That action ignited his ardour and herded him towards an insatiable urgency.

Alice groaned. The fires lit began to envelop. The raiding cane carried her rapidly towards the sublime. Her stomach was alight. The supernova approached.

Tap, tap, tap, tap, tap, *whack!*

The scald ripped through those agitated dunes, fomenting the inferno, throwing the girl headlong into an orgasm. Alice fell to her knees, hands thrust between weakened legs, fingers clutching at that disturbed fissure. She surrendered unequivocally to the carnal bliss, head bowed, expression concentrated.

Jonathan smiled, pleased the strategy had succeeded. He tended his own distraction, rubbing the considerable erection stretching his trousers.

'Oh God, Jay,' Alice mumbled. 'It happened. My bum is glowing. My sex is on fire. I feel so content. Almost as if an enormous weight has been blasted from my body.'

'And what a lovely body it is, Ali,' he said. 'Almost too much. I want to eat you, Ali. I want to suckle, kiss, sink my teeth into that magnificent body. I want to lick you from head to toe.' He unfastened his trousers. 'I don't give a fuck about repercussions any more, Ali. I'm a red-blooded male, and if I don't have you, make love to you, fuck you, then I shall regret it for the rest of my life.'

Katy reeled to the sixth detonation. She felt for her best friend. She sympathised with the dreadful pain she must have suffered. Harry used a wand of fine ends, nothing as brutal as that manufactured by Richard Barker, but still the hurt proved atrocious, her tormentor impervious to the suffering.

Harry whipped with force, the twigs unbelievably harsh stinging a wide area, an intense hell that twisted her gut and jarred the mind. Tears soaked the sock that covered her eyes. Spittle wet the one that kept her silent. She would kill Harry when he finally deemed to release her. She would insist he face the same or the sack. Vengeance would be hers in one form or another.

A dozen having brought her bottom to an untenable sensitivity, the servant switched sides. The assault renewed, he flayed the opposite flank, the hurt there deplorable, extreme and sickening. Harry, however, had worse in mind. In the meantime he proceeded with the rough handout, the haunch marked, striped and spotted.

Alice had said Katy would not be able to withstand a true corporal punishment. She had remarked that faced with a flogging in some distant country Katy would crumble. The girl began to accept that. It was one thing to feel aroused and have your behind warmed, but another to be flogged without compunction.

Stagnant's caning, and her own father's flogging; both had hurt cruelly. Neither did she wish to repeat. Perhaps she wasn't the complete masochist she thought she might be. *Heptonstall* might prove to be hell rather than heaven.

Her bottom felt lacerated, and each lash plunged her further into despair. She mentally begged for Harry to cease. She had lost control. Harry beat her as she had always desired, but the outcome proved disastrous.

The man stood astride her. He gloated over those welted cheeks, coloured by the strap and rutted by the birch. He would relish taking her. Harry savoured planting his prick again, and the puckered anus invited.

Ignoring the girl's continued gurgles, shrieks and struggles, he proceeded to whip her from above, those supple lengths igniting buttock and thigh alike. Her position incited, those delectable flanks thrust up, the flesh as tight as a drum skin. Harry closed on fever pitch, his lashes more forceful in consequence.

Katy's backside blazed. It glowed, but unfortunately her sex did not. Harry stoked the other cheek, her thigh reeling to the affliction. She had lost count but guessed he must be close to finishing. The man paused. He dwelt on that division. The gentle curve of bottom to thigh and what lay between. He laid the rod to that unmarked valley, the stretch of cheeks offering a navigable path. The ends whipped about the contour and dealt misery to her vagina. The subsequent muffled shriek pleased. Deliberately he repeated the act, Katy writhing in agony. Two more took her to the brink and tipped her into the kitchens of hell.

Harry tossed the birch to one side and knelt beside the miserable girl. He undid her blindfold, brown eyes blinking, the sunlight blinding. She glared at him.

'Oh, what's the matter, miss?' he asked theatrically. 'Wasn't it as you wanted?'

She sniffled and shook her head.

'I'm sorry, miss, I thought you said you wanted birching. So I birched you.'

She grunted.

'Sorry, Miss Kate, I can't understand you.'

Her face filling with colour she growled, the fury evident.

Harry smiled and cleared the gag. 'What was that, miss?'

'You vicious pig!' she exploded. 'I suppose you enjoyed yourself, did you? Well, ex-chauffeur, I fucking didn't!'

The smile faded. 'But you ordered me to beat you, miss,' he pointed out simply. 'I only carried out your demands. You can't see a fellow sacked for carrying out his orders, can you?'

'I didn't say to fuck me, Harry. I didn't tell you to give me a portion first, did I?'

'But I didn't, miss.' He spread his hands innocently. 'When did I take advantage of you? When?'

'You went and cut the rod. Then you sneaked back here and had me. Don't say it wasn't you, Harry, 'cos I know it was. I'd know your cock anywhere.'

'I'm sorry, miss,' he continued pleading ignorance, 'I don't know what you're talking about.'

She seethed. Harry wouldn't admit his guilt, and that reminded her of someone else. For once she was on the receiving end of the lies. 'Well if it wasn't you,' she demanded, 'who the fuck was it?'

'Let me get this right,' he said coolly. 'You're saying while I was away someone, unknown, had you?'

'Yes!'

'I did warn you. I considered leaving you here all trussed up a bit risky. But you said you'd be all right.'

'It was you, Harry,' she insisted. 'And if I ever manage to prove it, I'll see you on the end of the birch!'

'So why didn't you like it?'

'Because it hurt!'

'That sort of treatment generally does,' he pointed out with annoying simplicity. 'But I thought you liked pain, miss.'

'No point in me trying to make you understand, is there? Just untie me, Harry. I want to go home.'

Chapter Three

Alice gasped with pleasure as his erection was exposed. She crawled to him, the wiggle of scarlet rump and breasts beneath that scant covering taking further toll of a man already beside himself with lust.

Alice seized that formidable member, gripping it with both fists. She slid the foreskin back and opened her mouth.

'No, Ali, not this time,' he stopped her. 'I will only settle for thrusting deep into your fanny, sampling the squeeze, the heat of your sensual body, the wet of that delicious vagina.'

'Oh,' Alice gasped, the sweet sound almost inaudible.

'But first, my dear girl…' Jonathan assisted the girl in rising and put both arms about her, seeking those velvet lips. She obliged, the contact fevered, tongues meeting, dancing, probing inquisitively. Hands roamed, sought intimate places. Fingers sensed, sampled the delights of restricted erogenous flesh. Bodies ground, chest pressed to breast, groin to groin, hips gyrated, male organ besieging female mound. Minds exploded with burning desire. Enthusiasm raged, their demands unbridled, seeking that beyond physical satisfaction.

Jonathan descended, lifted that meagre covering and pounced on an exquisitely formed breast. The moment Alice long awaited had arrived. Finally her idol made unconditional love to her. She hovered in paradise, coasted on air. His frenzied oral assault on her nipple launched that familiar knot of energy.

Face pressed to that succulent orb, Jonathan licked, kissed and nibbled the fleshy protuberance, the feel of yielding breast cool and supple. A hand rose and fingers cupped the other. Finesse beyond the man he sank the tips deep, enchanted by the youthful consistency, the supple elasticity.

He placed arms about her thighs and lifted. He carried her to the desk. There he lay her before descending, kissing avidly. Giddy with animal compulsion Alice clutched at those auburn locks, her back arched, torso thrust up, legs dangling.

Jonathan laboured lower, lips treating the flat of her belly, expert fingers absorbed with erect nipples, stroking and inciting, triggering their erotic connection to the girl's overwhelmed sex.

Beside herself she lurched to his oral handling of her pubic mound. Teeth bit into the soft tissue, nipping that knoll, exquisite pain flooding her genitals. She reached down and trifled with his hair, gasping her rapture, the intensity of pre-orgasmic activity acute.

Jonathan lifted a leg, cast that over a shoulder, her calf draped on his back. He leant to the thigh, lips attentive, tongue tasting, teeth nipping. A hand tended the hot buttock, delighting in the feel of it.

Alice enjoyed it all. She revelled in the explicit devotion. But she wanted, needed to participate. She yearned, was overcome by the urge to make love to him. With lithe limbs she ensnared him by the waist and drew him up, towards her waiting mouth. Hands clasping his neck she coaxed him forward, lips meeting, Alice demonstrating her delirious intoxication.

Both breathless she refused him escape, keeping him there, the embrace extreme. Finally she let him go. Emeralds met jet, love and lust combined. The gaze lingered, eyes searching, imparting dedication, misted with adoration. Then Alice used those agile legs to turn the tables – she on top, he beneath. She attended to his shirt, frantically unfastening buttons. The flaps she wrenched aside and descended on his chest. Prominent pectorals she savaged, returning the compliment. White teeth gnawed whilst nails clawed the flesh. That inflexible member jerked in response, hot against her belly.

Alice imitated his intimacy, roaming the torso until she reached that pole, the phallus ascending magnificently from the nest of pubic curls. That monument to the male libido she seized and depressed until Jonathan's torso arched to ease the discomfort. Thumbs pressed to the underside of the exposed dome she began a deliberate excitation, her fingers massaging, the susceptible organ speeding its vulnerability to the prostate.

Alice leant to it, licked the length, Jonathan revelling in the illicit provocation. The stem wetted she concentrated on its root, teeth biting without consideration. Alice worked her way along the length, alternately kissing and nibbling, the stem submitting to sexual torment.

What drove Alice she would never know; virtually chaste she summoned lechery that should have been alien to her. A madness lashed at her conscious, drove her to primeval debauchery, she responding unaware of the influence.

She fell upon that plum, the stiff column held, squeezed, her mouth treating its sensitivity. Teeth touched, began to compress. Jonathan raised a hand, hissing the desperate plea. 'No, *please*.' But she bit; uncompromising teeth sank intolerably into volatile cock.

The rigid length went into spasm, the jerks of excited penis uncontrollable. Semen spurted, gushed from the urethra, viscous saline fluid filling her mouth. Alice didn't recoil. She savoured the seed, held it in her mouth, the wilting member withdrawing. She swallowed then pursued the shadow, licking at the liquids, further exciting the flaccid organ and its owner.

'Jesus!' Jonathan exclaimed. 'And you say you're a virgin?'

Her contented face loomed over his groin, and she settled her chin on the pubic mound. 'Only because it's you, Jay. You inspire me. I lose all control. The tigress takes over. Now how long before you can give me that poke?'

Jonathan laughed and hoisted his muscular torso onto prominent elbows. He stared bemused at her. 'Remember you tried to seduce me by dancing?'

Alice nodded. 'I made a complete idiot of myself.'

'No, on the contrary, you were very good. Extremely provocative. Do it again for me. Pull your skirt down and beguile me. Don't strip this time. Just dance. Let me gaze upon you, feed my hunger.'

'To music?'

'Something stirring.'

Alice located a sensitive classical piece and placed it on the turntable. She began a rhythmic movement, her body expressing the score. Jonathan feasted on that gentle sway of nubile figure, Alice's flexibility astonishing. The exaggerated swing of hips entranced, her torso barely influenced. The clinging material of that immodest skirt accentuated the movement of flanks beneath, his excitement enhanced by the lack of underwear.

The stockings bewitched, their silken tops falling short of the skirt by some three inches. The suspenders ignited an unreasonable emotion, black lace descending alabaster thighs. Jonathan licked his lips, ardour fast returning.

Cheeks peeked suggestive from beneath the hem, creamy buttocks he'd coloured by hand. Legs lithe and athletic manoeuvred that divine body, limbs that could easily negotiate his waist and cross ankles behind. Jonathan sighed.

The exposed tummy, flat and silken, the button a mere dimple. The waist incredibly narrow, and those breasts, constantly moving behind that veil of red cloth, animating the garment, barely covered, tempting, begging the intrusion of grasping hands. Jonathan groaned.

She met his gaze, her smile seductive. Jonathan rose, unable to contain himself, Alice suddenly unsure. Wordlessly he pushed her to the wall and filled his hands, fingers groping those teasing breasts. His pole revitalised he reached down and cupped her buttocks. He lifted the girl, her legs automatically engaging his hips. He kissed her passionately. 'Now,' he uttered, 'finally Ali, we fuck.'

She felt that monster press to the gates of her sex. She reached down, holding him with one arm about the neck and parted her vaginal lips…

The telephone rang.

'Leave it, Jay,' she gasped.

It persevered.

'It might be important, Ali.'

'And there again it might not be.'

'Jenny or Katy might be in trouble.'

'They'll ring back.'

'I should?'

The ringing ceased, and Jonathan relaxed.

'See, I doubt if it was important,' she whispered in his ear.

The intrusive sound recommenced.

'Oh, for fuck's sake!' Jonathan hissed.

'Go and answer it, Jay,' she sighed resignedly. 'I'll wait.'

Semi-naked, the man rushed to the hallway and picked up the receiver. 'Howell residence,' he announced.

'Is that Mr Howell speaking?'

'Yes.'

'Sergeant Roxford, Buxton police station…'

'What's happened?' Jonathan's heart sank.

'We would like you to come to the station, sir. We have your daughter here.'

'Why? Has something happened to her?'

'Nothing injurious, sir. But we would like you present

when we interview her.'

'Why, what's she done?'

'I am not able to state that on the telephone.'

'I'll be there in a half hour.'

'Thank you, sir.'

He ran back to the lounge and feverishly began dressing.

'Who was it, Jay?' Alice asked, concerned by the tone of what she'd heard.

'The police, would you believe?' he told her, shaking his head.

'What's happened?'

'It would seem my errant daughter has been arrested.'

'You're kidding!' Alice gasped. 'What for?'

Jonathan shrugged.

'Can I come with you?'

'If you wouldn't mind; without Jenny I feel a bit lost.'

Jonathan and Alice trooped up the police station steps, both anxious – Jonathan for his daughter and his reputation, and Alice for her friend and her bottom.

Jonathan introduced himself at the desk, the sergeant offered a smile and bade them take a seat. He then made an internal phone call.

Some five minutes later another sergeant appeared, with a file tucked beneath an arm. He jabbed a thumb over a shoulder, saying, 'This way, Mr Howell.'

Both Jonathan and Alice rose, but the officer waved Alice back. 'Just Mr Howell, miss,' he said, and disappointed, Alice retook her seat.

'What's this all about?' demanded Jonathan as he followed.

'All in good time, sir,' the officer said. 'I'm sure you don't want the world to know what your daughter has been up to.'

'I'm not so sure I want to.'

He led Jonathan to an empty room, bar a desk and two

seats. Pointing at one he said, 'Please,' and took the other himself. Then, arms folded, the sergeant began. 'I'll be blunt, sir,' he said. 'Your daughter…' he opened the file and referred to the details, 'Kate Howell was arrested this afternoon along with a gentleman by the name of Harold James Wilkinson. They were participating in a lewd act in a public place.'

'A lewd act?' Jonathan echoed, utterly shocked. 'In a public place?'

The sergeant referred to the file again. 'The car park of the Bull Inn at Sparrowpit, to be precise, sir,' he confirmed. 'Apparently they'd been for a drive in the country and on their way home your daughter instructed Wilkinson to pull into the car park, where they…'

'You mean, they had sexual intercourse, in the *car park?*'

The sergeant shook his head sagely. 'Not exactly, sir. When PC Whitelaw arrived at the scene, Miss Howell was practicing fellatio on Mr Wilkinson. She was also stripped to the waist.'

'She was what?'

'Quite carried away, by all accounts,' the sergeant added, unable to suppress the glimmer of a smirk.

'What do you intend to do, sergeant?' Jonathan asked, shaking his head. 'Prosecution?'

The officer shook his head again. 'No, sir, the young lady will be cautioned, as will the gentleman.'

'Lady and gentleman, I think, are unsuitable titles, sergeant,' Jonathan pointed out wearily.

'If, however, we do find either party committing a lewd act in public again, then we *will* press charges.'

'By the time I've finished with them, Kate will not wish to sit for a month and that damned chauffeur will be fertilising the heather out on the moor,' Jonathan vowed.

'Murder might be a bit extreme, sir,' the sergeant pointed out.

'Not from where I'm sitting.'

'As a representative of the law, I have to warn you against physical assault,' the sergeant went on, 'but as a father of three teenage daughters, a punch on the nose with no witnesses and a good alibi wouldn't go amiss.'

'Can I take her home now?'

'Of course.'

A suitably chastened Kate was led from a room to meet with an exceedingly irate father. Head bowed she mumbled, 'Sorry, father.'

'Sorry?' he repeated incredulously. 'Sorry? Oh yes, Kate, you will be very sorry.'

'I've no excuse, father,' she acknowledged. 'None whatsoever.'

'And you think you can get around me with the remorseful approach?'

She shook her head. 'I guess I'm just plain bad,' she admitted.

Jonathan put an arm about her shoulder. 'No, Katy, not bad,' he comforted. 'More like misguided.'

Harry then loomed into view, and shaking with anger, Jonathan pointed a finger at him. 'You, take the Jag home and start packing.'

Deciding not to risk a thumping Harry departed hastily, Alice noting his rapid departure via the waiting room and exit. Jonathan appeared with Katy a few minutes later, and tearful, apprehensive and plain terrified Kate accepted the embrace offered, Alice hugging her tenderly.

The threesome then strolled to the Bentley, Harry having decamped.

'What are you going to do, father?' asked Kate, with a possibility in mind.

'A psychiatrist would seem in order.'

'I suppose I'm not all there.'

'It's all very well being contrite after the event, Katy. But somehow we are going to have to make you think before.'

'Jolly old bum slash, I suppose.'

'I think we need to talk first.'

'Jolly old lecture, and then the bum slash.'

'Talk because I care, Kate. See if I can't understand you. There must be a reason for your outlandish behaviour.'

Jonathan unlocked the car. He took the driving seat, the girls climbing into the back. As her father drove out of the police station car park, Katy leaned to Alice and whispered, 'I'm in the shit this time, Ali. Best get a super size tub of antiseptic. When daddy sees my arse he's going to go mental.'

'Why?' Alice asked. 'What have you been up to?'

'Harry birched me. I had a hankering to know what it felt like.'

'And?'

'You have my commiseration.'

'It hurt?'

'Who would believe that little twigs could fire your bum like that?'

'Perhaps Jay won't whack you today. He does like one to dwell on it for a while.'

'Perhaps if I own up he won't be too severe.'

'I wouldn't bank on it.'

'How did you get on?'

'It glowed, Kate. God, didn't it glow.'

'See, the right hand and it works.'

'He's just as proficient with the left.'

'And don't I know it?'

Jonathan arrived home to find Harry waiting in the study. 'I thought I told you to pack your bags and get out,' he said curtly.

'I thought we might discuss that, sir,' the chauffeur retorted uneasily.

'There's nothing to discuss.'

'I've not committed any crime as such,' the chauffeur countered. 'In fact, all I really did was follow orders.'

'You take your orders from me or my wife.'

'That's made clear now, sir. But Miss Howell is your daughter and without a directive, I felt I had to do what she asked.'

'Rubbish, Harry! Having sex with Kate is not in your terms of reference and you damn well know it. All you had to do was report her to me.'

'My word against your daughter's? I don't think I'd stand much chance, do you?'

'Words, Harry. You are a weasel. You'll say anything to save your skin.'

'And have you found fault with my work at all?'

'You wouldn't be talking to me now if I had.'

'I wonder how the labour exchange will view my sacking.'

Jonathan grabbed the chauffeur by the throat and pushed him backwards. 'Are you threatening me?' he snarled in the man's face.

'No sir, just an observation, sir. That's all.'

'Instead of doing what I pay you for, you were at it with my girl. I think the labour exchange would look upon that with detachment.'

'So, you're determined I should go?'

'What do you think?'

'I think you should give it some thought, sir.'

'And why would I do that?'

'Because, sir, servants are privy to certain knowledge. In a house such as this they see and hear things. Of course they talk about it to one another, but the fact they are paid for their loyalty as much as their work, stops the scandal from spreading further afield.'

'This is beginning to sound like blackmail to me,' Jonathan observed, and Harry smiled, a sly twist to the lips.

'No sir, not blackmail,' he said. 'More a case of indiscretions catching up with one. A bit like mine catching up with me.'

'So Harry, what do you know?' Jonathan asked. 'What intimacy do you think you have uncovered that might save your neck?'

Harry grinned malevolently. 'She's a pretty girl, that Alice. Wouldn't mind a crack at her myself?'

His temper spontaneous Jonathan landed a punch on Harry's jaw, the chauffeur knocked flying, the carpeted floor receiving him.

'Well?' challenged Jonathan, fists clenched, chest heaving. 'Are you going to defend yourself?'

'That all depends on whether I'm sacked, sir,' said Harry, propping himself up on one elbow and rubbing his chin ruefully. 'I'll be the first to admit I deserved that. And as such will accept it as due payment.'

Rage abating, Jonathan lowered his arms. 'Well, Harry, what do you think you know?'

'Your trusted servants aren't as stupid as you would hope. When you believe they are nicely tucked away, so you can carry on with a girl less than half your age, you're sometimes wrong. Mind you, none would dream of saying anything out of turn, provided they are treated well.'

'If I find out anyone has been talking out of turn, Harry,' Jonathan warned, 'or spreading malicious gossip, I will not only sack them, I will prosecute through the courts. Do you understand me?'

'Of course, sir, I just hope Mrs Howell will understand, too.'

'My wife trusts me implicitly,' Jonathan stated.

'Of course she does. And you want it to stay that way, don't you sir?'

'Harry, you are a piece of shit. A ball of slime.' Jonathan opened a drawer and took out a pair of garden secateurs. 'You keep your job. You stay away from my daughter.

You stay away from Alice. You mind that mouth in front of my wife. If you fail in your duties I will sack you. If I find you making eyes at either of those girls I will cut your balls off with these.' He held up the snippers. 'Do you find your knew terms of reference acceptable?'

The chauffeur rose from the floor. 'Almost sir,' he said, straightening his clothes. 'But the pay isn't all it could be…'

'Don't push your luck, man,' warned Jonathan.

Harry dusted his uniform, placed a handkerchief to a bloody lip and chose a tactical retreat.

'I suppose you're happy now?' Jonathan toyed with a fountain pen, drawing doodles on a blotter.

'No,' whined Kate. 'I didn't mean to get caught. I mean…'

'I know exactly what you mean, Kate. You provided the chauffeur, a family servant, with oral sex in a public car park. Two fingers to authority, to commonsense, and to your parents. Now you have a file in the local police station. Tongues will wag. Fingers will be pointed.

'"There goes that slag Kate Howell, she's good for a freebie". Where's it going to end, Kate? When you've experienced every male organ within a fifty mile radius?'

'I know you're upset, father, and you've good reason to be, but there's something in me that makes me take risks. I thrive on the excitement. I feel alive when I'm doing something rash. I don't mean any harm by it. I just don't want to end up a boring housewife whose never done anything exciting.'

'Did you order Harry to that car park?'

'Is that what he said?'

Jonathan nodded.

'Well I guess I did then. Sacked him, have you?'

'No. We have an understanding. So don't try to entice him.'

'He knows about you and Ali, then?'

The man stared long and hard at his daughter. 'There is nothing between me and Alice.'

'If you say so. So, are you going to cane me?'

'Will it do any good?'

She shrugged. 'Does it ever?'

'I'll tell you what, Katy,' he said. 'You have until the weekend to write me an essay, explaining your actions and the reasons for them. If you present your case well and persuade me, I won't discipline you. I despise beating you. I suffer for days afterwards. I love you, Kate. You are my daughter. I don't see why I should be made to feel that way, why I should hurt for your misdeeds.

'Now, you will recall that I spent many weeks away from home when I built this business up. You will remember who kept you in line then.'

'Harris,' she acknowledged. 'But I was younger then. I'm a grown woman now.'

'That is a matter of opinion. If you fail to impress, Kate, I shall ask Harris to resume that roll.'

Kate felt the flush rise. 'You can't, father,' she pleaded. 'He's got to be sixty if he's a day. You can't let him punish me, not on my?'

'You know how to avoid that. And yes, he will cane you on your bare bottom.'

She studied her feet, bottom lip protruding. 'He's worse than you,' she sulked. 'He's a mean sod. If I promise to?'

'No promises, Kate. You write me that essay. Put your heart and soul into it. Then maybe, just maybe, I'll be able to understand you.'

'Will you be there when – if – Harris punishes me?'

'That would defeat the object, wouldn't it? No, I shall leave him precise instructions.'

'I'm old enough to leave home, father,' she pointed out. 'I don't have to put up with this.'

53

'I wouldn't want you to do that.' He spread his hands. 'But if you decide to… you see, Katy, I can't have a delinquent living under my roof. One that does exactly what she wants without concern for other family feelings. You live here – you accept the conditions. You leave – well, you can choose your own path.'

'And you wouldn't keep me?'

'You choose that lonely path, you travel it alone.'

She stood up. 'I'll write your bloody essay, and I suppose I'll be taking that thrashing from Harris, because I *will* have a sex life. Whether you like it or not.'

'I have no objection to the sex, Kate. It is where and whom you choose to explore with you.'

'So if I get myself a decent young man and cavort in my own bed, you won't object?'

'No. I won't like it, but I will have to accept it, much as you have to accept my conditions of living here, and inheriting the family fortune.'

'Don't dangle that carrot under my nose. I could be an old woman before I inherit that.'

'That isn't my intention, Kate.'

'No?'

'If by the age of twenty-one you can demonstrate a certain responsible attitude to life, I will offer you a piece of the business, and a certain amount of capital to operate that.'

Thunderstruck, she asked, 'What part, father?'

'If you're up to it, the magazine side,' he told her. 'Which will leave me free to run the fiction.'

'You mean I will get to compile all those juicy photographs?' she asked.

'A free rein, Kate,' he told her. 'I believe you have the attributes, although raw and unsophisticated. It is up to you to demonstrate a creditable attitude.'

He sighed. 'That is why I have been so adamant about you toeing the line. I can't and won't hand part of my business to a questionable…'

'Tramp,' Katy finished for him.

'Exactly.'

'I'll do my best, father.'

'You can start by convincing me Harris shouldn't discipline you. All the reasons are in your head. All you have to do is prepare a persuasive paper.'

'And I have until Saturday?'

'Let us say Saturday, midday. Alice is off to see Barker then. Your mother will be out shopping. And if you fail, I shall go for a round of golf and leave Harris to it.'

'I'll fail,' she said ruefully. 'I always do.'

'Don't even think that way. You're bright, intelligent, capable. You merely lack application. You won't succeed in life without application.'

Kate dumped her bottom on Alice's bed, her expression petulant.

'What did dear daddy have to say then, Kate?' Alice asked. 'By the way you deposited your backside on my mattress he obviously refrained from physical chastisement.'

'I've got to write an essay by Saturday lunchtime, explaining why I ended up in that car park gobbling Harry,' Kate disclosed.

'Why so pissed off, then? Surely that's better than a whacking.'

'I get that on Saturday afternoon.'

'Oh, so the essay is an added punishment?'

'In a way. Daddy says that if I explain myself well he won't have me caned.'

Alice picked up on the phrase immediately. 'Have you caned?'

'By Harris.'

'The butler? You're kidding. Why?'

'He says it's because he hates doing it himself, 'cos he

55

loves his little Katy so much. But I reckon he knows I'll hate that even more than him doing it.'

'What's so awful about Harris? He seems such a dutiful man to me.'

'Dutiful is the word. He used to punish me when daddy spent long weeks away from home. Mother's nerves were bad then; they aren't too good now, come to that.' For the first time in Alice's eyes Kate looked desperately lost. 'Harris was brought up in an era when the rod was used liberally on the servants. As a young man he received many a devout thrashing. As a senior servant he used that bad experience to brutal effect. He firmly believes in corporal punishment, Ali. He whips with a bloodthirsty zeal.'

'So does Jay.'

'Father won't cane beyond a certain limit. Harris will. Besides that, he's old and reeks of pipe tobacco. There's a cold side to him that chills to the marrow. Ali, I'm petrified.'

'You know the answer, Kate; write that piece,' Alice advised. 'Write it with the same passion you make love with. Give Jay what he wants. Tell him you will never err again and why.'

'When, though?'

'What do you mean – when? You've got all week.'

'No, I haven't. I've got a full diary.'

'What's more important, Kate? Your social life or your backside?'

The girl grinned. 'It's only fifteen minutes of pain against a week of absolute boredom.'

'You're not even going to try?'

'Could you write it for me, Ali? You're the same as me. You could do me a terrific favour. You know, like the one I did for you.'

'What favour?'

'Enrolling at *Heptonstall*,' Kate pointed out. 'Getting

you away from Richard.'

'He'll know if I write it, Jay's not daft. And what if he asks you questions? You'll get it worse, Kate.'

'I'll take that risk. Will you do it, Ali?'

'What's so important anyway?'

'I've got a date with a gorgeous hunk,' Kate explained. 'He's twenty-three. He's tall, muscular and blond. He's got a sports car and is the son of some earl or something. Who knows, Ali, if things go right I might not have to face Harris anyway.'

'He'll wham-bam-thank-you-ma'am and you'll never see him again,' Alice said doubtfully. 'How did you meet him anyway?'

'He was at the party. You wouldn't have noticed him. You had your eyes glued to Giulio.'

'So when are you going out with him?'

'Tonight.'

'That still leaves you the rest of the week.'

'He's taking me to Blackpool tomorrow.'

Alice peered at her friend suspiciously. 'Does he know that?'

'Not yet.'

'Okay, what about Wednesday, Thursday and Friday?' Alice asked.

Katy shrugged. 'Who knows?'

'Okay, Kate,' Alice conceded with a sigh, 'even if you intend to leave me on my own all week, I'll write your essay.'

'At least you'll have plenty of time to do it.'

'You cheeky cow!' Alice squealed, grinning and picking up her pillow in a mock assault on her friend. 'But if you're going out with this Adonis,' she went on, lowering the pillow again, 'what's he going to say when he eventually comes across your birch marks?'

'I'll say I have a vindictive and nasty father. Who knows, he might whisk me off to paradise to take me away from the wicked pater.'

'Don't bank on it. He might see you as a spoilt brat.'

'Me?' Kate gasped with exaggerated incredulity. 'Spoilt? A brat? Whatever gives you that idea, Ali?'

'Me doing your essay?'

Chapter Four

With little else to occupy her, Alice jotted down some notes. She enjoyed writing and viewed the essay as a challenge. Kate busied herself in the bathroom, and hours too early she threw all her efforts into preparation, instead of attempting to save her hide.

Jenny returned and Jonathan went out, such was the way of the Howells. Alice hadn't assessed Jenny as the overwrought type, which demonstrated to her how poor a judge of character she was.

A knock on the bedroom door distracted her from her creative thoughts. 'Yes?' she called out, thinking it must be Odette, the maid. But the door opened and Jennifer breezed in, as Alice casually laid a blotter over her work to hide it.

'Homework?' enquired the woman.

'Sort of,' Alice said vaguely. 'How did it go at the doctors, Jenny?' she asked, changing the subject.

'Fine, nothing to worry about.'

'Oh, good. Jay – sorry, Jonathan – has gone out, hasn't he?'

'You can call him Jay, I don't mind. Really.' Jenny lifted the blotter. 'So what are you writing?' she asked.

Alice's mind reeled. 'It's… um… just notes at the moment, Jenny.'

'Why I like the cane,' the woman read from the pad. 'Do you, Ali? It's an odd inclination, isn't it?' She absently massaged a buttock.

'It's hypothetical,' Alice explained. 'I thought it would be a challenge to write something like that. You know, try and put yourself in someone else's shoes.'

'And there are people who are disposed to being beaten?'

'So I understand.'

'You've been reading Jonathan's magazines, haven't you?' Alice nodded, and Jenny sat, her intention to stay and chat quite obvious. 'Richard thrashed you, didn't he?' Alice nodded again. 'Hurt, did it?'

'They were awful experiences.'

'They? He beat you more than once?'

'Yes, while I was living with him he strapped and caned me on several occasions. And he gave me the slipper.'

'And of course I chastised you.'

'Yes, Jenny,' Alice said quietly.

'Was any of that less than painful?'

She shook her head. 'No.'

'So tell me, Ali, how can you possibly write about something you have no comprehension of?'

'That's the challenge.'

Jenny smiled and picked up the notes. 'Why I sucked Harry's cock.' She raised an eyebrow.

'I…'

'Read about it?'

'Yes.'

'Would you? Suck a man's penis, I mean?'

'I don't think so.'

'A challenge?'

'Yes.'

'You are still a virgin, aren't you? Apart from that business with Giulio.'

'Yes.'

'I think to write about something like this, you'd have to have some experience of sex, at least. I chastised you for cavorting with Katy. There were, I believe, sexual

60

undertones. Lesbian undertones. Are you a lesbian, Alice?'

'No,' Alice said indignantly. 'I'm interested in men.'

'So Kate licking your breasts revolted you, did it?'

'No,' she whispered. 'I love Kate. I'd let her do anything.'

'Anything?'

'No, I mean larking about. Not sex.'

'A woman can be a lot more attentive than a man, Ali. After all, she knows what another woman likes. A man tends to think of only one thing…'

'His penis.'

'Exactly. A woman desires so much more. She wants to be pandered to, cosseted. She desires to be wooed. She likes foreplay. Do you like foreplay, Alice?'

'I'm a virgin, remember?'

'You have fantasies, though,' the woman pressed. 'You explore on hot, sticky nights, don't you?'

Alice blushed.

'I'm trying to help you with your essay, Ali. Trying to make you think a bit.'

'I… um…' a knock on the door interrupted the bumbling reply.

'Yes?' Jenny barked, obviously ruffled, and Harris appeared.

'I'm ever so sorry to trouble you, madam,' he said piously, 'but I would like to have a word in private.' Alice noted the inveterate snobbery in the man's tone.

'Yes, of course,' Jenny said impatiently, following him out of the room and pulling the door to.

Alice strained to listen. 'It's Odette, madam,' she heard him say in hushed tones. 'I've caught her in the act of stealing.'

Jenny made light of the situation. 'Not the cream puffs again, Harris?'

'No, madam, some of your jewellery, as it happens.'

'Are you sure, Harris? She wasn't just borrowing, was

61

she?'

'No, madam, I extricated a confession,' he told his mistress with evident pride.

'Call the police, then,' Jenny instructed.

'Yes, but before I do, madam, I feel I should relay the explanation for her criminal activities.'

'It won't take all night, will it?'

'Of course not, madam. It would seem she fell in with a bad lot, and got herself in debt with them. They put her up to it, madam. They blackmailed her.'

'Stupid girl,' Jenny snorted.

'There is an alternative to the police, madam,' Harris went on. 'She is generally a bright and willing girl, and she has promised she will never steal again. I believe her; she is basically very naïve and easily led.'

'Get to the point, Harris.'

'She is willing to accept befitting punishment for her misdemeanour,' he explained. 'I personally think it will be effective.'

'So what do you suggest, Harris? We cut her hand off?'

'No, madam, of course not.' Harris retained no sense of humour. 'I speak of corporal punishment.'

'By your hand?'

'If madam wishes.'

'And does poor Odette know what she's letting herself in for?'

'She accepts it preferable to the police and a criminal record, madam.'

'Fine, well, it's okay with me. But Jonathan is out at the moment, so if you want to seek his approval then it will have to wait.'

'I spoke with the master before he left,' Harris disclosed. 'He said to consult you, madam.'

'Fine. Proceed. Though if it happens again she will face the police, make that plain.'

'I have, madam.'

'Very well… is that all, Harris?'

'No, there is one other matter, madam.'

'Yes?'

'I believe you should witness the punishment.'

'Why?'

'So there can be no accusation of misconduct.'

'Where's Mrs Hardcastle?'

'Out shopping.'

'Then I'll be down in five minutes.'

The matter concluded, Harris's footsteps faded and Jenny slipped back into Alice's room. 'Did you hear any of that?' she asked.

'Some, Jenny,' the girl admitted.

'Well, come on then. You can write something from genuine experience. I think you'll forget all about indulgence in the cane once you see Harris in action.'

Alice didn't object; a lurid fascination gripped her. An opportunity had been afforded to witness what Katy would inevitably end up receiving.

They went down to a basement. Alice tried to adjudge where Jay's rooms lay in direction, but disorientated, couldn't ascertain that.

Odette waited with Harris in the servant's restroom, and on seeing Jennifer she burst into tears. 'I'm so sorry, madam,' she cried. 'I promise I'll never steal again. Please forgive me.'

Jenny took the girl by the shoulders and stared into those large, blue, watery eyes. 'Are you sure about this, Odette?' she asked. 'It's going to hurt you.'

The girl nodded. 'I deserve it. And thank you for not having me arrested, madam.'

The jewellery in question lay on a table: three pairs of gold earrings, a signet ring with sapphire insert, and an imitation pearl necklace. Jenny scrutinised the pieces. 'You wouldn't have got much for them, Odette,' she said. 'It's basically junk.'

'Oh, madam, I didn't want to take anything valuable.'

Jenny frowned. 'Oh, Odette, you'll never make a master criminal, will you? What was the point if you didn't want to take anything valuable?'

'I thought you wouldn't miss them. I didn't want to upset you. I like you very much, ma'am.'

'Ah well,' Jenny sighed, 'let's get it done, Harris.'

Odette, a blonde girl of medium height, faced the butler, anticipating his command. Slim, but with a full figure, she wore the uniform of her trade; black knee length dress with white bib and apron, the sleeves embroidered with lace.

'Lift your skirts and bend over, Odette,' Harris instructed, calmly observing the fumbling as the terrified girl attempted to control her hands. Exasperated, tolerance not his virtue, he growled, 'Just bend over!'

He took the hem of the skirt between fingers and thumbs, handling it with care and neatly folding it over her lower back. He then practiced the same regard for the petticoat.

Alice, happy that she stood as an onlooker, viewed the uncovered bottom and legs with a disconcerting interest. Fine pink cotton panties, the 'V' depressing full buttocks before passing out of sight via the tight gap between her slim thighs, the flimsy material engaging a fine lace border and waistband.

Odette wore black stockings, suspenders running beneath the panties to facilitate easy removal. Her attire was very feminine indeed.

Harris cautiously delved the waist and drew the panties down over smooth, pale buttocks; a bottom that Alice guessed correctly had never experienced the wrath of corporal punishment.

Odette didn't complain, perhaps the ritual had been explained to her, but Alice could clearly hear the rapid breathing, a clear sign of the maid's mental turmoil. Two urges assailed Alice – one to turn and walk away, uncertain she wished to witness the barbarity, but the second kept her gaze fixed on that rotund posterior, curious to see the punishment inflicted, and sexually aroused by the prospect.

Harris, seemingly content with the offering, selected a broad leather strap from a table, and then examined the implement before taking up position to Odette's left. 'I am going to strap you first,' he informed the hapless girl. 'It is a kindness, in a fashion. The leather, although it bites, will encourage a general warming of your posterior. That in turn will reduce the bruising normally associated with the cane.'

A kindness? thought Alice. It was a kindness to have your backside battered with one of those? Who was he trying to kid?

'Now, legs together. Straight please. Touch those toes.'

Alice waited with bated breath. Jenny relaxed, arms folded. Harris concentrated on those tremulous cheeks. Odette screwed her face fretfully.

Harris filled his lungs. His arm rose high, hovered a second and then plummeted. The heavy leather struck vulnerable flesh, a volatile slap. The cheeks were violently motivated, her bottom stamped with the Harris brand. Silence reigned for an instant before being shattered by the girl's piercing squeal. Harris waited for the detonation to subside.

As the arm ascended again Odette's evident horror numbed Alice. Hands clearly longed to tend the hurt. Fingers pointlessly clawed thin air. The poor girl seemed to have a limited threshold of pain.

With a face of stone, his intention to decimate, Harris delivered an impressionable second helping, the crack so loud Alice winced. Odette staggered forward, hands held out in case she fell, then bravely she retook her place, her pretty countenance twisted in agony.

Harris, emotionless, levied another, broad leather slammed into stinging haunches. The maid squealed, two bands of deepening red traversing her hindquarters, bridging the cleft and firing flesh to the far hip.

The butler swung another vigorous stroke, the slap resounding, that brutal implement devastating. Odette reared, fingers clutching at the hurt, tears streaming, a stuttering groan expressing her suffering.

'Bend, Odette,' Harris ordered, his tone cold, intent, calculated, and with no option and no excuse for dispute, the girl reached for her toes. The muted sound of the hellish leather's approach caused a hesitation, then Odette began to rise as the scourge savaged her backside, and for the first time Alice noticed annoyance on Harris's face. Lips tight he leant and shoved the girl down, his hand on her shoulders. Then the strap rose and fell three times in rapid succession, the upper reaches of her taut bottom reeling to the assault.

The man stepped back to pursue the punishment, Odette whimpering, hands yearning to tend the fire. 'If you think that disagreeable, young lady,' he warned, 'then you are in for a shock when I cane you.'

Seven, observed Alice. How many did the old bugger intend to give the poor cow?

Odette's bottom bearing the painful fruits of the deadly strap, seven bands of heated flesh, Harris chose a path of unblemished cheeks. The leather hit, pulverised, and fell away. Odette rocked and sobbed.

The martinet ran a hand over those traumatised flanks, seemingly dusting, flicking here and there. Decision made, he straightened and landed another dynamic lash, the lowest and meatiest portion briefly flattened. The girl sang the song of torment and a prolonged yelp rent the air.

Alice cast a furtive eye at Jenny. The woman appeared unruffled. She showed no outward sign of either dismay or satisfaction. What was, wondered Alice, her attitude?

Another awful smack snapped her from those deliberations, the maid beside herself with anguish. Her bottom almost glowed, the cheeks spurred to the deepest crimson.

Again Harris inspected, his hand feeling the heated spheres. 'Two more, Odette,' he ruled, and they assaulted the assailed, beaten flesh trounced, the girl squealing to both explosions.

Harris replaced the strap with a cane, and turned to see Odette rubbing the damage. 'I didn't say you could stand, girl,' he snapped. 'I made it quite clear that you remain bending until the punishment is complete.'

Face tearstained she apologised profusely. 'I'm sorry, sir, I forgot,' she sobbed. 'I didn't mean to disobey you. I'm really sorry, sir.' The girl immediately bent forward.

Harris eyed her, deep in thought. 'My instructions were specific, Odette,' he informed her. 'You do not rise or touch your posterior until punishment is complete. It is not, and you were well aware of that.'

'I'm sorry, sir,' the girl iterated.

'That's not good enough. Perhaps I should have tied you down. You portray contrition, but your reluctance to obedience leaves me in doubt. You have no respect, girl. No deference.'

Jenny added her unwanted opinion. 'She forgot, Harris.'

'I'm sorry, madam, but we have only the word of a thief. What shall we expect in the future? "I forgot to make the beds"? "I forgot to polish the silver"? No, madam, there is no excuse. The girl was told and she disobeyed. She will not have the opportunity to do so again.'

Jennifer glanced at her watch. 'Well whatever, Harris, just get on with it.'

The man left the room, returning some minutes later cradling a wooden construction.

'What's that?' asked Jenny.

'This, madam, is a restraint not used for some years.' He placed the rectangular box by Odette's feet. 'It has apertures for the wrists and ankles, madam, and keeps the delinquent in the bending position.'

Jenny smiled. 'How quaint.'

'Now, Odette,' the butler went on, 'as an added punishment for your lapse, you can take a lesson in humility. Remove your uniform and undergarments.'

Astonished, thunderstruck, she questioned his right. 'You mean naked?'

Harris nodded.

'But you can't!' She faced Jenny. 'He can't make me, can he? Isn't it bad enough I have to bare my bottom, to be strapped and caned? Now he wants me to strip completely. Why, for heaven's sake?'

'You address him as Mr Harris or sir,' corrected Jenny, 'not "he". And I believe Mr Harris has explained himself. I am here as an observer. The deal was cut between you and your superior. It is his decision to make, not mine.'

'Do as I say, Odette, or I shall recommend you be sacked on the spot.' Harris waited.

Alice licked dry lips, the excitement in her belly undeniable. What the hell was it that stirred her so?

Her bottom lip trembling, shame heaped upon her, Odette unfastened the apron bib and then the half-dozen buttons of the dress bodice. She slid it from naked shoulders and urged it over sore buttocks, and snivelling, tears rolling in self-indulgence, she reached behind and loosened her bra. Then with one final protest she argued, 'This isn't fair!'

'Remove it, Odette.' Harris flexed the cane, the bow intimidating, the rod neither whippy nor rigid.

She let the garment fall. Arms and hands moved uncertainly, her only wish to cover herself; the outcome a squeezing of full and shapely breasts. 'Do you want me to take off my stockings and suspenders as well?' she asked.

Harris shook his head sombrely, clearly relishing the young maid as she was. He knelt to release the ankle stocks, pulling the board free, then motioned for the wretched girl to fill the requisite semicircles. Odette shuffled forward, standing on the lower board, her weight ensuring stability, and Harris closed and locked the sister plank, trapping her legs.

'Bend forward,' he ushered, and Odette doubled, inserting her wrists in the forward apertures. Harris snapped them shut and threw the clips, then struggled to a standing position, face flushed with effort.

Odette squirmed, the position untenable. Her knees gave to the pressure, bowing. Her bottom hovered, scarlet, so vulnerable. Harris, in no mood for anything less than perfection, struck her buttocks with his rod, the swish and whack emphatic. 'Straighten those legs, girl!' he barked.

'Y-yes, sir,' she stammered, her knees locked, her legs trembling. Her back ached and her body shook with fear. She suffered total humiliation, naked and unable to cover anything. Her breasts hung for all to see. Her ravaged bottom thrust out, awaiting Harris's retribution. The strap had proved dreadful, the cane, he promised, would be worse. How could she endure it?

Alice experienced a pang of envy. The bizarre piece of furniture aroused her. She dwelt on Jay whipping her, held in such a fashion. She would be so helpless, locked in it. Completely defenceless – that appealed to her. But Harris flogging her didn't. For Odette she retained the greatest sympathy.

'How much is the jewellery worth, madam?' enquired Harris.

Jenny shrugged. 'I haven't got a clue, Harris. Why?'

'Perhaps you know the insurance value?'

'Not really. Like I said, it isn't very valuable.'

'Would twenty pounds suffice, madam?'

'I don't know,' the woman pondered. 'Thirty is more like it.' She didn't realise, but that was what she had condemned the maid to.

'A pound a stroke, Odette,' the elderly butler decreed. 'Fair, wouldn't you say?'

'Y-yes,' she answered, but the sentence caused her to near faint.

'Keep your legs straight at all times, Odette,' he ordered. 'Should you bend at the knee I shall remind you with a stroke of the cane. That stroke, however, will not be part of your punishment.'

'I understand, sir,' she whispered humbly.

Harris wiped his hands on a handkerchief, his beady gaze not straying from the alluring target, her neat bottom framed by her stockings and suspenders. The rattan he bent and twisted whilst priming his resolution and inclination. Short and squat, he harboured physical strength along with a speed normally denied a man of his age.

He abruptly brought the rod up, and taking a step forward as it hurtled towards its objective emphasised the impact. It thumped expertly mid-buttock, cutting deep into her tender bottom, the last six inches wrapping and inflicting torture before springing madly. For a split second the maid didn't comprehend the hell that visited her. Then she yanked desperately on captive fists, the knuckles white, and with knees bent her stricken bottom dipped. She wiggled it as if trying to cool the fire, a guttural moan informing all on how much it hurt.

Alice had only witnessed Kate being punished, once by her own hand and once by Jenny's horsewhip. Odette's flogging was eminently worse, though. Harris practiced corporal punishment in the truest sense. No wonder Katy quailed at the prospect.

The cane flashed, denying the eye. The cut of air acute it struck within a quarter inch of its predecessor, those fired cheeks shuddering, another livid stripe left to mature and burgeon.

Harris retreated, readying himself for the third. Each

70

stroke would be acutely administered. Each lash would reap a similar toll of precious bottom. The next whipped with equal ferocity, a narrow strip of flesh scalded, the murderous fire penetrating deep, spreading and gripping like a red-hot limpet. Her mind defeated, Odette tumbled in a cauldron of perdition. She could only tolerate, there would be no mercy, but how she would survive proved beyond Alice's thinking.

Welts began to thrust from those lambasted buttocks, providing Odette's tormentor with evidence of his justice. The captive rear wandered from side to side, Odette's only physical means of demonstrating her ordeal. Four whipped violently, that rotund end stilled, another impression etched in carmine, a reminder for days to come.

Odette sucked air, a rasping inhalation. A growl burst from her throat, forced through clenched teeth. That in turn transformed, a scream renting the quiet.

Harris replied with the fifth discharge, tipping the maid into purgatory.

'I don't think she can manage thirty,' whispered Alice, her comprehension gained from experience.

'That's Odette's problem, Ali,' replied Jenny. 'Firstly she shouldn't steal, especially from her employers. And secondly she shouldn't enter into an arrangement she has not the grit to undergo.'

'You don't feel sorry for her?'

'To be painfully honest, Ali, I'm quite enjoying seeing her striped,' the woman confessed.

Although Alice had to admit she drew a certain satisfaction from the flogging too, she pressed Jenny for her reasons, curious about the woman's bias. 'Can I ask why?'

'What's this, for your essay?'

'And because I'm interested.'

'Understand, it has nothing to do with seeing the wretch

71

tormented.' They blinked in unison as six reaped an intolerable harvest. 'No, to be honest it is totally sexual. Putting the way I react into words though, is not easy.'

Seven ripped into lower flesh, the quiver considerable.

'It's the swish of that cane,' the woman tried to explain, her voice a mere whisper. 'The delectable slap of rod on naked bottom, the ripple of Odette's cheeks. It's a man, if you can call Harris that, dominating a female who has no alternative but to receive. It's Odette being exposed, her femininity on display. She does have a lovely body, doesn't she?'

'Yes she does, Jenny,' Alice agreed without thinking. 'She makes me quite envious.'

'Why, Ali? You have a gorgeous figure as well.'

Eight produced a shrill cry of protest.

'You think so?'

'I know so. You'll spend the rest of your days refusing offers.'

'Just refusing?'

Jenny winked. 'Not all of them, I hope. Seeing Odette incarcerated so, what a provocative position.'

'It is, yes,' Alice concurred wistfully.

Nine located the crease between burning rump and stockinged thighs.

'And what a colourful, striped bottom it is.'

'You say watching that is sexual?' Alice asked, tentative. 'Was that the case when you flogged me?'

Jenny shrugged. 'I think "flogged" is an inaccurate description. Punished, is more apt.'

'It didn't do anything for you?'

'I was too angry.'

'That intimates that it might.'

The solid smack of the tenth filled the room, as did Odette's pitiful wail.

Jenny thought for a moment. 'Yes, I suppose it does.'

'Would you prefer to see, say Harry, in that contraption?

You know, a man instead of a woman?'

'This is beginning to sound like the third degree, Alice. Would you be trying to delve my sexuality, by any chance?'

'I'm sorry,' Alice apologised, 'I didn't mean to pry. It's just that…'

'You need help with your essay?'

'Yes.'

'Men mostly have miserable behinds - all square and skinny. Not all, mind you. Women, on the other hand, tend toward full, well-rounded behinds. So, I suppose a woman's is more engaging. Having said that, I understand that our dear chauffeur has what one might term as an admirable specimen. With legs apart that might prove a cheering exposure.' Jenny laughed, a faint blush rising.

An illicit urge gripped Alice. What would it feel like to be caned by Jenny? She recalled her meeting with Stagnant in the school gymnasium; that proved very disagreeable. But there again, that was cold-blooded punishment. How could she possibly put Jenny to the test? And if she did persuade her by indirect means, how would she explain the stripes that currently occupied her own posterior?

Eleven left its calling card on upper slopes, Odette having long surpassed her level of tolerance.

A round dozen executed, Odette's bottom began to resemble a sheet of corrugated iron. The welts rose in proliferation, marking her from left buttock to right hip. The girl would not care to sit for some time, and sleep would be best taken facedown. Thirteen danced madly.

'I've heard there are people who like to be caned for sexual reasons.' Alice sought a reaction, preferably favourable.

'And there are those that take satisfaction from providing such a service.'

'You don't think either perverted, then?'

'No, Ali, it takes all sorts. There are all kinds of kinks.

73

Whatever turns one on, as they say.'

Fourteen added to the miserable state of one repentant maid.

Alice smouldered with illicit desire. She didn't want to lose the opportunity to press; approached another day such questioning could prove arduous. 'So, if someone asked you to cane them in that apparatus,' she nodded at Odette's stocks. 'You wouldn't think them mad?'

Jenny recognised the youthful uncertainty, the attempted initiative. She suspected Alice held a bias in that direction, and looked at Alice for the first time since the flirtation began. Fifteen resounded as she replied. 'No, not at all, Ali, it would be their backside.'

Relieved Jenny didn't condemn the concept, Alice smiled, unaware of the woman's own recent discovery.

Sixteen ripped into upper thighs. Odette sobbed, promising herself she would never steal anything ever again.

Both felt the need to delve a little deeper. 'So Ali, what does Odette's punishment do for you?' Eyes bore into the girl's soul. 'Truthful, now; *I've* been frank.'

Alice studied her shoes. Hands behind her back she shuffled awkwardly. 'I can't say I'm appalled. That would be a lie. There again, I hate to see Odette suffer so much. But I suppose truthfully, it's sort of stimulating. Terrible, isn't it?'

'It would be if Odette hadn't invited it. I'll lay odds she never steals again. So, as far as I'm concerned, I don't see why I should feel guilty. I've waived the right to have her prosecuted. She will keep her job. And the stupid girl chose to be caned. So I feel justified in taking a little satisfaction from it.'

Harris whipped her for the seventeenth time.

Alice accepted what Jenny said as gospel. 'So, what you feel is acceptable only in the case of someone deserving punishment?'

'I suppose that's how it sounds. Look, Ali, for what it's worth, and you must read between the lines here, waking up sexually is difficult. There are lots of erroneous feelings. One never knows if one is taking the right path. You found that out with Giulio. Confusion reigns. Making an approach is often fraught with fears of rejection, or worse – vilification. You must resolve your inclinations. Accept yourself for what you are and decide on that path. Regardless of others' prejudices you should try to be yourself.'

Eighteen raped the ravaged. Odette howled.

'Once one's burnt their bridges, there's no going back.'

'And unless one forges new ones there's no going forward.'

Jenny's constant gaze unsettled Alice, and the girl took a deep breath. 'Up until a few weeks ago I had never been beaten,' she disclosed. 'But I've more than made up for that since. Some of it was deplorable, sickening. Awful experiences I would never wish to undergo again. However, amidst all the fire and brimstone were flashes of ecstasy. Watching Odette is having a profound effect on me. I feel insane. I yearn to be there, receiving.'

Alice couldn't look at the woman. She kept her eyes riveted on Odette. 'It has to be sensual, Jenny. It doesn't work otherwise.'

Suspicions confirmed, the woman nodded at Odette's crucifixion. 'I take it that isn't?'

Alice shook her head. 'That would be a dip in hell.'

'I won't ask who made it sensual for you – although I have a very good idea. Wearing any stripes at the moment, are you?'

Alice bit her bottom lip and nodded.

'Oh don't worry, Ali. He never hides the fact that he loves to whip arse. If you get something out of it then fine. As long as he didn't corrupt you.'

Alice misunderstood. 'That's all that happened, Jenny.'

Nineteen punctuated the claim.

'Keep the wolf at bay. That's the golden rule. Once they've tasted the flesh they tend to lose interest.'

'You're very understanding, Jenny.'

'I can afford to be. Now tell me, why doesn't the prospect of Harris thrashing you arouse?'

Alice swallowed hard. 'He doesn't hold anything back, does he?'

The twentieth stroke cracked loudly on tight buttocks, extricating an unearthly howl.

'No, Ali, I think I can safely say he doesn't.'

'I think I'd prefer to give Harris a miss.'

'He'd probably like that.'

'What?'

'A miss – a young miss, if I'm not mistaken.'

'I don't think Odette would put her hand up, do you?'

'She's put her bum up.'

That brutalised sphere received the twenty-first stroke, Odette a sobbing wreck.

'So what's your preference, Ali? The cane? The strap? Maybe a paddling? Or perhaps you have a bias toward my horsewhip. There again, I could simply put you over my knee and spank you.'

That suggestion, the manner in which it was delivered, sparked a sensual detonation. 'I'm a complete novice, Jenny,' Alice gasped. 'I really don't understand the way I feel.'

Twenty-two cannoned in, the splat on violated buttocks harsh.

'I wouldn't try to. Just accept it as an interesting addition to those innocent urges you are no doubt experiencing.'

'I've heard you deal a mean cane.'

'So I've been told.'

'I know of a girl who likes the responsibility taken from her. That turns her on. Excess seems to arouse.'

The twenty-third stroke engraved the mark of the rod mid-thigh, and Odette nearly choked with the pain.

'Talking of excess.' Jenny nodded at the pitiful maid. 'And you'd like to try that?'

'Yes.'

'And why would someone want to beat you, Ali?'

'Richard didn't need much reason.'

'How about a wife's revenge?'

'If you like.' Alice tried to act brazen, but eye contact she found impossible.

'A vengeful wife who's discovered a young and beautiful girl seducing her husband – now that would provoke God knows what.'

Twenty-four whipped and wrapped, Odette's bottom unrecognisable. As the regular squeals died so the girl sought clemency. She couldn't take any more. Her behind throbbed, the sting continuous, the prospect of Harris's rod cutting into beaten flesh terminating her resolve. She begged. 'Mr Harris, sir.' She sniffed. 'Please, Mr Harris, I've had it. My bottom hurts so. I really can't take any... aaaaah!' Harris crushed her pleas.

'Bit of a bum deal that, wouldn't you say, Ali?'

'I don't suppose Odette finds it funny.'

'A vengeful wife might go beyond the stick.' The words cast a doubt about Jenny's intent.

'True, but it would only be playing, wouldn't it?'

Twenty-six briefly burrowed lower buttocks.

'I suppose so. How about an audience? Yes, perhaps Odette would like to watch.'

'An audience?' Alice stared, stunned. 'Odette?'

'That's only fair, Ali. You've watched *her* get it.'

And Odette did get it, number twenty-seven bouncing violently on upper thighs.

'Do you think she would understand?' Alice asked.

'She wouldn't know why. Odette would simply accept you were being punished and was required to witness it.

For your humiliation, of course.'

'Why not just ask the whole household in?'

'Whipped in front of everyone?' Jenny mused. 'What a splendid idea!'

'I'm going off the idea, Jenny.'

'I'm only trying to comprehend your inclination, Alice.'

Odette neared the end of her dire lesson in honesty. Twenty-eight striped upper reaches, a forceful downward slice, the limited flesh trounced.

Alice had mixed feelings, shame and arousal balanced equally. Jenny's attitude reassured but doubts nagged, her guilty conscience playing havoc.

The penultimate bit cruelly, the connection seemingly louder than ever. Poor Odette writhed in her limited fashion.

'Well, Ali?' the woman persisted. 'She's nearly done. Makes one mourn the end, don't you think?'

'She'll mourn *her* end, Jenny. For days to come, I suspect.'

Odette's woe pierced the quiet for the last time, and Harris withdrew. Alice scrutinised that whipped rear; making an excellent job of Kate's essay seemed like a very good idea – for Kate, that was. The welts stood proud, barely a strip of buttock flesh left unmarked. The comment by Kate about hanging one's hockey sticks on them rang true.

Harris released the girl. Cautiously she rose, wincing as she neared the vertical. With great care she sought the source of her discomfort, immediately wishing she hadn't. All concern for her naked state had been eradicated. Fingers slowly traced the mass of stripes, Odette's concern obvious by her expression.

'Well I hope you've learned your lesson,' declared Jenny, devoid of sympathy.

'Yes, madam,' said Odette, barely loud enough to be heard. 'I promise I won't ever take anything again.'

'*Steal*, is the word, Odette. You won't *steal* anything again.'

'Yes miss, I won't steal again.'

'You best get dressed then, hadn't you?'

'Not yet, madam,' Harris spoke, wiping the rod.

'No? Why's that, Harris?'

'In my day, madam, after a sound flogging one stood in the corner for half an hour, facing the wall with one's hands on one's head.'

'Excellent, I'll leave you to it, then,' the woman said, and left with Alice in tow.

The pair strolled around the perimeter of the house. 'It's not easy to admit your innermost desires, is it Alice?'

'Imagine if I had admitted that essay was me, and you found the act abhorrent,' Alice suggested. 'Living under the same roof, with you seeing me as a pervert, would be impossible.'

'If we all lived the truth, no matter what, life would be most intriguing.'

Alice laughed.

'What's funny, Ali?'

'Nothing, really. I just thought about the awful pickles lies save us from. Often it's easier to lie than to tell the truth.'

'To cover indiscretions, you mean?'

Alice recalled the seduction of Jenny's husband, failing to control her blush.

'What's the matter, Ali? Have I embarrassed you?'

'No,' Alice said hastily. 'I'm hot, that's all.'

'There are no other secrets you want to divulge while we're being honest?'

'I've taken a giant step, Jenny, I think that's enough confession for today.'

'So there are others?'

'Maybe.'

'Whenever you feel like talking, you know now I won't moralise.'

'I love being here.' Alice breathed in the fresh country air, the views of woodland and lawns stimulating. 'When mother and father died, part of me died as well. I couldn't even think about the future. It was too painful. And as for the past? It had been obliterated in a split second.

'Now though, a miracle has been performed. Perhaps the Almighty smiled on me. I have a sister, where I had no such like before. And my parents have been... not replaced, no. They've been almost resurrected in you and Jonathan. I couldn't possibly be happier, Jenny.'

She faced the woman, tears filling those emerald pools, one tipping and cascading, a track of moisture left as it meandered. 'God, I hope nothing ever happens to either of you.'

Jenny put her arms around Alice. She hugged her, stroked her hair, her head resting on a shoulder. She felt the press of bosom to her own; young, firm breasts. Guilt exploded; whatever was she contemplating? How could she seduce a surrogate daughter?

'Are these the tears of joy?' she asked as Alice sobbed.

'I miss them, Jenny,' Alice declared. 'I miss them so badly.'

'Of course you do,' the woman consoled. 'And I suspect you always will. But I expect they're watching over you. Perhaps your coming here was more an act of parental determination, rather than one from the Almighty.'

'More like an act of Katy.'

Jenny laughed softly. 'Yes, I'm afraid once my contrary daughter gets an idea in her head there is very little that will stop her. She takes after her mother.'

'I'm sorry, Jenny.'

'What for?'

'For not counting my blessings.'

Jennifer held the girl at arms' length. 'You're human,

Ali,' she said. 'A beautiful, loveable innocent. You get it out of your system. Don't bottle it up. I'm here whenever you need me.'

Alice abruptly shoved a hand in her jeans pocket. 'Oh bugger!' she cursed uncharacteristically.

'What, lost something?' Jenny asked.

'Yes, I must have dropped it down in the staff quarters.'

'Important?'

'The confession, Jenny,' Alice explained. 'I wouldn't want Harris to read it. He might get ideas.' She'd managed to extricate some notes from wayward Kate – points that would be covered in the essay. They were in Katy's handwriting, and Harris was the last person who should read them.

Jenny frowned, head to one side. 'Ali, don't tell me he configures in your fantasies!'

'No, of course he doesn't. But all the same, I'd rather he didn't see it.'

'Want help finding it?'

'Erm, no thanks,' Alice declined the offer, 'I'd best pop back and look for it.' She ran back the way they'd come, leaving Jenny to admire the sway of her neat bottom and curvaceous figure.

Alice reached the restroom breathing heavily. The door closed, she raised a fist to knock, but Odette's anguished objection stopped her. 'Isn't it enough you thrashed me, Harris?' Alice heard, noting there was no use of the word sir, or mister. 'Why do I have to be subjected to this?'

'If madam knew the depth of your larceny, Odette,' Alice heard the butler say, 'I'm sure she would not only sack you, but call in the police. Is that what you want?'

The maid's answer was barely intelligible, so Alice pressed an ear to the door.

'I'm doing you a favour, girl,' the man went on, 'a kindness. Saving you from a spell in borstal. You know what happens in borstal, don't you?'

81

'You said before.'

'Young delinquents like you receive the birch. They are strapped down on a bench and their bare backsides are subjected to several dozen strokes, carried out with the utmost severity before a number of witnesses. I've saved you from that, Odette, so I believe you owe me a favour or two.'

'But you're…'

'Sixty? An old man? Do you find me that repugnant?'

'I didn't say that.'

'I have experience, Odette, something a lad of your age would lack. I know how to please a lass. See, I don't squeeze and pummel your tits, do I? I enjoy. I pet. Close your eyes and indulge. You can imagine who you like making love to you.'

Alice knew what he did, the blackmail he affected. She longed to see, to witness the dictatorial butler in his lurid extortion. Opening the door would cause the worst embarrassment imaginable, but was there another way?

Alice tried the door to the left. It led into an enclosed storeroom. She turned her attention to one on the right, and found herself in a kitchen, but there was another exit on the far side. Barely daring to breathe she tiptoed over the tiled floor. The door led to a small office complete with desk and filing cabinet. Harris's office, she concluded. There was another portal there to the restroom, but it too was closed, so she faced the same problem as before.

On an adjoining wall hung two small black curtains. Curiously she peeped, expecting a chart or work papers pinned to a notice board, but to her absolute shock the curtains covered a small inspection window, most likely there for Harris to keep an eye on the staff.

The office in darkness, there being no other windows, she guessed the couple in the restroom would not detect her, so she peered though.

Harris stood behind the naked Odette. He had his arms

around her and his hands filled with her breasts, the salacious expression lighting his bulldog face sickening.

'You won't ever tell madam, will you?' Odette either sought confirmation or wished to occupy her mind with anything other than the liberties Harris took with her.

'As long as you do as I say, my dear girl, you will have nothing to worry about,' he slavered.

'That rule book you gave me, are you serious about the punishments in it?' she ventured.

'Of course, I wouldn't have written them if I wasn't.'

Rule book? Alice pulled a face.

'And I have to agree to them?'

The butler continued to paw her, not seeming to tire of those generous breasts. 'If you wish to remain in employment, yes.'

'Has Harry or Mrs Hardcastle got one? Or Robins the gardener? Or his son?'

'They weren't caught in the act of thieving madam's jewellery,' he said scornfully. 'You commit the crime, be prepared to pay the price.'

'I thought I had. Look at the state of my bottom. You really laid into me, Harris.'

'Toe the line and it won't happen again. Of course, you could always leave if you're not happy.' He dropped his hands to her caned buttocks. They wandered, fingers tracing the welts, the disgusting bulge in his trousers noticeable from where Alice watched in silence.

'But I've nowhere to go,' Odette whined.

'Don't fancy going back to that stepfather of yours, then?'

The girl shuddered visibly.

'No, I didn't think so,' he said smugly.

'How far are you going to go?' she asked tentatively.

'All the way, of course,' he told her patronisingly. 'When I'm good and ready.'

Alice couldn't see the girl's face, but she could imagine

her expression of abhorrence.

'You're no virgin, are you?' the butler goaded. 'Arthur saw to that, didn't he?'

'What if I refuse you?' she challenged bravely. 'Will you force yourself on me?'

'Of course not,' he sniggered, 'you misjudge me, young lady. But we'd have to have a rethink on those stolen diamonds.'

'You've got me right where you want me, haven't you?'

'I don't see it in that light. I believe firmly in you scratch my back and I'll scratch yours.' He urged her legs apart and reached between them. 'Nice lips, Odette,' he said huskily. 'So soft, but alas, so dry.'

'What do you expect?' she said, squirming uncomfortably in his mauling clutches. 'You're not exactly turning me on, you know.'

'The master does though, doesn't he?'

'I – I don't know what you mean, Harris.'

'Perhaps I should speak in the past tense, eh? Since that delightful redhead turned up he's been a bit preoccupied, hasn't he? No nooky for you, eh?' He chuckled throatily. 'Must make you a bit jealous.'

'I've never been with Mr Howell,' she claimed. 'I'm the maid and he's the master.'

'When Miss Jennifer is away, the wolf will play,' he chortled salaciously. 'I'm surprised he never spanked you. The master likes to slap a firm young bottom.'

'He's not the only one, is he?' she challenged.

'Would you care to feel the sting of my hand on those striped cheeks?'

'No…'

'Then mind your manners.'

The time appeared to have arrived, Harris having aroused himself sufficiently. He led her by an arm and pointed at the table. 'Lean over that, Odette,' he ordered. 'I'll take my pleasure from behind.'

'Are you going to wear something?' she asked nervously.

'I can't get on with those rubber things,' he stated, 'never could. Still, I expect my seed is long past nurturing babies. But don't worry, girl, I'll pull out at the last moment.'

Odette obediently lay over the tabletop, looking uncertain about what was to come, and Alice assessed the damage dealt to those inviting buttocks. The lividness had subsided somewhat, but the welts were more pronounced. Thirty-one puffy stripes smothered her globes, most of them reaching to the right hip. Harris had caned only from one side, the tails of those marks reared discoid, inflamed and mauve in colour.

Alice witnessed the lowering of trousers, the descent of shapeless underpants and the lacklustre exposure of an ageing bottom. His back to her she couldn't see the worm, nor did she really want to. Harris delved between Odette's legs, apparently guiding that worm. He thrust without consideration, his uninspiring cheeks tensed. Then began his payment for deceit. He had the girl in slow, forceful strokes, poor Odette suffering the debauchery.

Harris took his time, or maybe he needed it, the age it took him. He lunged back and forth for the best part of fifteen minutes, frequently encouraging his libido with a grope of breast or rump. Then he withdrew, his semen spurting, dripping to the floor, then his trousers pulled up he levied a hearty slap on those beaten flanks and told Odette to clean up the mess. Alice knew the girl's life would be a misery from there on; she would have to run to his sexual beck and call, the threat of exposure forever hanging over her.

Alice couldn't leave. She still had the problem of retrieving the incriminating evidence. So she stayed while Odette obeyed Harris's humiliating orders, nauseated by his leering, hoping he would soon return to work so she could complete her mission, but then the butler stooped and picked up a folded sheet of paper, and Alice groaned with dismay.

Chapter Five

Alice hesitated, and before she could collect her wits Harris disappeared into the maze of Howell Manor. If he read those notes before she could reclaim them, then poor Katy's life would be complicated beyond contemplation. The rough handwritten jottings echoed in the recesses of her fraught mind.

I gobbled Harry's prick because he's such a horny bastard. That was Kate's starter, a joke of course. *I'm of a legal age. I like sex and wish to indulge in it. I live for excitement. Spontaneous sex in a car park with a servant is thrilling. I've a right to go with whom I please. I'm not a child any more.*

There were other points Alice couldn't recall, but the killer was. *If that miserable, hardhearted old geriatric Harris is allowed to thrash me, then I might just offer him my fanny as well, out of spite.*

After what Alice had witnessed that paragraph might well give the butler ideas above his station, so whatever the cost Alice had to reclaim those notes, and as they had ended up in his trouser pocket, she would have to ask for them.

Fifteen minutes later Alice found the elderly butler sorting the outgoing mail. After addressing and sealing the envelopes he would pass them to Harry, who in turn would take them to the post box.

'Um, Harris,' she started tentatively.

The man glanced up. 'Yes, Miss Alice?'

'Did… did you by chance find a folded piece of paper in the restroom?' she ventured, trying to sound as though it wasn't overly important.

He frowned. 'Paper, miss? No miss.'

'Are you sure?' she went on. 'It must have fallen out of my pocket, while I was, erm…'

'Watching Odette's punishment?'

'Yes, um, that's right.'

'I'm sorry, miss,' he said with infuriating arrogance, 'I can't help you.'

'I must have lost it by the armchair,' she pressed, desperate to reclaim the incriminating notes. 'You know, where I was standing.'

'Perhaps Odette has it,' he suggested indifferently. 'Or perhaps she found it and threw it away.'

No Harris, Alice thought, you have it, you little turd, it's in your trouser pocket. She hovered, trying to connive another initiative. Harris smiled at her, emotion absent.

'I'll, um, speak with Odette then,' she said resignedly, trying to quickly think of another form of attack.

'You do that.' The butler returned to sealing envelopes.

Angry, frustrated, Alice left him to it. Perhaps he had thrown it away and didn't want to admit it.

Harris, however, had forgotten all about the paper. It still lay buried in his pocket. But being a chronic snoop he was now curious, and he wanted to find out what was so important.

The girl certainly possessed a magnificent bottom, he mused. One he would dearly love to take his cane to. Mentally he slowly unveiled it and imagined his rod biting deep into stretched, sensitive buttocks. The man shivered. What chance would he have?

He delved into his pocket and withdrew the all so

important scrap of paper. Carefully he unfolded it and read, failing to recognise the handwriting and placing the onus on Alice. He frowned, scowled, and then leered. 'Oh dear, oh dear, Miss Alice,' he mused. 'Maybe I will get my heart's desire, after all.'

Alice accepted the worst. Harris denied having the notes because he knew the contents. She had allowed it to fall into the wrong hands, and cursed her stupidity. She had two options as she saw it. The first was to make a first class job of the essay, the second was to try and recover those notes. Writing came naturally and she would indeed give it her best effort, but covert raids in the dead of night would be something else.

Jenny examined her cane marks. Certain she wouldn't be interrupted she lifted her skirt and slid the rear of her panties down. The reflection showed nine bluish stripes; she always marked easily. Why did she let him do it? The pain proved diabolical, and worse, she could face similar next time. Perhaps she should change her doctor.

A flicker of energy stirred in her groin. The welts intrigued her. Distinct and alien, raised on a background of pale hindquarters, they disturbed her. They should have worried, concerned her, but those intimately laid scarlet and mauve trademarks of the infamous rattan prompted an odd reaction.

Jenny traced one with the tip of a finger. The immediate soreness had dissipated, and she would be able to sit with her husband without squirming. But what would he make of the state of her bottom? Knowing her Jonathan, he would probably mount her.

Perplexed by her sexual response she covered those etched cheeks and let the skirt fall. Perhaps she might visit Alan again, after all.

Then Alice abruptly stole her thoughts. Perhaps the

masochist would cherish the marking of her lover's behind? Lover? Could she ever be that? Did she really want to be? She did find the girl highly attractive. But was she that way inclined? Was Alice?

Alan, her doctor, her lover. No, not lover; Alan treated her anxiety. She had been seeing him for years, and things had blossomed. They had kissed, intimately. One thing led to another, and certain Jonathan played around, she succumbed as a form of retribution. The pair had been having an affair for years.

Alan was persuasive. He had prescribed her suspicion of Alice and Jonathan as a form of envy. He had argued that her concern stemmed from lesbian tendencies, Alice the trigger. She couldn't contest the suggestion, for when she examined her feelings she realised that she did find the girl attractive… very attractive. Alan's recommendation was to follow her instincts and see where they led.

Often over the years he hinted at penance to relieve the anxiety. He maintained that reparation eased the burden of guilt, which in many cases was the prime cause of depression. Jenny always resisted.

Then that morning he had altered tactics. Silver-tongued, the man reminded her about her admission with regard to punishing Katy. He told her plainly that she happily dished it out but shied from receiving. He called her a snob, a self-centred brat, spoilt by years of self-indulgence. He wasn't objectionable, he simply stated his diagnosis. He made her feel so terribly remorseful that she vowed she would not cane Katy without first considering other avenues, and grudgingly consented to his prognosis – a spanking and the cane on her bare bottom.

For Jenny that was an ordeal, she was no martyr to pain, but what she didn't know was that thirty percent of Dr Johnson's female patients left that consultancy room with stripes on their backsides. She had to admit to an inner peace, though. Jenny felt relieved and subsequently mentally healthier.

Alice set herself to the task of persuasion. She had a feeling that paying Katy back for her favours could take some time. She accepted the debt, but would have bailed her out anyway.

Jennifer loomed large in her thoughts. Alice's revelation hadn't born fruit. The woman proved understanding, sympathetic, but that was all. She seemed to play with her, to intimate suspicion. To warn in a roundabout way what she would do if she discovered any foundation. The sad truth was, Alice was genuinely innocent. Not through lack of trying or Jay's reluctance, but through fate. Their affair seemed doomed.

That intimidation. Maybe Jenny used that to try and heighten arousal, but the threat delved deep into a guilty conscience. What if the woman incarcerated her in those stocks and then took revenge on her backside? Fear mixed with uncertainty, Alice's hide crawled.

Kate interrupted that desperate reasoning. She burst in, arms spread, seeking approval. 'What do you think, kid?' she beamed.

Alice examined the girl, seeing the woman. Kate wore, or had been levered into, a black suit with a low-cut crimson top. 'Your tits are hanging out,' she rebuked.

'As will his tongue.' Kate grinned, irrepressible.

'How did you get into that skirt, Kate? I don't think I've ever seen anything so tight.'

'Willpower.'

'You won't be able to sit without fear of splitting the seam.'

'I wasn't exactly banking on sitting, Ali.'

'It will take him a month of Sundays to work his way into that.'

'Are you being catty by any chance?'

'Wouldn't you? If I was going out with Mr Handsome Pound Notes and you were left here writing *my* essay.'

'I'm ever, ever, ever so grateful, Ali,' Kate gushed.

'Have you worked out how you're going to explain those birch marks on your bum?'

'He might be nice and not try it on.'

'But you aren't nice, are you? And think how disappointed you'd be if he didn't try it on. You'd be unbearable tomorrow.'

'Like you are now, Ali?'

'Sorry, Kate, things on my mind,' Alice said. 'You look great. Divine. Irresistible. Gorgeous. You'll knock him dead.'

'You apply such passion to your compliments, Ali. What the hell's the matter with you? What's on your mind.' Kate put her arms around the girl's waist and unfastened her jeans. 'Tell Aunty Kate all about it.'

'I wouldn't know where to begin.'

Kate sank a hand to the girl's pubic curls and played there. 'If you're that upset about doing my essay, then don't,' she breathed.

'And what about Harris?'

'I'll get through it.'

'You're only saying that because it's four days away.'

'Our friendship is more important than my bum.' Kate pushed further, fingertips reaching the warmth of Alice's vaginal lips.

'And I say, isn't that sweet?' Alice said, distracted and flustered by her friend's attentions. 'I couldn't possibly let you get caned now.'

A finger eased between those soft, inviting lips. Kate leaned to Alice's neck and nibbled the fragrant flesh. 'When I first met you, Ali,' she whispered in the girl's ear, 'you were so sweet, so naïve, so innocent. Now look at you. You're more like me.'

'On no, Kate, never like you,' Alice said indignantly.

'You see I care, whereas you don't give a damn about anything.'

The finger penetrated, Alice sighing but not complaining. 'Delicious, Ali,' Kate whispered huskily. 'Made for fucking. So tight… it even squeezes my finger. With your looks, your figure and this burrow, you could have whoever you please.'

Kate located a sensitive spot and Alice tensed. 'All… all you th-think about is… is sex,' the embraced girl stammered dreamily. 'I would never take… take you to the zoo. The bloody monkeys wouldn't stand a chance.'

'As long as they were well hung, eh kid?'

The day had proved a long one for Alice. Jay's attention to her bottom and the subsequent failure to gain satisfaction, along with Odette's caning and Jenny's fencing, had left her wanting. Throwing her usual caution to the wind she undid the buttons of the chequered shirt she wore, pulling the flaps aside to reveal her breasts; for a change she wore no bra. Alice said nothing as she raised her arms and placed her hands on her head.

'Oooh, Ali, an invite,' Kate enthused. 'Oh yes, please.' The hand withdrew from Alice's panties and joined its partner in embracing those naked, luscious fruits. Katy cupped and fondled, her touch subtle.

'Have you the time?' Alice breathed.

'As you have the inclination, of course.' Fingertips circled erect nipples, stroking, teasing, inciting. Alice, young and inexperienced, revelled in the obscure sensations, the intimate touching of her breasts firing her passions. She wallowed in the soothing, erotic caresses. She moaned softly, all cares lost to the sensual exploration.

Katy, sinking in her own mire of lechery, decided her man could wait. She had more pressing matters to deal with. Her hands squeezed firm breasts more tenaciously. Fingers delved the rich corpulence, the act amplifying both girls' ardour.

'Oh, Ali!' Katy hissed. 'You fucking turn me on something wicked!' She wrenched up her tight skirt and, parting her legs, pressed tight against Alice. 'Feel me, Ali. Feel my cunt. It's hot and bothered and sopping wet, because of you.'

Alice applied a hand, fingers pressed to the lustrous satin panties. Katy groaned, her own breasts pressing to her gorgeous friend, her cleavage maximised, those ample breasts thrusting.

Hips gyrating, legs trembling, Katy indulged. Alice worked her genitalia, fingers probing, the wet material restrictive. She urged Katy up, legs astride. She leant lower to the satin covered bush and exposing the abundance of curls beneath, sank her teeth into the supple flesh.

Katy held her there, begging. 'Bite me, Ali. Sink your teeth into my bush. Oh, wicked!'

With her face pressed to Katy's stomach, Alice mumbled, 'The door's not locked.'

'So?' Kate gasped. 'Daddy said it's okay in the privacy of our rooms.'

'But Jenny didn't,' Alice argued. 'Anyway, I don't fancy Odette or Harris walking in on us.'

'They'd knock. Live a little dangerously, Ali. It heightens the excitement.'

'We've both paid for that before, Kate.'

'Oh, lock the door, then,' Kate snapped, her frustration getting the better of her.

Alice moved away and fumbled with the key, her free hand holding her jeans up, when Katy launched herself, wrenched the jeans down to Alice's knees and sank her hands into the girl's thin cotton panties. 'Oooh, lovely arse!' she exclaimed, and supporting herself against the door Alice succumbed to the groping, Katy squeezing and mauling her cheeks.

'Oh marks!' she squealed excitedly. 'Tramlines!' Kate felt the stripes. 'Wow, you've had a whacking, Ali. Did it glow?'

'It glowed like a hot sun, Katy,' Alice admitted, 'and it torched my pussy, too. I've never experienced anything like it.'

'Good for you – *Heptonstall* will be a breeze,' she said, pressing even closer to the lovely girl trapped against the door.

'What about your suit, Katy?' Alice pointed out, squirming a little in her friend's hold. 'You'll crease it.'

'Trust you to worry about something like that,' Katy scoffed, but just then the skirt gave with an alarming ripping sound.

'Oh, hell!' Katy cursed, peering down over her own shoulder. 'That cost me an absolute fortune.'

'Cost you?'

'All right, cost father.'

'It's only the seam,' Alice observed, extricating herself from her friend's embrace. 'It'll only take a minute or two to repair.'

A knock on the door disturbed their exchanges. 'Yes?' called Alice.

'Is Katy in there?' Jenny enquired through the closed portal.

Kate pulled a face, and then giggled.

'Yes Jenny,' Alice confirmed, hastily pulling up her jeans and straightening her clothing, as Kate did likewise with hers. 'She's torn her skirt.'

Alice unlocked the door and opened it and Jenny strolled in. Katy moved away and sat innocently on the edge of the bed. 'Your young man is here, Katy,' her mother informed her, then looked at the skirt in question. 'A quart into a pint pot, eh?'

'I did manage to get it on,' Kate told her indignantly. 'Then it ripped.'

'I'm not surprised. You're a lovely girl, Katy, but you don't have to flaunt yourself in miniscule clothing.'

94

'I just wanted to look nice.'

'What were you intending? To creep out of the back door?'

'Why?'

'Because, Kate, you're dressed like a tart. Not the right message, is it? It looks like: come and take me you're invited. Go and change. Put something decent on. He seems a nice young man for once. Impress him with your intelligence and personality, not your body.'

Petulantly, Katy stormed out of the room.

'What was really going on, Ali?' Jenny asked when they were alone.

'She ripped her skirt, Jenny. I was going to see if I could fix it.'

'What with? Goodwill?'

'Ah.' Alice couldn't say with a needle and thread; she had none.

'Exactly. Was the locked door for modesty's sake, or because you didn't want anyone bursting in. Remember that incident in the changing rooms in Buxton? I do hope this wasn't a replay.'

'No, Jenny.' Alice gazed out of the window, desperately trying to connive an excuse. 'We were just talking.'

Jenny furtively digested the girl's delicious body; the tight jeans making her look utterly mouth-watering. Those come-and-eat-me curves. She recalled the description Alan had extricated from her: 'Beautiful green eyes, gorgeous auburn hair, the most delicate of noses, bright face and clear complexion, full lips, almost always pouting, body sylphlike but utterly curvaceous, skin so soft one had to feel it to believe it, breasts of perfect size and so beautifully shaped, tiny waist and narrow hips, the most scrumptious derrière, legs slim but shapely…' It was no wonder, on reflection, that he determined a latent lesbian inclination.

'And you needed the door locked for that?' she asked, gathering herself.

'What do you want me to say, Jenny?' Alice folded her arms and kept her attention on the gardens, hiding the guilt she knew reflected in her eyes. 'That Katy and I are having a lesbian affair?'

'Are you?'

'And what would you do if I said yes?'

Jenny closed the gap between them, and ran a hand through that silky auburn hair. 'If my daughter is that way inclined, then why is she going out with someone of the opposite sex?'

'So it's me?' Alice challenged. 'I'm leading Kate astray?'

'I just want to know if you're attracted to women, that's all.'

'Why not, Jenny? I mean, I like my bum being whacked. I must be a pervert.'

'No one has said that. You are what you are, Ali. You are what God made you.'

Alice shrugged. 'I like both, I think,' she said quietly, looking down at the carpet. 'Men and women.' She lifted her eyes to the woman standing beside her, stroking her hair comfortingly. 'There, I've admitted it. I suppose you want me to leave your house now.'

'And Kate?' Jenny went on, ignoring the last sentence.

'Ask her yourself.'

'No need. As I said, you are what you are. I understand. I'll not condemn. As for Kate? Well, it's best in the open. No shocks.'

Alice faced her, more confused than ever. 'You really are very understanding, aren't you?'

'I try to be.'

'Thank you, Jenny,' Alice whispered sincerely. 'Thank you for everything.'

Jenny smiled, kissed Alice affectionately on the cheek, and left the room.

Kate went out on her date before Alice could talk to her,

so Harris she would have to deal with alone. How could she call him a liar?

She worked on the essay, her friend's comments recalled but virtually useless to a valid justification of wayward conduct. Alice used imagination, limited experience and articulate persuasion to argue the case.

Then late that night, the household in darkness, and with no sign of Kate having returned, she read the draft. If Alice had been defending herself then perhaps, maybe, Jay would accept it. It was her work and she knew he would see that.

Resigned to failure she undressed and slipped on a pair of thin cotton pyjamas. Sleeping naked still felt foreign to her – at home, at school, and interned with Richard, she had been obliged to cover up.

Sleep refused her. She considered Harris and the man's barefaced lie. If he had read the notes then why keep them? If he hadn't, then why...? Of course, he hadn't, but by asking about them she had stoked his curiosity. Prying, devious, unreliable Harris; she could take it for granted he knew the contents now.

What would he do? What *could* he do?

He could show Jay, who would more than likely dismiss the written vindication and sentence Kate to unimaginable punishment. Alice sat up in bed. She had to get those notes back. Whatever else, she couldn't fail Katy.

It was one o'clock in the morning. Surely everyone would be asleep. Alice crept from her room, stealth exaggerated. The staff occupied the south wing second floor, and she hoped the room she looked for was marked *Butler*, or *Harris*.

Barefoot, Alice moved quickly and silently, the pink pyjamas hugging her figure. The pants clung to her hips, delved the partition of buttocks and moulded to her vaginal lips. They amplified slender thighs and hung loose from the knee. The top similarly embraced her torso, breasts mobile with her gait, the outline of nipples conspicuous. Had any man wandered into the corridors that night, they would have deemed themselves expired and caught a glimpse of heaven.

She made the upper floor undiscovered, but vexed, she peered at the half dozen doors. All appeared the same. No name plaques. No indication of who resided beyond each closed portal.

She would have to try them one at a time; there was nothing else for it. If caught, she could say she was lost; she'd been sleepwalking. That was one good reason for remaining in her pyjamas. As far as she knew all the servants slept on site – Mrs Hardcastle, Harry; she cringed at the prospect of disturbing him. The pompous ass would be certain she sought his arms. Then there was Odette. Robins senior and junior and finally, Harris.

She tried the first door, which opened with no dreaded creak. She peeped around it, and Robins senior snored noisily. Carefully she closed it and sought the next.

That revealed Mrs Hardcastle, wrapped in winceyette, barrel hips turned towards her. Shaking her head, Alice approached the third. Again unlocked, she suppressed a gasp of shock behind her hand at the spectacle of Odette and Harry huddled naked on the single bed.

With three to go Alice sighed with relief upon opening one and seeing the butler flat on his back, blankets drawn to his chin. She crept in, barely daring to breathe, and sought his trousers in the gloom. They were neatly folded and lay over the back of a chair. As quietly as she could she rummaged through first one pocket and then the other, felt paper and withdrew it, turning for the door.

Alice froze as the room abruptly lit up, then nearly died as Harris's austere voice penetrated her shock.

'What the devil do you think you are doing?' he demanded fearsomely.

Alice had no choice, so taking a deep breath she rounded

on him. The man sat up in his bed, one hand on the bedside light. 'I – I came for this,' she said, holding up the paper.

Harris scowled. 'Well, I have to admit you're audacious with it,' he said. 'Aren't you looked after well enough, young lady, that you have to steal from the servants?'

Alice's mouth fell open as she checked what she held aloft, and she groaned at the five-pound note clutched in her fist. 'Oh, no...' A hot nail of fear pierced her belly.

'Oh yes...' he said. 'I wonder what Mr Howell will have to say about this?'

'I didn't come for this,' she gabbled desperately, throwing the money down as though it was infected with some horrifying disease. 'I came for my notes. I know you have them.'

'I know nothing of any notes, miss,' he said smugly. 'All I see before me is a thief.'

'I saw you, Harris,' she argued. 'I saw you... you doing things to Odette, and then I saw you pick my notes up.'

The man smirked. 'Doing things to Odette? What do you mean by that?'

'You coerced her into having sex with you.'

'Did I?' He shrugged. 'You have a fertile imagination, I'll say that for you.'

'If I tell Jonathan what you did, you'll be sacked.'

Harris pulled back the bedclothes and stood, unabashed about his naked state, smiling at the way the girl instantly lowered her eyes and blushed. 'Nothing occurred, Miss Alice. Why should it have? How could I possibly have compelled a pretty lass to do something like that?'

'She stole more than you let on to Mrs Howell. You used that and threats.'

'What did she steal, Alice? I'm interested.' Harris took a pack of cigarettes from the bedside table, and placing one between his dry lips, he lit it.

'Diamonds.'

'Diamonds, eh?' he scoffed. 'Odd that Mrs Howell

99

hasn't either noticed or complained, isn't it?'

'You must have put them back.'

'Or they were never missing in the first place. Now, more to the point, I catch you in my room, your thieving hands in my pockets, stealing my money. When challenged you state, in your words precisely, "I came for this". Then you concoct some cock-and-bull story about me and one of the staff, in some feeble and desperate attempt to save your own scrawny neck. We'll ask Odette in the morning if any of this happened, and what do you think she will say, young lady?'

'She's terrified of you,' Alice blurted. 'You know damn well she'll agree with whatever you tell her to.'

'There you go again, making accusations.' Cocksure, Harris blew out smoke and smiled, his expression triumphant. 'Seems you are in a bit of a predicament,' he went on. 'I've worked for the Howells for forty-two years. I am a loyal servant. There are no doubts about that, I can assure you. You however, have been here a matter of a few weeks. And if I'm not mistaken, have managed to bring about the wrath of not only Mr Howell, but Mrs Howell as well. Then there is the matter of Mr Barker having to travel here to punish you.'

'How do you know about any of that?'

'It is my duty to know all that transpires beneath the roof of this house, young lady. You've been caned by Mr Howell twice, I believe, and disciplined by Mrs Howell once.'

Alice couldn't contest the facts. How he knew was beyond her, but he was right. The second caning by Jay had been a contrived sexual adventure, but to inform Harris of that would be suicide.

'I dare say your bottom carries a number of stripes at this very moment,' he pondered.

'What are you driving at, Harris?' she demanded.

'I was merely being considerate, miss.'

'Considerate?'

'Yes.' He stubbed the cigarette out in an ashtray on the bedside table. 'I thought you would like a couple of days for your current marks to heal.'

'Why would I need a couple of days?' she asked, bemused. 'What are you talking about?'

'You don't think your attempted theft will go unpunished, surely?'

Alice laughed nervously. 'Oh no, Harris,' she said, shaking her head and taking a backward step towards the door, 'if you think you're going to cane me, you have another think coming.'

'What's the alternative?' he mocked. 'I shout thief. All the servants rise from their beds. They witness you here. What would you tell them? That you sneaked into my room to retrieve some piece of paper? I am a servant. Why not simply demand it from me? Or perhaps you wouldn't want anyone to read that filth?'

'So you have read it.'

'It was certainly an eye-opener, young lady,' he said, sucking his teeth as his beady eyes gleefully devoured her. The situation was growing worse by the second. At that moment Alice would happily have killed Katy, but of course it wasn't her fault. Alice had permitted the notes to fall into Harris's hands, so she had to accept responsibility.

'They were purely jottings for an essay,' she said hastily.

Harris folded his arms, resting against flabby pectorals and upon a potbelly. 'An essay?' He tapped his chin pensively. 'Now, what were those leading words again? "If that miserable, hardhearted old geriatric Harris is allowed to thrash me, then I might just offer him my fanny as well, out of spite". What sort of composition are you writing?'

'None of your business. And aren't you at least going to put a dressing-gown on?'

'Does my humble body offend you?' he sneered. 'This is my room, miss. I didn't ask you to come in. I was happily tucked up in my bed when you crept in to ransack my trousers. Besides, I note that you are not exactly *dressed*. Your pyjamas don't leave a lot to one's imagination, do they?'

Abruptly self-conscious, Alice attempted to cover her breasts, the thin material only serving to inspire his fancies.

'You haven't enough arms, young lady,' Harris leered, his gaze crawling down to below her waist.

'What sort of a man are you?' Alice challenged indignantly, the butler disgusting her sense of morals.

'The sort of a man you tried to rob,' he replied glibly.

'Oh, I've had enough of this,' Alice said, reaching for the door.

'I'll shout for help,' he threatened

'You'll…?' Alice gasped, turning back to him. 'Why are you being so horrible to me, Harris. What do you want from me?'

'It's not what I want, miss. It is what I shall have. Just retribution.'

'Retribution?'

'Yes, retribution,' he repeated. 'Tomorrow morning, ten o'clock, in my office. We won't be disturbed, and I will do you the favour of keeping this strictly between ourselves.'

Seeing no other solution Alice grudgingly conceded. 'You know, don't you, Harris?' she said. 'You know I've done nothing wrong, and you know I have no option but to do as you say.'

'That is life, I'm afraid,' he said victoriously. 'Now before you leave, a written confession, if you please. Otherwise what's to stop you reneging on our little… arrangement?'

'You have my word, Harris,' Alice assured him. 'And my notes, which I want back.'

'And I shall have your confession, or I may insist on calling the police.'

Alice sighed wearily, sat at his small bureau and took the fountain pen he smugly handed to her. 'What do you want me to write?' she asked.

'I was caught by Mr Harris in the act of rifling his pockets and attempting to steal a five-pound note,' he dictated.

'And you know that isn't the truth.'

'It is what I saw. Now write it. My patience grows thin.' Alice reluctantly wrote what he'd told her to. 'Now sign and date it.'

'I want this back in the morning as well as the notes, Harris,' she said.

'But of course, my dear girl,' he sniggered. 'Once due chastisement has been executed.'

Her stomach in knots, still not certain how events had unfolded and consequently entrapped her, Alice left the old lecher's room and hurried back to her own.

Safely there she got into bed, ruffled and troubled. Her gallant adventure had become a nightmare. Recriminations plagued her. Perhaps confrontation from the first may have realised success. But from the beginning Harris held the whip hand, so to speak, and in the morning he would use that whip hand with brutal effect.

She should have ensured the notes were secure, but of course that wasn't the true source of her problem. Sneaking into his room like some amateur commando and getting caught red-handed, not only in the act, but assuming the feel of paper to be her notes. Harris had her firmly by the short and curlies. He held her confession. He possessed the notes. His assumption had taken her by surprise, though; Alice hadn't conceived the possibility that he would think she wrote the defamation.

She dwelt on Odette's chastisement, the severity still fresh in her mind. Odette had been caught stealing, taking jewellery from her employees. Did the man view that more discriminately than personal theft? But Harris knew Alice's true intention, so how could he penalise her so?

Then the truth slowly sank in. He savoured corporal punishment. He delighted in striping bottoms. Harris had been offended, and Harris would use the punishment as exorcism, to ease the frustration. Her only escape might be to point the finger at Kate, but that at best seemed a feeble and cowardly possibility.

She accepted the only recourse was to bare her bottom for him and take with integrity his hostile medicine.

Alice barely slept. She listened for Kate's return, and when she did drop off for the odd half-hour she awoke from fitful dreams, fantasies that saved her from the forthcoming ordeal, but with consciousness returning the awful truth hit like a sledgehammer.

But Katy didn't return. Alice checked her bedroom early the next morning, the sheets undisturbed. Perhaps, she thought, she might not be the only one tending a sore bottom that day.

A little after nine Kate made contact, and chance placed Alice near the telephone when it rang.

'Ali? Is that you?'

'Yes, Kate,' she said in a conspiratorial whisper. 'Where are you?'

'Blackpool. See, I told you he would, didn't I?'

'And what's Jenny going to say?'

'I'll worry about that when I get home.'

'And when's that likely to be?'

'Oh, tonight I expect.'

'I suppose you've explored him intimately?'

'Sex in the surf, Ali. You should try it. Stimulating or what!'

'You are impossible. What if you'd been caught? You already face Harris's cane. Are you after a double helping?'

'You'll get me off that, Ali. I have every confidence in you. Honest, I'll pay you back sometime. I'll do you an enormous favour, okay?'

'No need, Kate,' Alice said. 'I'll see you tonight.'

She couldn't tell her friend what was going on, not on the phone. In fact, there would be no point in relating the awful circumstances at all. An hour to go. Alice's stomach lurched continuously. She felt unduly dizzy and sick. But the contradiction was not lost on her; how could she relish a severe caning from Jay, and quail at the prospect of one from Harris. If only she could indulge herself, turn the misery to pleasure, but she knew her fear would prevent that. Being thrashed by Harris could under no circumstances be construed as sensual.

Alice kept her eye on the clock, the seconds ticking by in slow motion. Why did fate torture her so? Was it her own inept attempt at life? Wasn't it enough to be dealt the mortal blow of parental loss? Alice knew in her heart that she needed to think more carefully about foolhardy actions, but blaming God helped.

She wore a white blouse and pleated skirt, reasoning that it would facilitate the proffering of her bottom, all her other skirts being tighter. She wore white panties, in the vain hope that Harris would leave them in place.

At five to ten she knocked on the tyrant's door.

'Wait!' he shouted in a stern fashion that kept her there, wishing the trial were over.

The minutes ticked by. She massaged her rump through her skirt, her mind in shock, contemplation beyond her. Then at last the door opened and Harris, in shirtsleeves, bade her enter. Neatly laid on the desk were several implements, sending a shiver of horror up her spine. A large plimsoll lay first in line, a thick twin-tailed taws alongside. A thin, fairly short rod was placed adjacent to two others of normal length but greater thickness. Alice shuddered fearfully. What did he have in mind?

Expecting the slipper, she frowned as Harris picked up the thin cane. 'In the Middle East they punish according to an eye for an eye,' he stated. 'As it was your hands that looted my pockets I think it fair to punish those first.'

'With the cane?' The girl's face paled further.

'But of course,' he confirmed nastily. 'Six strokes on the palm of each hand. Hold your right one out first.'

Tears filled her eyes at the mere thought of it and her lip trembled. 'But I thought…'

'I would simply cane your backside? Oh no, young lady. When you leave my office I doubt you will ever consider theft again. Your hand, please.'

'This is so unfair!' she complained futilely. 'You know what I was looking for last night. You know it wasn't the money. You're just taking advantage of the situation so you can get some perverted kick out of beating me.'

'If you've quite finished, I'll have your arm horizontal,' he said coldly. 'Your palm upward, fingers straight.'

With no alternative she obeyed, her hand trembling, and Harris placed the cane across the palm, the rod cool to her perspiring flesh. Alice looked away as the cruel rod rose, her eyes closed tight, her face screwed up in dread…

She heard the brief slice of air, leapt to the solid slap and yelped at the dire consequence. She withdrew her hand, tucked it beneath her arm and sobbing, danced a tortured circle, the reaction meeting an insensitive demand.

'Put it back, girl,' he ordered. 'You have another five to come.'

She glared at the man, large eyes pleading. 'Please, can't you just cane my bottom instead?'

'Oh, I intend to, young lady,' he drawled salaciously. 'I intend to…'

She returned her hand to the required position, the pain still dreadful. Harris struck again, the rod scalding her palm, and this time Alice chose the comfort between soft thighs. She squeezed the smarting hand between them, an agonised wail venting her torment. Bowed so and offering a target to the impatient butler, he took advantage and brought the short rod down sharply, striking her shoulder. Alice straightened in an instant, the fire in her back intolerable.

'Now put your hand back and keep it there,' he growled, and with no choice she held it in place, her other gripping the wrist. Harris dealt the third, her flesh decimated, and appalled by the excruciating hurt she followed the fourth, seeing the rattan slash and buck, reeling to the dreadful burn. She managed the fifth and then showed him her back, the traumatised palm again between her legs.

Harris seized her by the neck, and holding her down stung her covered rump with several cuts. Snarling he grabbed the disabled limb, and holding it up with his left dealt a violent stroke with the right. Alice screamed. The man released her. She jigged, crying, trying to assuage the fire.

'The left, please,' Harris instructed, recomposed.

'Please,' she begged. 'Please don't cane the other one.'

Harris grabbed her left and lifted it into place. 'Your choice, young lady,' he said. 'Six on your volition, nine if I have to hold it there.'

The arm wavered, steadied and waited. Alice covered her face with the punished hand, fingers wiping her tears. The rod swished, flesh received and the abominable detonation crippled.

The arm remained in place, fingers curled. Harris waited, and the fingers straightened. The cane returned with venom and her shriek rent the air. Her sweet countenance flushed and damp, she cringed. Her palm reeled to the third, the stroke as exacting and painful as its predecessors.

Determined to exact a revenge, to make the most of a unique opportunity, he laid the last three with equal force, Alice's hands temporarily unusable.

Harris, quiet and unhurried, laid the cane back in its

place and picked up the plimsoll. 'Take off your skirt, please,' he said.

Alice was in no mind to argue, so she released the buttons and dropped the garment to her feet, picked it up and laid it on the desk.

'Now, bend over,' he ordered.

Alice stared at her knees, fingers touching the toes of her shoes. Harris lifted the hem of her blouse and laid it over her back. He eyed the brief white panties, the exposed areas of her buttocks and the tramlines left by Jonathan's cane.

He took hold of the elastic and pulled up, the material delving between her cheeks. 'You would seem to have a thirst for trouble,' he remarked. 'A mild caning, judging by the marks. Now I wonder what you did to deserve that?' He snorted. 'I guarantee my rod will mark you much more effectively.'

Alice remained silent, thankful he didn't guess the real reason for their application.

Harris placed a hand on the small of her back and pressed the plimsoll to the soft flesh of her right buttock. It couldn't possibly hurt as much as the cane on her hand had. Or she hoped it couldn't.

As he lifted the shoe clear he stepped back, swung, body and strength behind the missile. The thick rubber collided with surrendering flesh, flattened and then passed, a formidable sting left, harassing. Hands still aching Alice swallowed the bitter pill.

Again Harris made a meal out of indicating where the rubber would pulverise, and for the second time the implement cannoned into untried flank, his performance effective.

Alice found she could contend with that. The plimsoll stung aggressively, the fire lingered, but in comparison with the cane on her hands it was tolerable.

She felt him press the sole to her, the tread encompassing

both cheeks, the division bridged. It left, then returned abruptly, the slap loud, her buttocks trounced. The burn escalated.

Alice gripped her ankles tight, the lower half of her bottom stinging. The size ten delved upper heights, rose, descended, the crack on tight haunch thunderous. The impact knocked Alice forward and she straightened to save herself. The buttock feeling branded she took advantage and rubbed it, incurring the wrath of Harris.

Mouth twisted in bitter indignation he pounced, fingers seizing her neck he forced her over, snarling, 'Did I say stand? Did I say to touch your bottom? You remain bending. You keep that bottom accessible. You do not attempt to comfort it.'

Satisfied he had forced her down as far as she could go, he added, 'Now we must begin again.'

For an awful moment Alice thought he meant from the very beginning, her hands still throbbing. She would sooner throw herself on the mercy of Jay than suffer that again.

Harris swung the plimsoll, his full strength behind it, and the rubber struck a glancing blow, her left haunch outraged. The colouring cheeks tensed as fire swathed the flesh. Eyes wide, Alice gulped, the blaze galvanising.

Harris moved his position, and standing directly behind the girl he cracked the shoe hard on her right flank, the flesh butchered, the pain intolerable. She sucked in air, fingers clutching slim ankles.

The ogre hit that stricken flesh again, an angular sweep, the sole pulverising upper buttock, the immediate feedback mind-jarring. The footwear pounded Alice's bottom to cherry-red. Harris had the girl exactly where he wanted her, her gullibility heaven sent. With twelve administered, in addition to the false start, Harris lay the plimsoll back on the desk. 'Now you may rise,' he told her.

Her rear blazed. The last six had been sheer purgatory

and her hands wavered by her sides, longing to console her suffering bum. Harris watched, eagle-eyed. Should she dare he would slipper her again, so Alice resisted the temptation.

'Lay on the desk,' he instructed. 'On your back.' She anxiously eyed the polished furniture. 'I've cleared it especially.'

What punishment could he perform like that? Alice furtively reached down and eased her panties from her crotch, the material delving where Harris had pulled them up. The man noticed and leapt to the offensive, the twin tongues of the taws slapping her loins.

'Ow!' Alice winced.

'Now get on the desk,' he growled.

Alice lay back fearfully, arms by her sides, staring up at the ceiling. Harris loomed into view, looking down on her, gloating. 'Now I'll have to readjust things, won't I?' he said.

Her skin crawled as the butler curled his fingers beneath the cotton of her panties, clammy against her soft pubic curls. He delayed, taking lewd pleasure from the feel of her. Then with a tensing of his lips he abruptly tugged, the material sinking between her tender labia. Alice reacted, protectively covering the apex of her thighs with her two hands, but a hefty slap to one of those thighs induced their lowering again.

He placed his leering face close to hers, and with nicotine-stained teeth bared he whispered threateningly, 'You touch nothing during punishment, young lady. And I mean nothing.'

Alice nodded, his message plainly understood.

'Good, now raise your legs.' Alice obeyed immediately and lifted them to the vertical. 'Keep going,' he urged. 'You're supple enough. I want your feet above your head.'

Alice complied again.

'Excellent,' the man praised, sincerity missing. He gazed

upon her shapely form unabashed, Alice finding his lurid scrutiny repulsive. Then he reached out, the girl afraid his touch would prove indelicate. The hand settled on a taut thigh, wandered to a buttock, examining, feeling the trounced flesh. A faint smile on his lips, Harris seemed preoccupied, intrigued by the mottled imprint of his plimsoll.

The fingers traced the curves, crossed the division and stroked back up the opposite thigh. 'You see, Alice, I can be tender,' he said, wheezing slightly. 'I can be considerate. This is preferable to the smart of rubber, is it not?'

She looked away, not caring to answer. Revolted by the obvious sexual approach, she experienced a calming that unsettled her greatly. Taking pleasure from Harris's mauling sickened her, the lure unacceptable.

'I could be extremely considerate, Alice,' he rambled on, his fingers loitering close to her discomfited sex. 'You are a very attractive young lady. You could so easily turn a mature man's head.'

She knew his intimation, well versed by now in men's lechery. She sought a reasonable rebuff; there would be no point in angering him. 'That wouldn't be my choice,' she informed him.

'No, I suppose not,' he returned, unaffected. 'Pity. For you, that is.'

Harris removed those benevolent hands and stepped aside, gathering the taws. The leather ran across the palm of his left hand, and then he dealt a withering blow with the right. The twin tails slashed upturned thigh, the leather rousing an intense sting, a smart that even eclipsed the effect of the plimsoll.

Alice hugged her calves and pressed her lips to a knee to suppress the scream that would so delight her tormentor.

'Sensitive, isn't it, young lady?' he goaded. 'The thigh,

111

I mean.'

The scald consuming she ignored the gibe, her only thought to see an end to Harris's deplorable punishment.

'What were those scurrilous words?' he mused exaggeratedly. 'Ah yes: miserable, hardhearted old geriatric, wasn't it? Well, Alice, that first stroke was for the misnomer miserable. I am not miserable. I am what one would term as stern. Remember that, girl, stern.'

He deliberately prolonged the agony, waiting for the burn to ebb, indulging in his pompous lecture, twisting the knife of mental torture.

The taws hit again, the smack sickening, the pain worse. A second vivid stripe matured, her thigh hooped. 'Hardhearted? No, strict, girl. Out of necessity I am strict. I will not tolerate the vagaries of immature brats.'

Dreading the violent revival of unbearable pain, Alice cowered as the man brought the taws in a brisk arc, the strain in his face obvious. She squealed as the leather bit, the sensitive flesh ignited.

'Old? Maybe in comparison to someone as callow as yourself, a smug urchin quick to hurl vitriolic abuse with regard to her betters. A vain baggage who I suspect spends more time before the mirror than she does in hard toil. Do you study your reflection, Alice? Do you dwell on misguided fools who drop at your feet, the blind idiots who see the façade but not the rotten inner? Do you stand naked and cup your breasts, believing them irresistible to mankind? Do you gaze at your bottom, considering it perfect? Do you, young lady?'

Alice ignored the hostile suggestions.

'Answer me.'

She refused, so Harris placed a finger and thumb on either side of her sex lips and squeezed. Alice bit her lower lip in anguish, her torso arching with the pain.

'Well let me tell you, young lady,' he went on. 'You will age. Youth is but a fleeting moment on the road to oblivion.

It is gone in the blink of an eye. The lines and wrinkles will ravage. The flesh will lose substance. But inside you will feel the same. The soul is eternal, the body brief. You will be trapped, undesirable, your figure bloated and ravaged, but still hunger for the joys of youth.'

Harris stepped back and swung the fourth. The tails bit, missing her vagina by a hair's breadth. Alice rolled on her back, sweet face wrought, the smart pure agony.

'Geriatric? Do you have any comprehension of the word? Well, do you?' Harris placed a finger at the entrance to her sex. 'Well?'

'Yes,' she answered hastily, frightened of what he might do.

'You surprise me.' Deftly he pushed the flimsy white material aside, his finger pressing. 'Do I dribble?'

The fingertip touched her clitoris, and Harris applied pressure. 'You will answer, young lady.'

'Um... no!' she squealed.

'Does my mind wander?' Again the fingertip agitated the sensitive nub.

'No!'

'Do I wet myself?' He twisted the finger and Alice writhed.

'Ah, no, Mr Harris,' she said desperately, rolling her head on the desktop.

'Then there's no substance to your aspersion, is there?'

'No, sir.' Alice was tired. A whacking was one matter, but his verbal assault vexed her.

He levied another rigorous stroke, the leather scalding lower buttock and thigh alike, and then he leant close to her, hands resting on the desk on either side of her breasts.

'Please, Mr Harris, I've had enough,' she said contritely. 'I'm sorry. I apologise. Please don't go on.'

'I am merely trying to comprehend the inner workings of your mind,' he said. 'Obviously they are simplistic. No reasoning. No logic. Still, I am sure your mind comprehends the sting of the taws.'

Harris navigated the desk, and then levied five unrestrained strokes in rapid succession to the other thigh, pronouncing each offensive word as the leather lambasted her leg. The limb on fire, the hurt untenable, Alice sobbed. She writhed, begging the burn to desist, not daring to offer physical comfort.

'Now, young lady, you may have a respite,' he said, surprising her. 'Dress yourself and then be back here for two o'clock.'

Alice rolled from the desk, indifferent to what she might show him. She tended her stinging legs, fingers caressing, attempting to soothe. Harris watched, aroused. She stooped, massaging beaten flesh, her back to him. He drank of the scarlet buttocks, the tread of the plimsoll quite plain, the panties still caught between the two taut globes of flesh. He smirked at the livid bands that plagued her thighs, fine welts evident where the taws had devastated.

'Come on, girl!' he barked. 'Clear my office. I have work to do.'

Sobbing, sniffling, she collected her skirt and stepped into it, and having buttoned it about her slim waist she gratefully left.

Alice fled to her room. There at least she could vent the frustration. She lay facedown on the bed, tears streaming. Her pride had been shattered; self-esteem that had taken years of effort to compile. No wonder Katy didn't want to face the martinet. Harris punished in the truest sense of the word. His strokes were scathing, his attitude overbearing. He instilled terror. He had a way about him that made her feel as if she was nothing. He leered and ogled, made her feel cheap. For the first time she felt ashamed, not merely embarrassed.

A few hours would see her back there, him whipping her backside with those dreadful canes. How many? How hard?

Curiosity settled, and Alice undressed to view the damage. She offered her naked back to the mirror, her rear seemingly sunburned. Tentatively she stroked those beaten dunes, the tread pattern visible in places. Sore was definitely the word.

Her loins and thighs fared no better. She could easily pick out each strap mark; fine ridges either side highlighting them.

What a mess, in more than one sense of the word. She could refuse to return to his office at the appointed time, but what would the butler do? Alice didn't want to invoke something no one could turn around. And what if Harris refused to give back her confession and notes? What then? Another whipping whenever he felt inclined?

She would have to divulge all to Kate. She needed a shoulder to cry on. At least her friend she could trust. She might even be able to extricate her from further trouble. Alice hoped that Kate might even settle the score.

She had no doubt that the interval was purely for Harris's pleasure. The plimsoll had numbed her somewhat, the man's arm a lot stronger than she would have given credit for. This was psychological punishment. He wanted her to sweat. He wanted her a nervous wreck. Fear was the key. It controlled the suffering. The more apprehensive she was, the worse it would be.

For the last hour or so Alice wandered the gardens, praying for the throbbing in her bottom to subside. But at two o'clock she was again in Harris's office, standing before the ogre, head bowed, fingers interlocked at her front.

'If the Howells knew you crept about the house at night stealing, they would no doubt see you in a very different light.'

'Except I wasn't stealing, as you well know,' she said with more defiance than she really felt.

115

Harris picked up the mid-sized cane and bent it between his fists. 'All I saw was you making off with my money, and for that you will suffer the consequences. Take off your skirt.'

Wanting nothing more than to get the ordeal over as quickly as possible, Alice obediently unfastened the button at her trim waist and let the skirt fall to her feet, Harris intent on her every move.

'Now place your legs together and bend forward,' he went on.

Alice reached down for her toes and waited, stomach churning with nerves, breathing difficult.

'So far so good,' drooled the fiend. 'Let's hope you can keep it up. You know the rules. You do not rise. You do not attempt to comfort your bottom. Should you do so I will simply begin again until you show restraint.' He flexed the rod, chest out. 'You will receive twelve with this cane.'

Harris admired the stretch of her white panties over firm cheeks. The old cane marks were camouflaged by imprints of the plimsoll, subsiding, a sprinkling resisting. Her thighs bore the fruit of the taws, now dulled but still discernible.

Harris savoured the evidence of corporal punishment almost as much as inflicting it. He lay the rod to those tortured haunches, the cold touch significant, a warning of commencement of hostilities. The girl tensed, the slight tightening of buttock flesh discerned by the tyrant.

Then it began. Hell rained on her. The arm rose, the rod sliced air and bottom, delved deep, susceptible flesh pulverised. It wrapped and tore into vulnerable haunch. Pain jolted, wracked, consumed. Her stomach revolted and heaved. Lungs went into spasm, the grip of the inferno preposterous.

The fibrous wand revisited, doubling the gut-wringing ire, the recipient tumbling psychologically, mayhem loosed in her backside. An anguished cry rent the ether. There was no fanfare of saviour trumpets. No charge of shining armour. Nowhere to run and limbs that refused. So the bending subordinate to pain remained transfixed, purgatory laid by strokes of daunting strength, the pelt of conquering scourge pitiless.

A dozen energetic and harrowing lashes dispensed, her rump in turmoil, Alice monitored the switch of rattans, Harris replacing the medium with a thicker version. The unpleasant brute returned her gaze, an icy smirk, his calculating eyes inhuman. He drank of livid decorations, grim testimony to expertise and strength of arm.

'That was but a mere taste of what is to come, thief,' he warned her. 'I'll have those panties off now.'

Alice slipped thumbs into the elastic waist and eased the underwear down, the contact with fresh stripes disconcerting. Having removed them she resumed that ignoble position, degraded, her naked bottom welted and abused and offered for further sacrifice.

Grief wet her face. Tears spilled and dashed to the floor; those tiles as cold as her tormentor's soul. Alice winced at the cool touch, panic rippling through heart and lungs. She shook impulsively as the wand massaged, the slide of polished vine unnerving.

'See how I deal with a thief,' came the man's intimidation, and then hindquarters reeled to the explosion of heat. Molten lava applied, flesh shrieked beneath the blast. Scalded flesh fled the impact, the solid rod burrowing in earnest. The knot of anxiety tightened, its grip choking, and saline droplets fell faster.

The rod penalised, cut after exacting cut. With her pain barrier far exceeded, and with no sexual retreat, Alice closed on abject submission, her buttocks branded and torched.

'Well, thief?' Harris demanded, laying the cane down. 'Do you not wish to beg for clemency and tell me how you will never steal again?'

The welts raging, her behind etched and pleading relief, she sniffed and answered the only way she could, pride still not totally vanquished. 'I'm not admitting to something I didn't do,' she told him grimly. 'I accept this punishment only because I behaved stupidly. I allow myself to think the best of people. I should have reported you to Mr Howell.'

'For what, exactly?' he scoffed, flexing the last implement in the arsenal, the bend limited, the cane dark and solid.

'For what you did to Odette and for not giving me back my notes.'

'I see,' he mused. 'And you think Mr Howell would believe you and not me?'

'I should have done it anyway.'

'Unfasten the top few buttons of your blouse.' His voice penetrated, tore into her heart, his every whim a further torment.

Alice fumbled, fingers ignoring command. Harris waited impatiently, idly tapping the cane against his leg.

She managed the buttons and reached again for her toes. Harris seized the blouse's hem and folded it up her back, but not content he pulled it over her head, the garment falling to be caught by her wrists. With a deft flick of finger and thumb he released the catch of her bra. Alice fretted; surely he wouldn't use the rod on her back, would he?

Harris vent his anger. Without warning the rod bit beaten backside, the thump pronounced, the burn unquestionable. Aching fingers clawed air, an anguished sob delighting Harris. The movement loosened the grip of the bra and one cup fell, dangling, exposing an enticingly suspended breast.

Savouring the beautiful vision he cut again, the slash low, the joint of bottom and thighs stunned. The jolt to

118

her lower anatomy sparked a tremor in her fleshy breasts, not missed by the lecher, encouraging him to further acts of savagery.

Alice wallowed in a fever, her mind unable to take the dreadful shocks. Harris eclipsed Jonathan in the ranks of execution – Alice understanding why Katy dreaded being reunited with his austere hand. She felt skinned alive, her fertile imagination perceived her buttocks flayed, that once delicate hide stripped.

A vertical slice penetrated those forced defences, the spasm of pain excruciating. Her strangled shriek signalled the effectiveness of that bombshell, the announcement the cream topping to Harris. The bra surrendered completely, treating Harris to the spectacle of unobstructed pensile orbs.

Alice hovered between the bent and the horizontal, fingers wanting to give comfort, but she fought the urge and sought her toes. Harris added the last and most vicious stroke of all, the inflexible brute bowing to her rump such was the force used. Alice fell to her knees, hands on the floor, the fire rampant, worse than anything she had ever suffered.

Harris grinned and lay the cane down, then gazing upon the crushed soul he said sarcastically, 'You may lick your wounds now, girl. Or perhaps I should do that for you.'

Alice knelt and cautiously placed a hand on her battered haunches, too drained to worry about the restrictive blouse. She touched and recoiled, the aggravation too much. 'C-can I go now?' she asked.

The man did not answer. Alice climbed slowly to her feet, her bottom complaining at every movement. She stood heedless of her naked state, blouse hanging before her, bra balanced about her middle. Harris ogled what he saw.

Wincing, pretty countenance fraught, she asked, 'Can I have my notes and confession now?'

119

'You've been rightly punished for your wrongdoing,' he decreed. 'But you'll have to earn the return of your writings.'

Her tearstained face fell further. 'How?' she asked anxiously. 'Surely you don't intend beating me any more?'

'No, Alice, there are other ways of paying.' He advanced, and Alice retreated until the wall stopped her. With gnarled hands held chest height he sneered.

Alice shook her head in denial. 'Oh no, you keep your disgusting hands to yourself. I'm not Odette.'

'Nice tits, Alice,' he drooled crudely. 'What's a little feel in comparison to being thrown out of the house?'

'You piece of scum,' she said, holding the blouse protectively against her front, her enticing breasts covered. 'I've paid in full, and you're not getting anything else.'

He stopped six inches short, his breath on her face. 'Then you can forget those incriminating papers. I'm sure the Howells would be very interested in them.'

His hand pulled hers away, the blouse falling from her breasts. Fingers grasped the opportunity, probing without care or finesse. Breathing heavily he leant close, watching her intently for any sign of rebellion, his tongue tasted, loose lips suckled, the other hand squeezed. Alice stared at the ceiling, trying to banish the ordeal from her mind, contempt etched on her face.

Harris pleased himself, slavering over her youthful breasts, gratifying his lust. Having ridden the wave of lechery so far he deemed it his entitlement to satisfy himself. He unfastened his flies and eased his erection clear, his intention not lost on the cowered Alice.

She shook her head, dismay on her face. 'No, no, you're not doing that! Please, I'm a virgin!'

'You, a virgin?' he sneered incredulously. 'Don't make me laugh. You've been fucking Mr Howell since you arrived here.'

'I haven't,' she denied, shaking her head again. 'Believe

120

me, I haven't!'

'Well there's only one way to find out, isn't there?' He prised her legs apart and pressed a hand to her soft curls. 'We'll see just how intact you are.'

Alice recovered her courage, and born of desperation she warned, 'You put your finger inside me, Mr Harris, and I'll tell Mr Howell everything. And I mean everything.'

'You'll be thrown out of the house,' he countered.

'I'll risk that. As it stands, you give me back my papers and we'll call it quits. Otherwise I'll take you down with me. Fancy trying to find another job and somewhere to live at your age?'

The hand withdrew. Harris stepped away. 'Another time, Hussey,' he vowed vehemently, 'I'll have you. That's a delicious arse and you haven't felt the last of my cane yet.'

Alice quickly put on her bra, blouse and skirt. The panties she held in her hand, the trial of wearing them too much. She left without another word, each step misery, Harris eyeing her stilted gait.

She made her way slowly back to the stairs leading up to the ground floor, and there Harry barred her way.

'Been looking for you, miss,' he said.

'Why?' She felt in no mood to brook his tiresome rhetoric.

'I was just wondering about you and Mr Howell.'

Her arm attempted to push him to one side. 'I'm in a hurry, Harry, if you don't mind.'

The chauffeur stayed put. 'But, miss, I could save you a lot of hassle.'

'Oh, and how will you do that, Harry?'

'By minding what I say to Mrs Howell.'

Jaw set, her eyes glazed. 'Don't talk in riddles. If you've got something to say, then say it.'

'Such language from the landed gentry!' he mocked.

'But I'm not, am I, Harry? I'm the uncouth brat from

the poor side of town. I'm merely seeking Mr Howell's fortune.'

'If you say so, miss. Been busy, have you?'

'What?'

'You're carrying your knickers. You've not been pleasing old Harris, have you?'

'Get your brain out of the cesspit.' She glared at the young man. 'Was there something else?'

'Like I was saying, Alice, Mr Howell virtually admitted there was something going on between you and him.'

'And why would he tell you?'

'Old buddies, me and him. He tells me a lot, he does.'

'Get to the point, Harry.' Her bottom plagued her. All she wanted to do was lie down, preferably on her front.

'Well, I was wondering what it would be worth to mind my p's and q's when talking to Mrs Howell, that's all.'

'Oh, I see,' she said, nodding. 'So you won't tell her I'm shagging her husband, you mean?'

He grinned smugly. 'Sort of.'

'So what exactly are you after, Harry?' she asked wearily. 'I mean, I've no money.'

He ogled the mouth-watering shape of her breasts, filling her blouse so enticingly. 'A piece of the action, maybe?'

'Oh, you want to screw me,' she said with mock surprise. 'Why didn't you just say so?'

'I don't want to take liberties.'

'Well, Harry, there's no time like the present.' She threw her arms around his neck and stared longingly into his eyes. Harry tentatively placed his hands on her trim waist.

'Where would you like to do it to me, Harry?' she breathed seductively.

'Oh blimey, I didn't think you'd agree so easily,' he gasped hoarsely.

'Why not, Harry?' she asked innocently. 'Aren't you irresistible?'

'I don't have any complaints.'

'No?'

'No, miss, I always aim to please.'

'So do I, Harry…' she whispered, 'so do I…' Her smile tensed, her emerald pools glazed, and a sickening pain erupted in Harry's groin. He groaned and sank to his knees, fingers gripping the agony. She glared down at him with contempt. 'You go and tell Mrs Howell. Tell her everything you think you know. Then pack your bags; you'll be out of here so fast your feet won't touch.'

As an added act of bitter intolerance she punched the hapless chauffeur in the mouth, and as a trickle of blood coloured his chin she shoved him aside and waltzed by, deliberately rolling her hips and shaking her hand, the knuckles fired.

Chapter Six

Alice tossed her panties onto the bed, then leant on the windowsill and indulged in the summer landscape. Her lower lip trembled and brine filled her eyes. It was such a wonderful place, but what was it with her that incited and encouraged the likes of Harris and Wilkinson?

She could understand Katy being on the wrong end of the rod, for she walked the tightrope and didn't give a damn. But all Alice tried to do was please, and a caned bottom was becoming the regular payment for that kindness.

It seemed that everyone in the world wanted a crack at her arse, or to maul her body. Even women found her irresistible. Was that all that life had to offer, a constant whirlwind of beatings and fighting off suitors? She sincerely hoped not.

She was due to see Richard on Saturday. Would he round on her for trivialities? Would he take his turn in the queue and chastise her? Even the Howells' main interest in her seemed to stem from a desire to mark her derrière. Jay resisted sex but always leapt at the chance to spank and cane her. Kate kept offering and even Jenny seemed tempted.

What if Richard did continue to find faults with her? What if he did loose a cane on her behind? Would four days be sufficient for Harris's thrashing to heal? He'd see her stripes, assume the worst, and probably lay into her with more gusto. That prospect did little to cheer the hapless girl.

And that damned butler still kept her notes. He retained the evidence. Would he attempt another assault? She had little doubt he would, some time.

Perhaps she should throw herself on the mercy of Jay. After all, she'd done nothing wrong. But there again there were the notes. Should he read them he would know who wrote them, Katy would receive worse, and Alice couldn't live with that.

She studied her reflection. What the hell was it about her? What drew the scum of life to her in particular? Was she stupid? Did she inadvertently invoke their wrath? Was she one of life's unfortunates who acted like a magnet to the vindictive?

She turned and cautiously drew her pleated skirt up, the view in the mirror shocking. She tentatively investigated a welt, raised and puffy. It stung to her touch, her bottom smothered, decimated cheeks reminiscent of a ploughed field. Sitting to tea would be impossible. She would have to feign a headache and go hungry.

She heard footsteps outside and let the skirt fall. Katy burst in, her usual self, full of unsuppressed energy. 'What a night and day!' she beamed.

'Nice to see someone happy.'

'Oh, you've been crying, Ali. What's happened?'

Alice shrugged. 'I don't know where to start.'

'You never do. Can't I leave you for five minutes without you finding a heap of trouble?'

The irony of the question tickled Alice, and she giggled.

'What's funny?' Kate asked.

'You, Katy, calling the pot black. I'm a mere novice at trouble compared to you.'

Kate failed to see the humorous side, and then Alice blurted the truth. 'The notes you gave me, Kate,' she said. 'Harris has them.'

'Oh shit!' her friend gasped. 'You're kidding! So why have you been crying? It's my bum, not yours. And more to the point, how did he come by them?'

'I'll show you why I've been crying.' Alice revealed her flogged rump.

'Shit!' Kate exclaimed. 'Who did that? It looks like Harris's work.'

'It is.'

'The wrong man to upset, Ali,' Kate said sagely. 'He's a mean swine with a cane.'

'I lost your notes watching Odette get a caning from him.'

'Odette was caned too? What for?'

'Stealing.'

'Stupid cow! Trust me to miss it.'

'I asked Harris if he had seen them and he denied all knowledge. But I saw him pick something up, so like an idiot I sneaked into his room last night and went through his pockets. He caught me. Worse, I thought I had the notes, but I didn't. I had some of his money, and the short of it is I ended up writing a confession. He used the plimsoll and split strap on me this morning and the cane this afternoon. Kate, he really hurt me. He caned my hands. I've never felt pain like it. And he's still got your notes and my confession.'

'Oh, Ali, you silly sod,' Kate admonished affectionately. 'Why didn't you just go and see father?'

'I wasn't sure he'd believe me. And the notes, well, Harris thinks I wrote them. And with your impending thrashing on Saturday I thought it best he carried on in that belief.'

'So you took the blame for my jottings?'

Alice nodded.

'When are you going to learn the first rule of life, Ali?'

'What's that?'

'Look after yourself before anyone else.'

'Would you have? In the same circumstances.'

'I wouldn't have sneaked into the butler's bedroom. And if I had, I would have got the right piece of paper.'

'But would you have taken the blame for me?'

'Probably. But there again, I've got a cast iron bum.'

'What can I do, Katy? How can I get those incriminating notes back?'

'Leave it to me, Ali.' The girl smiled. 'You'll have them back. I promise.'

Chapter Seven

Kate left it until the following morning before confronting Harris. As the daughter of the house she could have justifiably searched his room instead, but the prospect of facing the butler offered the opportunity to exorcise old ghosts. The man intimidated her. Since childhood and those ferocious beatings she had never been able to challenge his questionable authority.

Where Harris menaced, Katy cowered. The man's demeanour frightened her. Like one of those tyrants that proliferated in schools, he had the ability to silence her with a warning glance. Never sure of his capability she shrank from retaliation, uncertain of what he might do.

He worked as a butler, but that didn't mean the man lacked intelligence. In Katy's experience she found him to be wily, clever, plausible, calm, but worst of all, he drew no boundaries. As with a psychopath nothing deterred his resolve. Harris proved frighteningly unscrupulous.

Katy felt mature enough to put him in his place, to assert herself as lady of the house. Upset about his treatment of Alice, she determined to take the man on his own ground. She knew he would be in his office at eleven and set off there a few minutes before.

'Ah, Miss Kate,' he said with his usual arrogant air, 'what a pleasant surprise. Did you enjoy your night out?'

The inference was there. It hung in his voice like tolling bells.

Kate tried to hide her shaking hands and speak, but at the crucial moment words failed her.

'Come about Alice, have you?' he egged.

How did he know? As a youngster she believed him to be in league with the devil.

'You should choose your friends more carefully. I did what I could under the circumstances. I tried to relieve you of the burden. I would never have laid the weight on your young shoulders. Your friend, however, pretty as she is…' that disarming smile, the death mask, she used to call it, '…obviously does not share my consideration. I dare say she has made me out to be the villain?'

Katy opened her mouth, but Harris went on. 'She tried to steal from me, Miss Kate. She attempted to take my hard-earned wages. What was I to do? Had I called the police in your father's absence I could have been assessed as indelicate. If, on the other hand, I had informed Mr Howell,' his words hung menacingly as always, 'then he would have been forced to expel the girl. Now you wouldn't want that, would you, Miss Kate?'

'I want to…'

'No need to apologise,' he interjected. 'The young lady and I came to an agreeable conclusion. I offered a lesson on the error of her ways, and I believe, genuinely believe, she has digested it.'

'You shouldn't have…'

'The rod has always been the way of this house, miss. You have fallen to its embrace on numerous occasions. You accepted your punishment as a lady of breeding, but I should have seen that a girl of lesser grace would seek to upset the tradition.

'Did I ever, on any occasion, flog you without just reason?'

Kate reluctantly shook her head.

129

'No, of course I didn't. I am an honourable man, a loyal servant to your family.' Knowing Kate was no match for him he eyed her up and down, the look derogatory. 'Now, was there anything else, miss? I have work to do, so if you don't mind...'

'The notes and the confession,' Kate blurted, 'I want them back.'

'What notes, my dear?' he said, the picture of innocence. 'What confession?'

'Alice lost some notes, she says you have them,' Kate persisted. 'And she says you made her sign a confession. Harris, I want them, please.'

'I don't know anything of any notes, miss. And why would I demand a confession? Alice agreed to a caning in just recompense for her attempted pilfering.'

'Harris!' A knot of anxiety made Kate feel sick. 'I wrote those notes, not Alice. It was me who wrote those things about you.'

'You, miss?' Harris feigned shock. 'But why would you do that?'

'Because,' she said, taking a deep breath, 'for matters that don't concern you, father has me down for a thrashing this Saturday, and he informed me that if I didn't persuade him in writing in the meantime, then he would have you execute it.'

Harris leered at the enticing prospect and licked his teeth.

'Those notes were for my essay.' She wrung her hands nervously.

'And writing insulting things about me would persuade your father to cancel your punishment?'

Kate saw the pit opening and felt herself teetering on the crumbling edge. Harris could always leave her way behind in a war of words. 'W-what do you want, Harris,' she asked tentatively, knowing exactly what he wanted, 'for the return of the notes?'

'If I did possess such notes, then it would merely be

for a safeguard,' he said. 'A safeguard to prevent certain people pointing a finger of lies at me. I would need to feel secure.'

'I guarantee there will be no further mention of them,' she insisted.

'Accepted,' he acknowledged, his eyes crawling down to her legs, and back up again. 'There would also have to be an appeasement for the defamation of character.'

'I will accept your punishment,' she said, fully understanding his meaning.

Harris puckered his lips thoughtfully. 'And perhaps while we're having this cosy little chat, you might explain the meaning of, and I quote, "I might just offer him my fanny".'

'Out of spite.'

'Would you?'

'No.'

'Well, that is the price for the confession.'

'You're not serious!'

'You should be careful what you write, Miss Kate,' he advised unnecessarily. 'You never know who might see it.'

'You'll use the confession, won't you?' she accused him. 'You'll use it to beat Alice over and over.'

'You know me, Katy,' he grinned salaciously, 'do you think I am capable of that?'

'I'm surprised you haven't demanded sex from her.'

'Oh, too many complications,' he said, tutting and shaking his head. 'I don't know her like I know you. Difficult to say what she would do afterwards. Besides, she's a virgin, isn't she?'

'Okay, Harris, I agree. But I want those notes afterwards, or I swear I'll raise the roof.'

'I wouldn't renege on a deal.'

'What's it to be? The jolly old cane?'

'No, I think I'll reserve that for the weekend. See, if

I'm right, your father will send you to me on Saturday.'

'Gives you something to live for, doesn't it?'

'Manners, Katy,' he admonished mildly, fully confident in his victory. 'I can ensure the cane bites with severity, you know.'

'You do anyway.'

'But today I shall spank you. Over my knee. An unruly brat warrants a thorough hand-spanking, don't you think?'

'Now?'

'Is that my style? No, this afternoon at two o'clock. Bare bottom and paddle.'

'You'll give me the notes then?'

'You have my word,' he said self-righteously, his eyes lingering on her breasts.

'I've seen Harris,' Kate told Alice. 'He's going to give me the notes later.'

'Can you trust him, Kate?' Alice asked, worried.

'I'll get them, don't worry.'

'How did you manage it?'

Kate smiled, a tired curl of the lips. 'Persuasion, Ali,' she said without conviction. 'Just you make sure I don't have to see him again on Saturday.'

'I'll work on it for the rest of the week.' Alice threw her arms about Kate and hugged her. 'Thank you for everything,' she whispered.

Those three hours crucified, Katy on tenterhooks. A sexual thrashing was one thing, a prospect to relish, but a cold-hearted spanking from Harris she dreaded. That paddle, a vicious V-shaped swat of dense leather, the ends weighted with flat metal studs. She recalled how he would 'warm' her buttocks first with his hand, raining hard slaps at a ferocious pace. He would cover her from the small of her back to her knees, not relenting for a second, the fire instilled proving untenable and persistent.

Then he would use the paddle, first beating her over his

knees and then over the desk, the final explosions impossible.

Her only saving would be in her ability to turn the pain, to envisage it as a sexual encounter. But on this occasion that would prove nigh on impossible, for Harris understood how to instil fear in his victim.

Katy didn't dwell on the other payment, rejecting it from conscious thought. She did have a choice – war. She could point the finger and wait on the outcome. Who would her father believe? Dear old Harris, butler to the family since time began, or his wayward daughter, inveterate liar and troublemaker. She didn't have to ponder too long on the probable outcome.

Perhaps it was her comeuppance. Since of legal age she had been pleasing men and herself. Father had warned that she would inherit a tag, that rumour would proliferate, and now even old Harris fancied a dip, as everyone else had.

He would do it and leave no trace. That was the way of the man. Cover his tracks. There would be no proof, no later recriminations. Again, it would be his word against hers.

Two o'clock neared and Kate made herself ready. She knew what Harris preferred; a dress code that might alleviate some of his rancour. She dug deep in her wardrobe seeking clothes she hadn't worn for years. Perhaps they wouldn't fit her now.

Surprisingly the skirt and blouse did, for their design had altered little since she'd last worn them.

Outside Harris's office the girl checked her attire. She pinched her facial cheeks to produce some colour; terrified she might be, but Harris perceiving that wouldn't help her at all. She knocked, desperately trying to quell the shake in her arm. As usual he let her wait; the war of nerves began.

Mouth dry, she listened in that dreadful silence to the

blood rush, a pulsation generated from a thumping heart
that sounded in her ears like gushing water. Her body felt
numb, all except, of course, the area reserved for
punishment. That seemed to be overly sensitised. Although
covered it felt naked, vulnerable, an irresistible target.

'Enter,' Harris called.

That voice, the tone so reminiscent of a headmaster,
and it carried the same weight, the same intolerance, the
same terrifying implication. She placed her trembling hand
on the doorknob, twisted and pushed. Harris sat straight-
backed, a fountain pen in his right hand, attention on the
papers before him. Kate waited meekly.

He attended to the last detail, closed the ledger and settled
back, elbows resting on the arms of the chair, hands
clasped together, fingers steepled to his lips. 'Miss Kate,'
he eventually said, having scrutinised her for a few tense
minutes, 'on time, I see. That's very good. You've now
had time to mull this matter over, and you are suitably
anxious, I take it?'

With little expression or emotion, not wanting to give
him the pleasure of seeing how he was winning the mental
battle, she retaliated, 'I'm ready.'

'Good, I'm pleased to hear it. Lock the door,' he ordered,
a sadistic sneer unseen by her as he eyed the sway of her
hips.

Harris took up position on an armless wooden chair.
'Now, take your blouse off,' he said, when she was again
standing before him. 'Let me see how you look since the
last time I had the pleasure of punishing you.'

'That wasn't part of the bargain,' she complained.

'Ah, just as I thought,' he said, looking amused by the
futile, mini-rebellion. 'You seek to distract and then barter.
Do you honestly think I will concede? I do still hold the
whip hand,' Harris chortled at his own pun, 'and I can
punish.' He smiled cruelly. 'Or I can crucify.'

Knowing there was no other alternative, Katy

134

surrendered and began unfastening the buttons of her crisp white blouse, and Harris ogled lecherously.

The garment undone and hanging open from the tips of her large breasts offered the first glimpse of her cotton bra, breasts bulging within the undersized allotment. Harris coloured and his ardour rose.

Katy shucked her shoulders and let the blouse fall, and Harris's eyes crawled all over her voluptuous form, his expression understandably appreciative. 'My, my, doesn't that bring back memories,' he wheezed quietly.

'What memories, Harris?' Katy attempted further distraction, trying to warm that granite soul.

'Of my youth,' he said. 'But that is beside the point. I believe we have a spanking to execute.' He patted his lap, and the abrupt reminder jarred Katy and her heart sank as following his relentless orders she meekly lay across his elderly thighs, knowing intense pain would soon follow. Almost ritualistically he lifted her skirt and folded it over her back, and she heard his snort, the Harris approval.

'So firm and yet so soft, Miss Kate,' he drawled, and she felt his cold hand run over her bottom. 'You do realise that the tightness of your panties will accentuate the sting rather than protect against it, don't you?'

'I?'

'Oh yes,' he carried on, disregarding any response from her. 'Buttocks that are compacted such as these are more liable to feel the full severity of my hand, and severe it will be. I can guarantee that.'

The man's left arm pinned her down, and she stared at the floor and waited anxiously.

Harris continued to run his hand over those cotton-compressed buttocks, the cheeks strenuously confined. The appearance, the feel, the promise, all had their effect on him. With his cock rising to the occasion he raised that hand, and with severity in mind brought it down hard.

With her backside well versed in disciplinary assault,

Kate barely winced. It stung, burned, but could never approach the gut-wringing hurt of the rod. She held no dread of his hand. No, it was that demon paddle, the bite of those metal studs that Katy remembered so well.

Harris slapped left and right haunch repeatedly. He moved up and down, her bottom continuously in motion, the fire gathering strength. Minutes later, her bottom a rosy sphere beneath the taut white of her panties, the pain began to approach shocking.

Harris sensed and felt the tension in her. He noted the attempts at evasion; subtle rolls of her hips. He managed a more rigorous palm, the slaps noisy, intense, rapid. Katy seized the chair legs and clenched her jaw, her face contorted.

Her bum blazed and she could see no end in sight. Harris always took discipline to the limit of endurance and beyond. Where another might accept the victim had suffered enough, that ogre would punish in the truest sense of the word.

Pride battled suffering. Dignity demanded her silence and refused to offer the voice of appeasement. Distress begged total surrender. Kate compromised. She whimpered to each violent detonation. She kicked as the hurt ripped through her hide. She sobbed as an expression of contrition.

But her declarations of discontent did little to persuade. Harris continued with his rough hand, Katy guessing he would. The demon persevered until she fair shrieked at each ruthless slap, one hand hovering close to that tortured posterior. 'I assume,' he said, intellect calculating, 'that the force of my hand has faded in your memory.'

'No, Harris,' she replied, sniffing, 'I remember only too well.'

'Discipline should not only chasten but deter,' he decreed piously. 'What good is the insincere scolding? The miscreant will only offend again.'

Harris picked up his paddle and laid it on that scalded hide. 'Now, Miss Kate, we will spend a little time in contemplation. While I beat you I would like you to consider all those other misdeeds. The ones you have managed to evade punishment for over the years.'

'What misdeeds?'

'You want a list?'

'Not really.'

'You have grown into a disgrace to the Howell family. You have no morals. You are wanton. Your manners are appalling. You drive your good parents to distraction. You may think you are clever, but I can assure you, you are on the road to ruin.'

The paddle struck with sickening force, the studded V biting into her buttock. Kate rose to the horizontal, kicking desperately, and Harris, content with the reaction, dealt another blow. How anyone could hit so hard with such a short stroke dumbfounded her. And that degrading posture meant, unless she reversed the position, all the blows would rain on one flank.

Cheeks smarting, tender and hot, she floundered as those twin tails cut again. How much she could take she wasn't sure. The dilemma, though, was incidental, for she could do nothing about it, except suffer.

And she did. Those agonised dunes complained bitterly, the leather and metal pounding, continually intensifying a raging smart that edged her closer to despair.

And yell she did. Screams she let fly. Whimpers and squeals bombarded the ether. She kicked wildly, legs in perpetual motion. Arms waved in desperation. Hands clutched at chair legs and brace. They wrung each other. Fingers clawed the air, tore at tresses and made forays toward that throbbing backside.

Harris knew no mercy. Those tormented cries and thrashing limbs served only to feed an insatiable appetite. Her twisting, writhing torso quenched his thirst. The man

137

thrived on others' misery. His sadistic lust ripened to Katy's wretchedness.

Then at last his words penetrated the haze of oblivion. 'Get up, Miss Kate,' he ordered. 'We'll complete this over the desk, as we used to.'

She stood, back arched, bust thrust out. Her hands wavered, hovered over those fired, burning dunes. Harris shook his head and the girl knew not to touch. No comfort, no matter how minimal or futile, was permitted.

She bent over the desk, adopting the position etched into her memory. Face and breasts to the wood her arms formed the crucifix. Legs firmly together she tendered that raw behind.

Harris took one last admiring glance before tucking fingers in the elastic and tugging those panties down. He bared her rump, the division deep, the buttocks full, crimson, mottled and showing the marks of the studs.

'A dozen to each cheek, Kate,' he told her. 'And you will count them, please.'

Face drawn, grimacing in anticipation, she dug her nails into the desktop. Harris drew the paddle right back, his arm horizontal. The atmosphere so tense it proved claustrophobic, he dispensed an absolute stinger, the clap of weighted leather on haunch stupefying. Her thrashed behind shuddered traumatically beneath the volatile impact.

Kate leapt to the detonation. Her head cleared the desk, expression startled. A groan swiftly changed to a throaty roar, the agony vent. As Harris's arm hovered for a second she gulped and blurted, 'One!'

As that obligatory statement faded so the second struck, the crack loud, the consequence mind shattering. Katy rolled her face on the table, tears filling those brown pools, teeth clenched in reply. Spectres raced from the past, flitted through her mind's eye. Horrors resurfaced. Violent encounters from the past. Floggings that surpassed the acceptable, whippings that left her sobbing for hours, stripes that would keep her from sitting for days.

'Two!' she shouted, her voice nearly taken by pain.

That ample rump shivered to another paralysing discharge, the scarlet flesh rippling, an excruciating burn driven deep into her flesh.

With father away and mother in another world Harris had governed with a free hand. There had been no one to run to, no consoling love to seek solace with. No person in the world to end her torment. 'Three,' she squealed.

Oh, Harris had commenced hostilities with a fair hand. Those first meetings had been for discipline only. Unwarranted chastisement in her mind, but of course Kate was a free thinker, and what she saw as right others did not.

Her sickeningly raw bottom shuddered. Kate screamed. Pride lost to the leather and savage conduct she only cared to release her frustrations.

Beaten with the slipper to begin with, she could shrug it off. Then when no criticism was voiced he slowly increased the threshold.

'Four!' she gasped.

The slipper became a plimsoll. The half-dozen advanced to twelve, and the man's excuse? Katy refused to learn her lesson.

'Five,' she yelped, sunk beyond despair.

Then the hand spankings began.

'Six,' she hissed.

Over his bony knees, skirt hoisted, his paws groping her buttocks. His reason? Judging the strength of delivery. Then he began, slapping her bottom, a slow, deliberate crucifixion. Then when she thought he had finished, he pulled her panties down.

'Seven!' The tears rolled freely.

The embarrassment. The humiliation. Her face took on a hue as red as her behind. She protested, but he struck her with force in reply. So began her initiation, her introduction to the world of corporal punishment, suffering for his pleasure.

'Eight!' Ranks of tears flowed.

He led her onto the path of masochism and confusion. She failed to comprehend the excitement of exposure. She took those bursts of energy to be directly attributable to the promise of chastisement, although that in itself could never be deemed as pleasurable.

'Nine!' The fury eased, a general numbness infiltrated.

He spanked her for what she recalled as seemingly endless. He slapped those soft dunes until she begged forgiveness, and then he soothed, fingers stroking the agony. She considered that an affectionate kindness.

'Ten!' Those ends ripped into untouched flesh, biting deep into the buttock division, the metal scalding. Hell briefly revisited.

The butler watched her every move. He noted every breach of discipline, always ready to beckon, to levy a toll for transgression. Gradually he widened the range and scope of corporal punishment.

'Eleven! Oh!' Delving her buttock crease again.

Kate began to live in dread of waking, careful of every move. Even then Harris would find reason and she would visit his office. The strap superseded the plimsoll, on her naked rump nauseated. The intervals of inspection humiliated more than ever. Foolhardy by nature she sought some evidence of his brutality, combing his office for a written corroboration. A diary, maybe.

'Twelve!' She panted, gasped for breath. Perspiration wet her face. Pain burned in her eyes. Her bottom blazed, the lick of fire continuous.

She discovered no testimonial. Instead she uncovered an envelope full of old photographs. Young women dressed in their underwear. Some shots were ancient, in sepia. The rest mainly monochrome. Some had been tinted, hand finished to imitate the flesh tones.

'Thirteen!' A switch of sides, her other cheek bore the brunt.

Katy realised the import of those prints – Harris had a thing about bloomers.

'Fourteen! Aaaah!'

So out of her allowance and after much searching she procured a pair. Harris's face when he uncovered them for the first time – she robbed him of all breath, she felt his penis rise and dig indecently into her belly. He stroked and petted her for ages, the feel of warm buttock flesh beneath cotton bloomers absorbing him completely.

'Fifteen! Aaaah! Ah! Ah! Ah!'

However, Katy hadn't foreseen the obvious. How could she know? It was hardly coincidence, so he interrogated her. He wouldn't desist until she admitted her indiscretion. Harris sent her away, telling her to report the following day.

'Eeugh! Oh! Sixteen!'

Petrified she returned at the allotted time to find Harris waiting with a new implement. She quailed at the prospect, the sight of that rattan instilling terror. He caned her on her cotton-covered haunches, the hurt worse than she had ever experienced before.

'Oh, please! Ah, Harris, it's killing me. Seventeen!'

Worse still, the man convinced himself that Kate had attempted a seduction. Why else would she dress in a fashion that she knew would kindle his libido? So she had to endure his unwanted and unwarranted attention, although thankfully he never attempted anything outrageous.

'Aaaaah! Eighteen!'

Thankfully her father's return full time, and his decision to send her to *Carters*, saved her from worse.

Countenance soaked with tears, her body wracked with pain, Katy suffered the nineteenth.

No wonder she grew twisted. No wonder she sought

physical punishment. She had been brought up in her most impressionable years with the rod as her only source of attention. She chased sex because of that lack of affection in those susceptible years. She had been jaundiced. And that bastard was solely responsible.

Twenty cracked cruelly and vindictively on upper haunch, and taking as much as she could, Kate sprang from the desk, a veil of red mist before her eyes. She swung her right fist and caught Harris hard on the jaw. The man staggered, the paddle hitting the floor with a thump, and with expression astounded he voiced no protest as Katy pulled up her panties.

She pointed a finger at him. 'Now Harris, fucking servant,' she cursed vehemently, 'I want those fucking notes and Alice's confession!'

Speechless, he pulled open a drawer and handed the sheets of paper to Kate. She put on her blouse, and shaking nearly out of control, managed to fasten the buttons. Then offering nothing else she lifted her chin and left.

Harris rubbed his jaw and slumped disbelievingly back on the chair. He shook his head, the abrupt violence beyond his comprehension.

Kate handed the confession to Alice.

'You did get it back!' Alice squealed delightedly. 'Wonderful! But how?'

Kate sat on Alice's bed, her mind temporarily on her smarting knuckles. She winced, and lying on her back, lifted her tortured buttocks from the mattress.

'What's the matter, Kate?' asked Alice, concerned. 'Oh, Katy, you didn't? Tell me you didn't.'

'I didn't,' whispered the suffering girl.

'Then what's wrong with your bum?'

Katy laughed. 'There's a price to pay for everything, Ali.'

'Harris flogged you, didn't he? You paid for this with

your backside.'

'It was nearly my cunt, as well,' she said, as usual her crudity more acceptable than inoffensive.

'What?'

'My arse for the notes, and my pussy for the confession.'

'What happened?' Alice pressed. 'I don't understand, Kate.'

'Oh, I paid for the notes, all right,' Kate disclosed.

'So what stopped him getting payment for the confession?'

'My right hook stopped him. I hit the cunt, Ali. I punched him in the face. Then I demanded those papers. He was so dumbfounded he gave them to me without a word.'

'He wants sacking,' Alice snorted.

'I couldn't agree more. The trouble is father thinks the sun shines out of his arse. If I complain he'll blame me. I am, after all, the princess of trouble, aren't I? He'll think I'm just trying to dodge the Saturday whacking.'

'What about that? If Jay doesn't accept the essay, then what's Harris going to do to you?'

'I don't want to think about that, Ali. Whip the skin off my back, I expect.'

'He wouldn't dare.'

'Perhaps I've left an impression. Maybe he'll tread carefully from now on.'

'Oh, I do hope so, Katy,' Alice said, albeit with a lack of belief. 'I really hope so…'

Alice put her heart and soul into the essay. She spent most of the rest of the day in thoughtful repose, placing every emphasis on why Kate shouldn't be punished. But at the end of the day she still couldn't justify what she'd done in a public car park with Harry.

Eventually she offered the piece to Kate while she inspected her rear for the umpteenth time.

'Any better?' she asked.

'It will be,' Kate said, with her usual cheerful resilience. 'Good job I mend quick, ain't it?'

Kate read the essay, and handed it back to Alice. 'Fine,' she adjudged. 'That should set daddy thinking. For a man that loves whacking arse, he has a very limited understanding.'

'He just wants what's best for you.'

'You would say that.'

'No, Kate, I'm not defending him. But gobbling the chauffeur in broad daylight in a pub car park is pushing your luck. And think of the titters down at the police station. I bet Jay felt humiliated.'

'So, you're saying I deserve what I get?'

'You're a wild child Kate, and I don't think you'll ever change.'

Chapter Eight

James collected Kate just after noon the next day, and Jonathan left the house shortly after. Alice considered the day ahead. She had Odette and Jenny for company, if needed. Harris still terrified her and after crushing Harry's manhood, she thought it best to avoid him too.

Alice took a walk. It was a beautiful day and she strolled down to the lake. She missed Kate. She longed for companionship. Perhaps she should curtail the chase, Jay persistently elusive. Perhaps, like Kate, she should find herself a young man nearer her own age, a man with no ties, no complications.

There again, maybe she should ignore her constant urges and concentrate on her finals. A return to the principles of her religion wouldn't be a bad idea. She had let matters get out of hand recently; the sordid business with Giulio, her fault as much as his, her pursuit of the married Jay and all the risks that went with that, the flirtations between her and Jenny and the possibility that Harris might get wind of it and blackmail her into... no, that didn't bear thinking about.

Alice neared the chill waters of the Howell estate's lake, the sun hot on her shoulders. Relief intimated in the form of grey cloud edging over the horizon, mere shadows barely discernible through an enveloping haze.

The summer's growth had dried to a harmonious gold

amidst a profusion of diverse greens. Nature's whispers hindered an otherwise serene hush, man's clamour unknown there.

Only a few months had passed since being tipped into the abyss of despair. That dreadful loss compounded by the uncompromising Richard. Days best forgotten. Memories best erased. If only she could. Were matters any better? She rubbed her bottom. Harris's rod had left its impression, but that was gross stupidity. It didn't have to happen.

No, life was better, infinitely so. She only had to face discipline when she erred. Jay and Jenny were caring and generous. Katy was better than a real sister. All she had to do was avoid trouble, work hard and the world would be her oyster.

Alice reached the stony shoreline, and feeling hot, the cool waters offered temptation, so she kicked off her sandals and settled her feet in the refreshing lake. She paddled, deep in thought.

Three days would see her back at college, not *Carters*, but the daunting *Heptonstall Moor*. Thank goodness Katy was going too. A trouble shared, they say. And she was seeing Richard on Saturday. Hopefully the last ever connection with the abhorrent little man.

Alice breathed of the vitality about her. Some days it felt good to be alive. She gazed at the still waters, recalling how she and Katy had skinny dipped there. It was so hot, an encore beckoned.

Eyes scanning the banks, seeing no signs of life, she waded further. Immediately she felt cooler, a sudden breeze embracing. Alice spread her arms, gazing up at the azure sky, basking in that comforting zephyr.

She waded deeper, her buttocks enlivened by the wet coolness. Eyes closed, Jay was there. Her hands were his hands. They explored her body. Jay cupped her breasts, feeling the sensuous orbs through the thin cloth, the subtle touch sparking the first wave of sensual activity. Those attentive sensors roamed the firm spheres, kindling, exasperating the passion. Fingers feverishly unfastened buttons that terminated at the waist, rose to seek entry, slipped beneath the covering and delved succulent flesh, goading, a preliminary to more earthly devotion.

She sensed his breath, his lips, and met them with her own. Lightning passed between them. The subsequent roll of thunder, the pounding of her heart. Fingers encompassed erect nipples, toyed, stroked, tweaked, exquisite pulsation heightening the arousal.

Those explorers withdrew, descended, followed the contours of ribs and belly. There they divided, navigated hips and fell upon the plumpness of erogenous derrière. They absorbed the firm constitution, fondled and pleasured.

Alice slipped beneath the placid waters, kicked from the bottom, swum adjacent to the bank. She wallowed in the bracing shroud, dipped her auburn hair, savouring the stimulus. She glided, arms sweeping, graceful legs kicking.

Alice stood and shook off the surplus water, spray spattering the serenity. She perused her body, smiling. The thin cotton clung semitransparent and evocative. Breasts thrust and disclosed their youthful substance where the cloth parted. That material clung and wrinkled over the flat of her belly, then chased the dip of her groin, highlighting irresistible legs, traversing shapely thighs and laying explicit to pronounced buttocks.

Hands roamed, gliding over lush haunches. Fingers sought the sodden contact of dress and precious triangle of groin, where lay the crop of silky curls.

As she bowed, fingers tracing the inner surface of her thighs, her expression in blissful content, her breasts shivered with the motion.

Her hands moved, cupped her buttocks, the tramlines concealed but still quite prominent. They wandered up, sensuality left in their wake, to mount the apex of hips and move steadily across her tummy. There the fingers met, clutched the fleshy plateau of belly and held her.

Jay stood behind, muscular chest to her back, ticklish groin to her rump; erection nestled between her thighs. Alice threw her head back and sighed, his hands falling, seeking and finding the prominence of her pubic mound, fingers delving the soft knoll. If only. But he did, in her imagination.

Spurring wild sensations the forefingers marked the path, drove sedulously towards their goal. The fires ignited, blazed rampant, her breathing laboured.

They touched and cajoled, lifted the saturated skirt, her thighs parting expectantly, facilitating access. A hand slipped beneath her wet panties, teased the curls there, manoeuvred between the silken limbs, bejewelled by sparkling droplets and petted that susceptible slit. Alice gasped, and teeth clenched let the scrutiny explore the softness of folds, the gates of euphoria.

Panting, bubble close to bursting, a finger parted the sensual lips and slid the length of her sex and then slipped in unimpeded to probe, her vagina oiled with anticipation.

The bubble exploded. Alice straightened, hands clasped to her sex she rolled her head from side to side, the expression of sublime pleasure relating the rapture within...

Then her sigh of satisfaction was crushed by the sound of a slow handclap. Eyes opened in alarm and Alice stared in shocked disbelief at the source crouched on the bank.

'Nice one was it, Alice?' enquired a delighted Harry.

'You...!' She fumbled for words and with buttons, desperate to cover herself. 'How long have you been spying on me?'

'Bit late for that,' he remarked, nodding at her saturated cloth enshrouded body. 'What a lovely display of masturbation; a real eye-opener. Tell me, who was the lucky fella in there?' He jabbed a finger against his head.

'You filthy shit!' she shouted. 'Enjoy yourself, did you?' Alice plucked at the dress, attempting to reduce the emphasis.

Harry sat, stretching legs out before him. 'And I thought today would be just another day. When I saw you strolling down here and decided to follow, I would never have dared to even think you might... well, play with yourself. You've a lovely body, Alice, like I imagined. Especially when your boobies decided to air themselves. A pair it would be a pleasure to fill my hands with, that's for sure.'

Alice backed into deeper water, submerging her lower half, and with both arms defending her breasts she asked angrily, 'So you've had your peek, now what?'

He picked up a small stone and tossed it at her, splashing a foot away. 'Not just a peek, Alice,' he taunted, 'more of a full-on eyeful, I'd say.'

Alice, still concealing her breasts with one arm, reached into the water and fought the floating hem of her dress down with the other.

'Seems we got off on the wrong foot, Alice,' he went on. 'I made the wrong move and you flattened my balls for it. Perhaps we can start again.'

'And you think sneaking up on me like this is the right way?'

'Human nature, is that. If you were some great wedge of flab, well it would be different. But you're not. You're about the sexiest bird I ever clapped eyes on.'

'So now you've clapped your eyes, will you just go?' she pleaded. 'Do the decent thing for once, Harry.'

Smiling greedily, he shook his head. 'I like it here, Alice. It's such a lovely day and all.' His eyes crawled over the wet material clinging to the lower swell of her breasts, just visible to either side of her slender arm. 'And such a good view, too. It's not as if I have to rush back. I've not much to do, you see. But sitting here I can watch one of the wonders of creation. I'll tell you straight, girl, that dress don't hide much in its current state.'

'If you don't let me out I'll have a word with Mrs Howell,' she warned.

'You whine like a brat in nappies, Alice. Could it be that you have more to hide than that sexy body?'

'What makes you say that?'

'Well, rumours abound. The smack of cane on shapely bottom carries in that house, and the trouble is, you never know who might be listening. Or watching, come to that. Take that time Mrs Howell took a whip to your delightful backside, for example. Such a teasing ripple of buttocks to behold. I was quite transfixed. I know Katy got worse, but her arse can't compare to yours.'

'You peeping Tom!' Alice accused. 'You pervert!'

'Ooh, language, young Alice,' he admonished, tutting animatedly. 'Swearing doesn't suit your innocent image. Or perhaps you aren't so innocent. Maybe you're a fake, putting on the little-miss-innocent act purely for the Howells' sake. So they won't guess what you're really up to.'

'I'm getting cold, Harry,' she said, pouting, ignoring his gibe.

'So come out. Or maybe you could generate some more heat with those industrious fingers of yours.'

'I warn you, Harry, I'll speak with?'

'Yes, yes, you said,' he interrupted impatiently. 'I'm impressed, as you can see. So did Harris cane you too?'

Alice refused to answer, her teeth beginning to chatter as the cool water began to chill her.

'I know he did,' Harry answered his own question, 'and the only reason I can think of is because he knows something about you. Is that the case, Alice?'

'Why don't you ask him?' she challenged petulantly.

'What, old misery guts?' he scoffed. 'He wouldn't piss on me if I was on fire, let alone let me share the goodies. What's he got you down for, eh? A whacking a month to keep his silence? You see, that's the old duffer's fancy. He relishes spanking and caning a nice ripe bottom. Now me, I prefer something more normal, though I could put you over my knee if you so wished.'

'I'm frozen, Harry,' Alice tried the pleading approach again. 'Will you *please* go away so I can get out?'

'Depends if you're nice to me, Alice. Then I could make sure I didn't say anything untoward to the Howells.'

'It's not going to happen,' she insisted. 'You can say what you like. You can make all the accusations that come into that feeble brain of yours, but it won't happen.' Angry, cold and tired her patience snapped. 'I'm sick of morons like you. I'm sick of everyone thinking I'm here for their convenience. What is it with this place? You're all a bunch of perverts!'

'Rumour has it that is exactly what you are, miss.'

Alice snapped. 'Right, that's it! You are going to eat those words.' She waded determinedly forward, splashing water with her hands, not caring about the subsequent exposure. Harry attempted to shield himself, eyes glued to those firmly mobile breasts moulded by wet cotton, trying to digest the voluptuous vision that was Alice.

As she drew closer she kicked instead, a shower falling on the startled man. Then she cleared the water and marched up the bank, a fist raised.

Cringing, acting, Harry peered up. 'You ain't half sexy when you're mad,' he beamed.

'Mad?' she echoed. 'You bet I'm mad!' She kicked him, her bare foot having little effect. Harry hugged himself, laughing, and she kicked again, her ankle caught in a strong fist as it neared the target. Easily too strong for her Harry lifted and toppled her over, his arms catching the helpless girl as she hit the ground.

'My, my, you're the biggest fish I've ever caught in this lake,' he chuckled.

'Let me go!' she spat.

'No, I think I'll have a closer look at that sweet arse,' and he turned her effortlessly and pinned her over his lap. She kicked, struggled, but Harry fought the soaking dress up her thighs and over her tensed buttocks. He leered at the glistening limbs, the vision provoking a reaction, the stiffening of a certain part.

'This is sexual assault!' she shrieked. 'I'll have you arrested.'

'My word against yours, missy,' he said, cocksure of himself. 'And if I'm right then I'll point the finger. I reckon from what I've heard that you're fair game.'

The wet material successfully drawn over wet buttocks, Harry ogled those panty-covered cheeks, the water rendering the panties virtually transparent. He could easily discern the plethora of stripes beneath, stretching either side of the panty-line. 'Well, well, what a whipped bottom we have here,' he leered. 'That's definitely Harris's work; I recognise the trademarks.' Harry chuckled. 'So why did he do this? What reason did he have? Stealing like Odette, was it?'

'Let me go, you swine!' Alice cursed, wriggling desperately in his strong hold.

'You've a lovely bum, girl,' he drooled, each hand full of firm buttock. 'Mr Howell must be having a whale of a time with you.'

Alice wriggled back, Harry accepting that he dare go no further, but indulged in the feel of her breasts against his arm, and then she sank her teeth into his shoulder. The man cussed and released her.

Alice quickly scrambled to her feet. She pulled her skirt down and pointed a warning finger at him. 'This doesn't end here, you creep,' she vowed. 'I'll see you sacked if you try anything like this again…'

Harry was about to respond, when Jenny's voice stunned them both. 'What is going on?' she asked. 'Harry, what are you doing here, and Alice, why are you soaking wet?'

Chapter Nine

'Ah, Harris, I'd like a word in private, if you don't mind,'
Jenny said, having located the butler in the kitchen.

'I'm rather busy at present, Mrs Howell,' he said
snootily. 'Can it not wait?'

'Harris, you will do as I say.'

'It obviously cannot, then,' he said, his snootiness
undiminished.

The butler followed Jennifer to his office, to the very
office he had whipped Alice and Katy in. She closed the
door and told him to sit.

'I want to talk to you about your responsibilities,' she
began. 'About your duties, Harris.'

'Those I take very seriously indeed, Mrs Howell,' he
insisted.

'Yes, I'm sure you do,' she allowed. 'However, you do
not seem to realise where your duties end and mine begin.'

'I'm sorry, Mrs Howell,' he said, with believable
innocence, 'I don't follow you. Please explain further.'

'Alice – you caught her in your room apparently
stealing,' Jenny stated frankly. 'Why didn't you report
the matter to me?'

'Oh, that,' he said, apparently unperturbed at being found
out.

'Yes, Harris, that. Do you think there is anything that
goes on in this house without me knowing?'

'It was late, Mrs Howell. Miss Alice is a friend of your daughter, so I didn't want to cause trouble or embarrassment for her. I'm sure she won't repeat the episode.'

'You arrogant old man,' Jenny said.

'I beg your pardon, Mrs Howell?'

'I said, Harris, that you are an arrogant old man. Perhaps you've been the head of this household for too long. You've acquired an attitude. You believe yourself faultless. You have no right making such decisions. If Alice truly was a thief you should have brought the matter to my attention.'

'As I said, Mrs Howell, I tried to keep the matter quiet for everyone's sake,' he said smarmily. 'I apologise if I did wrong, but it was for the right reasons. In your father's day corporal punishment would have been the only acceptable procedure.'

Jenny laughed, the humour lacking. 'In my father's day? This is no longer my father's day, Harris. And you know that full well. You run the house and you discipline the servants. You do not flog one of our guests.'

'She agreed to it?'

'I don't care if she went down on bended knee and begged you, to be honest,' Jenny cut in impatiently. 'You do not beat our guests, under any circumstances. Now, do you understand that?'

'Yes, madam,' he said obsequiously. 'I am very sorry, madam. I only tried to protect the family.'

'No, you blackmailed her, Harris. You used the notes she'd written to blackmail her.'

'I certainly did nothing of the kind,' he denied, almost convincingly. 'In my opinion the girl is a common thief, nothing more, nothing less. I merely dissuaded her from further illegal ventures. And punished her for the act as well, of course.'

'How long have you been employed here, Harris?' Jenny asked, finding his attitude increasingly tiresome.

'Forty-two years, Mrs Howell,' he stated efficiently.

'So you've never sought National Assistance before? Still, it is only a matter of form filling, so I understand. But then there's the problem of finding somewhere to live. Hmmm... now that would be a different ballgame entirely.'

'Are you... are you *sacking* me, Mrs Howell?' he asked, getting to his feet and for the first time taking the situation seriously... very seriously indeed.

'Maybe...' Jenny folded her arms and tapped her chin pensively. 'I'll have to give the matter some serious thought.'

'Jonathan.'

'Yes Jenny?'

'What happened between Harry and Kate?'

'I don't follow you.'

'Yes you do. Are you ever going to stop protecting that daughter of yours?'

'No.'

'So what occurred in the car park?'

'Who told you?'

'It doesn't matter who told me,' she said sternly. 'Stop prevaricating, will you please?'

'She provided our randy chauffeur with what's commonly known as a blow-job,' he informed his wife frankly. 'Unfortunately she chose the car park of a public house to perform the deed. A shocked member of the general public rightly reported her, the police attended and she was taken to the station, along with Harry.'

'Good lord! Whatever are we going to do with the little trollop? She's going to bring shame upon our name, if she hasn't already. And this essay you set for her; what's the point of it?'

'I'm offering Katy the chance to act with some responsibility,' he informed her. 'If she succeeds in persuading me that she isn't completely off the rails, then I won't have her punished.'

'But I suspect she *is* completely off the rails,' Jenny said. 'And what do you mean by "have her punished"?'

'Well, she dreads the thought of Harris disciplining her, for obvious reasons. So it seems a particularly appropriate punishment.'

'No, Jonathan,' Jenny said, shaking her head. 'No Harris, and no essay. I will take the matter in hand.'

'Oh dear, poor Katy,' he mused.

'If you ask me there's been too much poor Katy around here. Perhaps that's why she is so fractious. She is showing all the signs of being a spoilt little rich girl. She needs, in my opinion, a severe snapping of the reins.'

'And you believe that a thrashing will pull her up?'

'You obviously did, or you wouldn't have considered Harris for the job.'

'A means to an end, that's all,' he said, defending his decision. 'An incentive to persuade. I wanted her to sit and write that explanation, in the hope she might see the folly of her ways, that she might begin to analyse herself.'

'And did you think about that when you chastised her for that episode at *Carters*?' Jenny challenged. 'Or after the Giulio affair?'

Jonathan shrugged. 'Perhaps I should have.'

'I'm not entering into this lightly, Jonathan. Katy couldn't even take your request seriously. Having a high time is far more important to our beloved daughter than either family loyalty or impressing you.'

'What do you mean, couldn't take my request seriously?'

'She has persuaded Alice to write the defence for her.'

'Alice told you that?'

'I squeezed it out of her, yes.'

'Then there's something else you should know,' he confessed. 'A matter that I suppose disposed me toward

156

the logical approach. Our daughter harbours masochistic tendencies.'

'What are you telling me, Jonathan? That my daughter enjoys being chastised?'

'To a degree, yes,' he confirmed, nodding.

'So if I do punish her physically, I would be wasting my time?'

'Not exactly, but I hoped the essay would explain all. But that's obviously not going to happen now.'

Deep in thought, gazing out of the lounge window at the garden, Alice didn't hear Harris approaching behind her, and leapt as the man loomed and asked, 'Is Miss Kate all right?'

She gasped and spun around, her hand on her heart. 'Harris!' she complained. 'You startled me!'

'Is young Miss Kate all right?' he asked again, his head to one side in mock concern.

'Yes, she's fine,' Alice told him.

'She's become more brazen since you arrived here.'

'I beg your pardon?' Alice was dumbfounded and hurt by the unjust inference of his comment.

'You and her are a bad combination,' he clarified his patronising opinion.

'Haven't you learnt your lesson, Harris?' Alice asked, unsettled by the fact that his boss's warning of dismissal clearly hadn't deterred him. 'I thought Mrs Howell made your position clear, so please mind your own business.'

'But it's not that simple, is it?' he persisted annoyingly. 'I've seen Kate grow up. I have an enormous affection for the young lady. A verbal warning won't deter me from seeing she doesn't come to any harm.'

'What is that supposed to mean?' Alice demanded indignantly.

'Oh, you can be audacious now,' he scoffed, 'believing you have the protection of Mrs Howell. But that doesn't alter the fact that you are a worthless troublemaker. The Howells will come to see that eventually, probably sooner rather than later, and then things will be different.'

His ice-cold tone, so confident, so sure, unsettled the girl. 'You've been caught out, Harris,' she said, trying to gain the upper hand. 'You wouldn't dare repeat what you did to me.'

'You're quite correct in that assumption. I wouldn't repeat that. But you will make a mistake sooner or later and I will be there, waiting, Alice Hussey. I will watch you like a hawk. I will always be somewhere in the background. And when you do err you will feel the wrath of my arm. Not a mere tickling like the last time, no, a flogging that will make you regret the day you ever came to this house.' A hand rose slowly and he ran a forefinger possessively over her breasts, unerringly finding and tracing the outline of her nipples. 'I'll have you, Alice Hussey,' he rasped threateningly. 'Mark my words, I will have you.'

He turned and ambled to the door.

'Empty words, Harris,' she called after him with little conviction. 'Idle threats. You don't worry me.'

The old man stopped at the doorway, and without turning he warned, 'Those notes, young lady. I took the precaution of photographing them before I handed them over. The prints are quite legible.'

Chapter Ten

Harry dropped Alice off at the train station, and she caught the nine-twenty to Southport. She reckoned on being at her uncle's by mid to late morning and home again by mid-afternoon. Home? Yes home. She had settled comfortably at the Howells' house, and she had taken strongly to her surrogate parents. Despite the age difference between her and them both, Jonathan she adored, and Jenny proved to be a good friend.

She could see who Katy took after, and it wasn't Jonathan the level-headed businessman. No, the girl had a lot of her mother in her, if not in looks, certainly in temperament. The woman's obvious attraction to Alice worried her a little, though. Although Alice certainly found her attractive too – which continued to confuse her emotions no end – she wasn't sure about the wisdom of allowing anything to develop in that way.

Where would it all end? Tucked up in bed between Jay and Jenny? Taking them in turns? Making love to them both? Her substitute father and mother? She thanked fate for *Heptonstall*, as boarding would give her a breather from the increasingly complicated situation. It would provide time for matters to calm, for her to ponder the dilemma, her feelings, and how to shape her future.

From now on she would have to steer well clear of Harris, though. The look on that man's face was pure unadulterated hatred. And that threat? Have her? What exactly did he mean by that? Did he mean to punish her soundly given half the chance, or carry through what he tried before? That possibility nauseated her, but she was well aware that being a scheming old lecher, he might well fabricate an opportunity.

Would Katy really behave herself and knuckle down? Was the girl capable of that? If she did then life, Alice realised, would be quite dull attending *Heptonstall* with a reformed goody-two-shoes. Kate did breathe excitement into her life, even if at times it proved downright dangerous, and most often than not, extremely painful.

Alice listened to the rhythmic rattle of steel wheels on iron rails and watched smoke waft past the window she gazed out from. Lancashire offered a beautiful countryside, even if the towns were coated in industrial soot and grime.

She wore her pastel pink skirt and matching blouse. The skirt hugged her bottom, emphasising the line and curves of exquisite buttocks. The blouse similarly exhibited beautifully the swell of firm breasts, the top three buttons innocently left undone and offering glimpses of an enticingly tight cleavage. She wore white bra and panties beneath, trimmed in delicate lace, the panties possessively cosseting her delectable rear, as the bra did her breasts. On her feet she wore a pair of light sandals, the lovely summer weather too warm for anything more. But just in case it did turn a little cooler she wore her adored cherry-leather bolero as insurance, the warmth making it unnecessary for her to do it up.

Alice had applied a little make-up. Delicate sage coloured her eyelids and frost-pink glistened on rosebud lips. Mascara darkened her lashes and black liner emphasised the large, sparkling pools that were her emerald eyes.

Alice had it in mind to intimidate Richard – to turn him inside out and put him on the back foot. She had revenge in store: retribution for the abominable manner in which he had treated her. She would vex the frustrated tyrant and leave promptly with her exam results.

Jonathan, ever protective, had given her ten pounds before she left. 'Get a first class ticket,' he said. 'At least the oiks will leave you alone then. And if the little worm doesn't feed you buy yourself something to eat. Oh, and hail a taxi from Southport station.' He admired her, standing before him ready to leave. 'And Ali,' he added, 'you look absolutely gorgeous. You're an independent young woman now, so don't you take any of that man's shit.'

What would he do if Richard did turn spiteful towards her? Pay him a visit and beat him up? That was a pleasing possibility.

She was alone in the compartment for most of the journey, enjoying the peace and quiet of her own company, but a young man did bustle in at Appley Bridge. He took up residence opposite her and smiled in an amicable manner. Alice politely returned the smile, and then went back to gazing out of the window.

'Are you travelling far?' he enquired.

'Um, Southport,' Alice replied, not sure if she wanted to engage in a conversation with a complete stranger.

'Business, or pleasure?' he went on.

'I'm just visiting someone.'

'It's lovely weather we're having.'

'Yes, it is. And the countryside is so green.'

'Our green and pleasant land, eh?' he quoted, beaming happily.

Alice smiled again, and then went back to the passing views.

'I'm sorry,' the young man suddenly apologised, apparently just noting her lack of enthusiasm for communicating fully. 'I didn't mean to be a nuisance or intrude on your privacy.'

'Oh, no,' Alice said quickly, suddenly feeling guilty for

perhaps coming across as rude, 'you're not, truly. I've a few things on my mind, that's all.'

He nodded graciously, accepting her comment, and silence reigned for a while as they both gazed out of the window. Then he seemed to gather himself for something of great importance.

'I get off at the next stop,' he stated without being asked, and Alice waited for him to continue, wondering what his point was. 'I shall most likely never see you again.'

'Oh,' she said, somewhat flustered by the unexpected comment, 'no probably not, I don't suppose you will.'

'I would like to, though. I would like to very much.'

'Oh.'

'I suppose I'm a cheeky blighter for saying so, aren't I?' he went on cheerily.

'Impetuous, probably, yes,' she said, still taken aback.

'The way I see it is that if one doesn't grab the opportunity one loses it,' he ploughed on regardless. 'Nothing ventured, nothing gained, as I always say. I'm a solicitor. I come from good stock. I am single. I have a future, I hope.' He took a business card from his pocket and handed it to Alice, and she realised he was actually putting himself forward as a potential suitor, asking her to be his girlfriend in a very unorthodox, and cutely endearing manner. She was shocked by such an unexpected approach from someone she'd only just encountered for the first time, but touched and flattered too. 'If you would consent to a date...' he continued regardless, '...dinner, perhaps?' He coughed, suddenly looking bashful and embarrassed. 'Well, anyway, if you do, then please ring me...'

'But you don't even know my name, or where I live, or anything about me,' she pointed out. 'I might be an escaped convict or reside in the Outer Hebrides.'

He laughed. 'I'd drive to the ends of the earth for you.

162

My name's on the card, by the way.'

She looked down at it and noted the name printed there. 'My name is Alice…' she introduced herself, suddenly feeling somewhat bashful. 'Alice Hussey.'

The train began to slow. 'My stop, I'm sorry to say,' he said. 'It's been lovely to meet you, Alice Hussey.' He stood, took her hand and bowing, kissed it. 'I really hope we might meet again.'

She watched him getting off the train, her confidence bolstered. Whether she would take up his offer or not, she didn't know. Almost certainly not. No, she would never see him again. But it was nice to be asked.

At Southport she got into a waiting taxi, and as the vehicle made its way to her fateful destination she reflected with apprehension on her imminent meeting with Richard. And the nearer she drew the more her conviction failed her. Severe doubts resurfaced. Old fears and scars returned. Perhaps she should have worn something less feminine, less attractive – like a sackcloth, maybe. Richard despised her looking pretty. Her chosen outfit would likely send him into some puritanical rage.

Had she the wit and courage to face him? Would she fold at his first verbal assault? She lived with the Howells now. They cared for her, and he had no rights over her at all. She had no doubts that if necessary Jay would pay for her education as well, so she tried to suppress her nerves by convincing herself that she could tell her uncle exactly where he might stick his adopted responsibilities.

The taxi pulled up outside his house, and unhappy memories flooded back. The only consolation being that she would never have to see the vile bastard again, hopefully.

Shaking irrationally she paid the fare and approached the front door with a feeling of real dread, knowing what a vicious sadist lived beyond it.

She knocked, and eventually Richard opened the austere portal. 'Yes?' he enquired, sarcasm dripping from his voice.

'It's me, Alice,' she said unnecessarily.

'Alice?' he said condescendingly. 'I didn't recognise you. You look, erm, *different*.'

'Can I come in, uncle?' she asked, trying to ignore his snide gibe, knowing exactly what he was getting at.

'Yes, yes of course.' He stepped aside. 'Before anybody sees you.'

He followed the girl to the parlour, his attention immediately absorbed by the sway of shapely hips and the roll of firm buttocks.

So far so good, thought Alice, her confidence gradually on the increase.

Discomfited by his draconian morals, Richard tried to ignore a red-blooded impulse, his experience with women still limited.

She perched on the edge of an armchair, her graceful legs neatly together, her hands settled on her lap. The hem of her skirt slid up and highlighted dimpled knees and a portion of smooth thighs, unwittingly provoking the ogre with the vision. The emphasis of sculptured leg severely tested his mettle.

'How are you, uncle?' she asked courteously.

The delicate scent of feminine perfume influenced him, promoting salacious unrest. 'Me?' he said, drawing his eyes to her lovely clear face. 'Oh, the same as usual, I'd say. But you certainly seem to have landed on your feet, young lady.'

'The Howells have been very kind to me, I must say,' she told him.

Richard's gaze flickered furtively upon the area of her blouse that was innocently undone, an inch or two of cleavage just visible to his eagle eye. 'But they don't share the same responsible expectations that I do, it seems.'

'I'm sorry?' she said, unsettled again by his tone. 'I'm not with you. I?'

'And that's a shame,' he said. 'If you were, you would dress more to your age and tender position.'

'Oh, I see, uncle.' Alice leant forward, determined not to be intimidated by the man, the restricted display of the creamy upper slopes of her breasts lying within the blouse deliberate. Katy's words rung in her ears: *'Richard would dearly love to fill your pussy, Ali. Don't tell me he wouldn't. He's a frustrated old man, who's never going to find a woman because he is what he is. And he knows it. You're all woman. Gorgeous figure. Beautiful looks. Oh, he wants you, Ali. He wants you all right. The trouble is, he can't. So he beats you instead. Frustration, you see. At least that way he can get an eye full, without forcing himself on you. So Ali, sex hangs in the air. Electricity buzzes between you both. See yourself for what you are, and tease the bastard. Egg him on. Think how you'll frustrate him further. Feeling sexy, you see. That's the answer.'*

'You find my choice of clothes offensive, uncle?' she challenged.

'It is not the clothes, Alice,' he said. 'On a woman of the world they would be acceptable. They extend a communication. They extol the female form. But a girl of your youthful years should, in my opinion, refrain from such explicit messages.'

'A woman of the world?' she echoed. 'I admit I'm not that experienced, but isn't it the right of a free woman to wear what she pleases? I mean, we have only in the last decade defeated the Nazis for such reasons.'

'You are quite correct,' he acknowledged. 'And I fought them, remember? And you are also quite correct about your inexperience. So perhaps you need me to tell you that you look like a common tart. That you are dressed more suitably for a street corner in Kings Cross, or on Clapham Common.'

165

'How dare you?' Alice gasped. 'Jay didn't say anything so cruel.' She felt hurt. She should have expected little else from such a narrow-minded little man such as he, but the criticism still hurt immensely.

'Perhaps he didn't feel in a position to,' Richard sneered. 'Did he attend your spending spree?'

Alice shook her head.

'Exactly. Polite. A girl of your age should never be allowed to choose her own wardrobe.'

'Perhaps I should take my exam results and go,' Alice suggested, exasperated by the man. She realised she'd been hoping he'd changed, but quite clearly he hadn't, not one jot.

'You mean run away?'

'It's obvious we will never see eye-to-eye, uncle,' she said diplomatically. 'So perhaps it's best that we see as little as possible of each other.'

Richard eased himself into the armchair opposite her. 'Do your blouse up, Alice,' he said quietly. 'I might get the idea you are trying to goad me. Now we have matters to discuss, and there will be no leaving until they are resolved.'

Despite wanting to defy the man and his preposterous prejudices, Alice found herself reluctantly conceding to the order. 'What matters do we have to discuss?' she asked, fastening the three offending buttons, still perched demurely on the front edge of the armchair's cushion, her knees still neatly together, Richard's eyes again flitting to the few inches of smooth thigh exposed to them while she was distracted with adhering to his authoritarian wishes.

'Your welfare and education,' he said, his eyes lifting as she looked back up at him from the now fastened buttons. 'Whether I will permit you to live with the Howells or not, long term. Your outlook on life, and the way you conduct yourself. And your exam results.'

'But none of that,' Alice complained, 'has anything to do with you now?'

'I take my responsibilities seriously, even if you don't offer me the respect I consider due,' he went on, arrogantly dismissing her flow. 'I put that down to my upbringing.' He studied Alice closely. 'You see, I was raised in less liberal times. Children were reared to a set of socially acceptable principles. Deviation in any shape or form was not tolerated.

'But…' Alice tried again.

'A girl such as yourself would have been construed as recalcitrant, if not flighty. Steps would be taken before you could descend completely into a depraved lifestyle.'

Richard raised an eyebrow, challenging, awaiting a reaction.

Alice began to regret her choice of clothes, and question the wisdom of visiting him at all. Too short a period had elapsed since escaping the man's thrall. She had hoped she could confront and even defeat his brutal arrogance. But as Richard spoke, she felt her confidence rapidly draining away.

'I just wanted to look nice, uncle,' she said, knowing she was almost apologising for herself. 'It doesn't mean I'm off the rails or looking for a career as a street girl. And as for my welfare, the Howells care for me very well. I have no complaints whatsoever. Quite the opposite, in fact. My education you have kindly taken care of, so I would like very much to stay with them. I feel comfortable there. It's not as if I will spend a lot of time with them. I'll be at *Heptonstall* for the best part.

'As for my outlook on life, my conduct and what you term brazen attitude, I don't understand what I've done wrong to make you despise me so much.'

She returned his level stare, her self-doubt increasing. 'Are my exam results so bad? Has that something to do with the way you talk to me?'

'All in good time, Alice,' he said, deflecting the last question. 'I took you in. I certainly didn't have to. I fed you, clothed you. I made arrangements to secure your future. I began the torturous process of preparation, to ensure you embraced the necessary attributes to forge a successful path through life.

'I accepted liability for a spoiled brat – an undisciplined, disobedient and rebellious orphan. I made allowances for your unwarranted behaviour. And although I held reservations, I tenaciously sought the means of helping you?'

'You beat me!' Alice snapped, tired of his damning rhetoric. 'You used any excuse to be cruel to me! How can you sit there and say you tried to help me?'

'Do you honestly think I wanted to do such things?' His tone hardened. 'You left me little choice in the matter. You refused to toe the line. You were up to mischief every time I turned my back. You wouldn't listen to reason. You're spoiled and arrogant. Yes, arrogant! Alice Hussey knows it all. Alice Hussey is above discipline. All should bow to Alice Hussey. The world should fall to its knees for her…'

He calmed a little, and then his sarcasm pierced the tense atmosphere. 'Perhaps I have it wrong. Maybe you are the Second Coming. Should I prostrate myself before you? Should I hail you, pay homage to you?' He laughed, the sound derogatory. 'No, you're more like the anti-Christ.'

'I may have had problems, uncle, but it's hardly surprising, is it?' she said defensively. 'Losing my parents so suddenly.'

'Problems?' he scoffed. 'I don't think so, Alice. You can't hide behind that one. Children are bereaved every day. It is a sad fact of life, but most face that fact and get on with their lives. It's the weak and pampered who have problems.'

A vindictive smirk settled on his face. 'A disposition to being stripped and bound is hardly connected to loss, is it? More to an inborn perversion.'

Alice blushed. Richard had chafed a raw nerve.

'But I won't linger on that matter,' he went on. 'You were justly chastised for that outrage. However, I now see before me a girl in the guise of a vamp, a girl who has used the opportunity to demonstrate her flawed character. What am I to think?'

'Be happy for me,' she pleaded.

'Be happy for you? What sort of sentimental claptrap is that? Outraged, more like. You breeze in here, every inch of your body emphasised by the most salacious of clothing.'

'*Salacious?*'

'You then begin conversation with your chest all but hanging out of your blouse, and I take it that your underwear is not what I prescribed.'

'Uncle, I don't live here now,' Alice pointed out, trying to keep her cool. 'You cannot tell me what I may or may not do or wear.'

'I have an agreement with Mr Howell,' he announced, 'whereby I retain certain control over your development. I'm surprised he hasn't mentioned the fact. I made it quite clear from the start that that was to be a condition of your move.'

Alice inhaled a deep breath. 'You have no rights over me. You can't threaten to throw me onto the streets now, can you? Jay pays my keep, not you.'

'You seem to be very conveniently ignoring the fact that I have paid your school fees.'

'I thought this anonymous benefactor did that.'

'Same thing.'

'No, uncle, it is not. I thank you for putting a roof over my head when I needed one. I thank you for the food and clothing you provided for me. When I am able to I will refund your expenditure. But I'm not going to sit here and take your vilification.'

They rose together, then Richard closed the gap between them and pushed Alice back down into the armchair. 'You ungrateful little bitch!' he growled. 'You are not walking out on me again. I know your game, young lady. Take what you can and then turn your back on the gullible wretch. But not this time. Oh no. Not until I have instilled in you a regard for decency.'

She recalled his temperament well. Cold hostility. Forcibly savage. Certain in his contemptible approach. Violence he would endorse with religious argument. Catholic principles would justify his actions and vindicate any feelings of guilt. In the face of such a threat, Alice chose placation.

'Uncle, what are you going to do to me?' she asked, her knees drawn up and her arms crossing her breasts defensively.

'You see, Alice?' he said, as though not hearing her. 'You see how authority summons respect? You see how you cringe before propriety? You know you have sinned. You know, in there…' He leant over her and jabbed a finger at her scalp, Alice wincing under the aggressive action. 'And you know in there…' His hand knocked aside an arm and pressed over the soft breast beneath which lay her heart.

Alice held her silence, not daring to remove the offending hand, not daring to even ask for its removal. The feel of it sickened her. Even through her blouse and bra it felt cold. She thought she felt it move a little, as though enjoying the feel of her breast… but that could not be…

She decided to play for time, to try and appease him whilst awaiting any opportunity to bolt.

'Wickedness eats like acid,' he preached, his eyes bulging fanatically. 'It is the cancer of the soul. And the young are the most susceptible. They have not the experience to

170

recognise or battle the demons.' The cold hand remained, cupping her breast, rising and falling a little with the movement of her slow, anxious breathing. 'But you know, Alice. You know that you have breached God's laws. You conceal the devil. You offer him a place to hide. Evil cannot win against the staff of righteousness. That's why Satan employs insidious methods.'

He smiled, satisfied with the rationale. 'Your temperament, bearing, opting for immodest clothing, your impudence, immorality and sudden disregard for your faith are all indicators.'

The accusations struck Alice like hammer blows. Perhaps truth flowed from those vitriolic words after all. She was suddenly filled with doubt. Images filled her mind. Memories flooded that guilt-stricken conscience. She recalled the teachings, instruction she once accepted as sacred. Once virtuous she had stumbled, taken the wrong fork at the junction of adolescence and womanhood. Since losing her parents she had at times doubted her sanity.

Richard's demeanour calmed, and taking a deep breath he crossed himself before a crucifix on the wall. 'I'm sorry, Alice,' he said. 'That's not much of a welcome, is it?'

The girl couldn't believe her ears. Was he some sort of a schizophrenic? Such rapid mood swings were deeply disturbing. 'Th-that's okay,' she whispered forgivingly. 'Perhaps there is something in what you say.'

Still apologetic, he continued. 'It's my upbringing, Alice. Modesty is so ingrained I find it difficult to overlook clothes like those you are wearing. Too long on my own, I suppose, no one to contest my opinion.'

'You are entitled to that, uncle,' she said, taking the opportunity to straighten her blouse.

He faced the girl again, offering a smile, his eyes still cold, unfeeling. 'In my defence, I suppose I'm trying to do the job perfectly. What your dear mother wanted prays on my mind. If she can see you, and I'm sure she can, I want her to be proud.'

'So do I, uncle,' Alice said with heartfelt emotion. 'So do I.'

'Have you visited their graves recently?' he asked.

'No, I've been remiss,' she said, feeling ashamed of such an admission.

He nodded pensively for a few moments, gazing at the crucifix. 'Forgive me, Alice, I'm being such a poor host,' he said, snapping himself out of his thoughts. 'Would you like a cup of tea, or something?'

'Please let me make it,' she offered. 'I'm sure I can remember where everything is.'

Alice rose and made for the door, relieved that the initial barrage was over, although nothing was certain, and with Richard's temperament that could so easily be re-ignited. She noticed a sixpence lying on the floor by the door and bent to pick it up, unaware that the man was studying her legs as she did so. She presented the perfect bottom to him, encased in hugging material, the line of her panties teasingly discernable through it.

'I've missed you, my dear,' he suddenly said, so quietly Alice wasn't sure if she'd heard him correctly.

She straightened up, turned, and offered him the coin. 'Did you say you've missed me?' she asked dubiously. 'Missed me in what way, uncle?'

'Your company of course,' he said. 'What other way could there be?'

Unsettled by a Richard she'd not seen before, she smiled and said, 'I'll make the tea, shall I?'

He followed her out into the dingy hall, his eyes riveted to her voluptuous, teasing bottom. 'You're a very attractive girl, Alice,' he said. 'A very attractive girl indeed…'

The prey became the hunter.

Still very much unsure of herself or of him, but certain that his latest change of mood gave her the creeps, she

172

ignored the comment and longingly eyed the front door as they passed, wishing she was on the other side of it and fleeing down the street.

In the kitchen Alice filled the kettle, Richard standing close by. 'Perhaps I've been a bit too hard on you in the past,' he said. 'Losing your parents must have been very traumatic.'

'Yes it was, *uncle*,' she replied, the emphasis on uncle.

'You see, I was brought up very strictly.' Alice didn't like the way he repeated himself, as though he didn't realise he'd just told her that. 'My father had a penchant for the belt.'

'Then... then you should know how much it hurts,' she said carefully, not wanting to provoke him.

'It's ingrained, not that easy to ignore. Plus I have a temper on me.'

'I always did my best, uncle. I didn't deliberately look for trouble. I was disturbed for a while. Perhaps you take your religion too seriously. Perhaps you shouldn't be quite so zealous.'

'It's all I have. I must take it seriously. What would be the point of ignoring part, merely because it demands the uncomfortable?'

'Does it?'

'As a young man I spent some time in a monastery. I held prospects of becoming a brother. That building lay adjacent to a convent. The nuns taught boarders. I can assure you, Alice, that in both establishments penance was levied by pain and humiliation.'

'It's not always the answer, though,' she said, putting the kettle on to boil.

'I agree with you. At *Carters* you received corporal punishment for your misdemeanour. You accepted that as just. All schools generally run a similar regime. If the rod were banished where would we be? Children would run amok.'

'Yes, children,' she concurred, 'but not adults.'

'So at what age would you like to see the rod put away?' he questioned. 'What determines an adult? Age? Or responsibility?'

'I don't know the answer to that,' she acknowledged, unsettled by his close, lingering proximity. 'But I don't believe it right that a man should cane a girl reaching her majority.'

'But that's the humiliation, Alice,' he countered. 'That is part of the punishment. In the religious communities it is not unusual for a nun to flog a brother and visa versa. In especial circumstances a novice or two may beat a senior monk. The whole idea is that the psyche is punished as well as the body.'

Alice poured boiling water onto the tealeaves in the pot. Then squeezing around him she assembled two cups and saucers and waited for the beverage to brew.

'I suppose I agree that sometimes people need it,' she said, wanting to keep him talking. 'If they err then they should be punished.'

'Aren't you hot in that?' Richard indicated the jacket.

'I wasn't going to stop too long,' she said, by way of a reason for not taking it off.

'Why don't you stay over?' he suggested. 'You can go back tomorrow.'

'Um no, uncle, but thanks for the offer.' The invitation unsettled her even more, and she decided it was getting increasingly wise that she bring her visit to as swift a conclusion as possible. 'Um, you said you wanted to talk to me about some matters.' She poured the tea. 'Like not staying with the Howells.'

'I don't think they're good for you,' he said coldly.

'You don't?'

'No, Alice, I don't. I can tell that since you've been living there you've changed.'

'Yes, uncle, I've grown up,' she said.

'No,' he said, shaking his head. 'You've learned to flaunt your body. That's not growing up. Growing up is acting responsibly. Tell me, was your journey without intrusion?'

Alice recalled the young solicitor. 'How do you mean?' she stalled.

'Did you manage the journey without comment or wolf whistle?'

'I was asked out, it that's what you mean,' she admitted. 'But that doesn't mean he thought I was a tart.'

'And if you'd been travelling in the *Heptonstall* uniform – white shirt, tie and pleated skirt – would that have happened, do you think? Would he have looked at you twice, let alone speak to you or ask you out?'

Alice knew he was cornering her, but her honesty condemned her to an answer. 'I suppose he might have thought I was older than?'

'Exactly!' he snapped. 'Wearing such clothes at your age,' he flicked a hand at her blouse, his fingers just sweeping up against the side of one breast, 'elicits dangerous attention. What if the man had been a rapist?'

'Then I don't suppose he would have been concerned about my age,' she said defiantly, noting with a chill of dread how he held those fingers with some sort of reverence, as though he could still feel her against them.

'Still prone to flippancy, I note,' he said flatly, his tone alarming her again. 'What I am trying to impress upon you, young lady, is that clothes like yours are likely to inflame a man.'

'I see,' she said, casting an anxious glance over his shoulder at the open kitchen door. 'And are you inflamed, uncle? Does my body affect you?' Alice cringed, wishing she'd not said either of those two things.

'That, young lady, is neither here nor there,' he said slowly, and Alice sensed that her forthright questioning of his manhood had knocked him onto the back foot somewhat. So without weighing up the possible consequences but sensing the chance to press home an advantage, she went on the offensive.

Alice, acting utterly impulsively, undid those top three buttons of her blouse again and pulled the material apart, bearing the upper slopes of her breasts and her squeezed cleavage, the lacy top edging of her bra cups just visible to his stunned eyes. 'Do these inflame you, uncle?' she demanded. 'Do they? Does the sight of my tits inflame you?'

Stunned, Richard's face slowly grew bright red, and for a moment she feared his head would explode. 'Do yourself up immediately, you damned trollop!' he hissed dangerously, and Alice nearly faltered.

'Why, uncle?' she pressed on regardless, too late to go back. 'It is only my body, and if I remember correctly you once said there is nothing wrong with the body. I should be proud of it. You told me that nudity between relatives was acceptable. Why, you even stripped and bathed in front of me to prove it.'

'I'm wasting my time with you, aren't I?' he spat, but his eyes remained glued to that teasing glimpse of those glorious, fleshy globes that offended him so much. 'What's the point of trying to reason with a wilful obscenity like you? The only logic you understand is the rod on your backside!'

Alice moved even closer, determined to unsettle him further, to defeat him once and for all, the precarious situation strangely exhilarating. 'Your words, uncle, not mine. Surely you don't see me as a sex object. I'm your niece, after all.'

'Don't push me, Alice,' he warned. 'You may live with the Howells, you may believe yourself beyond my jurisdiction now, but I will do what I think necessary, regardless.'

With his bark now seemingly ineffectual, the madness out of control, and considering herself at last beyond his manipulation, Alice impulsively put her arms around his neck. A shapely leg ascended his, the limb firmly in contact. 'I thought you wanted my company, uncle?' she purred. 'After all, I am a wanton slut, aren't I? Why else would I choose to wear these clothes?'

'I warn you, Alice,' he growled, 'you are playing with fire here.'

'Oh, I don't think so, uncle,' she said, moulding her youthful litheness against his rigid, scarecrow-like stance. 'No, I gauge you to be a pitiful excuse for manhood. A pathetic, frustrated lecher who has gone too long without a woman.' Alice attained new heights of boldness. Pent-up frustrations flowed, relieving the hatred and hostility she had never dared to vent. She felt good, and she had not finished with him... not by a long way.

Richard, aghast, mouth gaping, veins standing proud on his forehead, watched in disbelief as she stepped back and turned around.

Alice caught the hem of her skirt and peeled it up. 'Is this what you want to see, uncle?' she teased, peeping at the speechless man over her shoulder. 'Toned legs, smooth white thighs. Or this?' She inched the hem slowly higher, over those divine buttocks. 'You took every opportunity to get a glimpse of my body before, when I lived here, didn't you?'

Richard studied those perfect flanks, and noted the fading tramlines of Harris's cane. With some effort he cleared his throat. 'Oh, it seems I stand corrected,' he managed. 'It would seem the Howells do engage in discipline after all.'

'The stripes?' Alice provoked him mercilessly, feeling herself gaining an unassailable stranglehold on the situation. 'No, that wasn't because I was naughty, uncle. That was because I wanted to be caned. I asked Jay to do it to me, and I loved every second of it.'

'You're sick!' he erupted. 'I'm better off without you!'

'I'm no more sick than you, uncle. I enjoy receiving, whereas you wallow in giving.' Alice bent gracefully from the waist and touched her toes, her bottom rounded and stretched… inviting… beckoning… 'Wouldn't you just love to lay a flexible, whippy cane to it right now? Couldn't you savour the slap of rattan on my tight cheeks?'

His face scarlet, the rage exploded. The shameless girl enraged his twisted sense of decency, outraged years of sexual frustration. 'You abomination!' he yelled. 'You filthy slut!'

Realising far too late that she had gone much too far, Alice hastily straightened up to face his wrath, hips swaying as she quickly pushed the skirt back down and pulled the top of her blouse together. Richard jabbed a finger at her, stabbing her shoulder and edging her back until her bottom was blocked by the work surface behind her.

'You are the devil's own instrument!' he growled. 'You are the catalyst of a vile entity. Satan chooses well. You are temptation! You are a temple of immorality. You are filth!'

The finger provoked her, angered her again. His tirade exasperated her and the bile of outrage rose in her throat. A veil of scarlet obscured her reason. Alice reacted to the defamation. She seized that prodding digit. 'Don't be ridiculous!' she spat. 'I'm a normal, healthy teenager. I?'

'Normal? What sort of label is that for a tart who seduces the oaf next door? A Jezebel who has him tie her naked to a chair? A strumpet who basks in the pawing of her body? A near stranger's hands groping her chest, fumbling with her…' Richard faltered and Alice flinched, the reminder hurtful.

She had spent many a long hour ruing that misadventure, regretting the dalliance, mentally punishing herself for such outlandish behaviour. His gibe did little to admonish. Instead the girl rose to the bait. She spotted that character flaw and launched her own derision.

'Vagina, uncle,' she stated coolly. 'It's called a vagina. Some might refer to it as a fanny, or pussy. But its accepted label is vagina.'

The man recoiled, the vernacular slicing pompous bearing. Richard couldn't handle crudity, the focus on sexual difference. A virtuous rearing had deprived him of worldly expression. Pious morality repressed, the primate in him confused.

But instead of exploiting the advantage, Alice felt guilt. She had snuffed the venom and deflated the bluster. But any apology to him beyond her, seeming inappropriate and undeserved, she made to leave.

'I think it best we don't see each other again,' she voiced her opinion, brushing past the man.

'You haven't yet got what you came for, Alice,' he reminded her, an eerie undertone to the statement.

'My exam results, you mean?' She stood by the kitchen door, fairly confident, looking over her shoulder at him.

Slowly Richard turned, a malevolent snarl warping that doleful countenance. 'No, no,' he whispered unfavourably. 'I mean, a lesson in attitude.'

Grasping the glaze to those soulless eyes, the set of his jaw, the tension of his frame, Alice fled. She dashed for the front door. Frantically she fumbled with the catch. Desperately she pulled on the latch. The door opened an inch, and then slammed shut with a frightening finality as Richard's fist hit it.

'No!' she screamed, tugging on the latch again as an arm coiled snakelike around her waist. 'Let me out! Let me go!'

A fist gripped the collar of her treasured bolero, hauling her back into the gloom of the dingy hallway. Alice lost her footing and fell to her knees, losing both sandals in the process. She made no attempt to rise, breathing heavily as she crouched there, anticipating the madman's next move.

'Ostentation!' he barked. 'Lavish costume does not maketh the person.' He reached down, and gripping the jacket he tried to wrench it from her body.

Alice struggled, falling to her side, arms defensive, hands trying to beat him off.

'Satan's guise!' With cold grey eyes manic, he growled. 'But I see the festering within. The noxious eyesore cavorting as woman.'

'You're mad,' the cowering girl protested.

Richard slapped her head, Alice unable to defect the blow, and with a hand seeking to ease the smart she offered the ogre the chance to renew the assault. Utilising her auburn hair he forced her facedown on the floor, then kneeling on the small of her back he tugged until the leather pulled free. With a grimace of distaste he tossed the garment aside.

'Mad, am I?' he spat. 'Enraged, more like! Offended in my own home! Nauseated by this tumour of depravity that masquerades as an innocent. Sickened by this blasphemous brat who flaunts the divine gift in a lewd and despicable way. You insult the Almighty with your promiscuity, for it is in His image you are made.'

He grabbed her flailing wrist and forced her arm up her back to her shoulder, the pain unbearable. 'Ouch, you're hurting me!' Alice begged. 'You'll break my arm!'

'You dare to complain?' Spittle coated his lips. 'A tramp who brandishes her chest, her legs, her bottom? None of which are modestly covered. A godless guttersnipe who parades marks of the rod and boasts of her liking for the pain? I will give you pain. Then see if you care to brag about the marks I leave.'

'I'm sorry!' she screamed. 'Uncle! I beg you. Don't beat me.'

'Exactly what I expected,' he sneered, seething. 'The worm turns. Where's the swagger now, eh, Alice?

180

Where's the foul bravado? Those disgusting descriptions of your private anatomy?'

Her mind fraught, realising she had stupidly pushed Richard too far, Alice tried placation again. 'All right, I am what you say I am,' she appeased. 'I have a temper. I only said it because you intimidate me. Please, Uncle Richard, let me go. I promise I will be more like you want me to be.'

'Acquiescence at the threat of suffering?' he mused. 'What kind of a fool do you take me for?' He straightened up, looming over her, careful to keep the arm-lock in place and hauling the unfortunate girl up with him.

He curled an arm around her throat and drew her head back, saliva-coated lips to her ear. 'We will remedy this flaw in your character once and for all, today, Alice,' he murmured vehemently. 'You will learn respect. You will comprehend morality. You will surrender to obedience.'

Holding her nubile curves tight to his wiry form, he urged her forward into the kitchen. 'W-what are you going to do to me?' she asked, terrified, the first tears of dread meandering down her flushed cheeks.

'I'm going to help you of course, Alice,' he crooned. 'I'm going to do the responsible thing as your guardian. That is all I have ever tried to do. I will drive the malignancy from you. Bring you to your senses. Place you back on the path of righteousness.'

'If I'm not home by five Jay will come looking for me,' she threatened in desperation.

'But Alice, you are home. That is if I decide you can stay.' His body pressed tight to hers he forced her forward, the feel of her buttocks, their lithe movement pressed to his groin, tantalising him. 'I remind you; I am officially your guardian. The fact that I allow the Howells to look after you is irrelevant. Now tell me, why should Jonathan be so enamoured by a slut like you?'

Slowly, grudgingly, Alice gave ground and allowed him

to edge her deeper into the kitchen, ever further from the front door and escape, Richard not relieving the pressure for a second.

'Well, Alice?' he persisted, his voice hoarse in her ear. 'Has he some interest other than to look after you because you are the friend of his daughter?'

Alice knew not to bait the man further, and now wished she'd learned that lesson earlier. She was tempted, inclined to say they were lovers purely to vex the righteous bully, but this time she foresaw the repercussions. 'Of course he hasn't,' she claimed. 'But he's very protective, that's all.'

'And would he ignore your blatant provocation, your foul use of dialogue, your immoral attitude?'

Answering yes or no would not gain remission. Yes would ensure he fought her return to the Howells. No would afford him reason to persecute her further. Alice felt him lean back with one foot and kick the kitchen door shut, the sound a harbinger of misery.

'No, of course he wouldn't, Alice,' he answered for her. 'Mr Howell is an honourable man, isn't he? He would condone correction of your disgusting behaviour, wouldn't he? I suspect that is how you came by those marks. He's seen through you already, hasn't he?'

Alice remained tacit, but Richard increased the squeeze on her. 'Hasn't he?!'

'Yes!' she squealed, and the man relaxed the bear hug.

'So what did he cane you for, Alice? What depraved act did he catch you performing?' At last he released her and, without taking his eyes from her, reached back and fumbled for the key in the kitchen door, turning it in the lock, and secreted it in his trouser pocket.

Alice backed up until a work unit again halted her retreat, her bottom resting against it as she warily watched him, ashen-faced.

'I'm waiting, Alice,' he went on threateningly. 'Why

were you caned?'

She rubbed her arm, soothing the ache he'd inflicted in the limb. 'Do you want every gory detail, uncle?' She could have bitten her tongue off.

He settled himself at the kitchen table. 'Yes, Alice, every detail.' He didn't bite. Instead he sought to humiliate her. 'I want to know why, and whether you were covered or not. And just how much it hurt.'

Maybe, just maybe he might prove sympathetic to an injustice. That would be preferable to a lie that might involve her in worse. Alice couldn't tell the whole truth. That would implicate Katy. She had to be sparing with that commodity.

'I wrote an essay of a confidential nature,' she told him. 'There were some notes. I mislaid them. I had good reason to believe that Harris the butler had found them, but when confronted he denied it. So stupidly I sought them in his room. He discovered me there and accused me of thieving, so rather than let the matter get completely out of hand I let him cane me for the imagined infraction.'

'It was Harris the butler, you say, and not Jonathan Howell?' Richard looked even more interested in this development.

'Yes,' she confirmed.

'Is that usual in the Howell household? The butler caning a guest?'

Alice looked down at the dull flooring, and shook her head.

'Why let him do so if there was no crime?' he interrogated. 'You must have had something to hide.'

'What does it matter, uncle? I paid and that is an end to the matter.'

'No, I'm afraid it isn't. My niece a thief? Does Mr Howell know about this?'

'No, but Jenny does. And she wasn't very pleased.'

'I'm not surprised. She takes you into her house and

183

you steal from the servants.'

'She wasn't pleased with Harris,' Alice corrected him. 'She nearly sacked him over it.'

'You mean the man had to suffer your pilfering without redress?'

'I didn't steal anything, uncle. He used that as an excuse. Jonathan was away at the time. I wanted to save everybody the embarrassment of police involvement. Otherwise I would have gone straight to him.'

'Not Jenny, your ultimate saviour?'

'It was complicated. But it was sorted in the end.'

'But Harris still works for the Howells?'

'Yes,' she confirmed. 'But please understand, uncle, the man is a devious sadist. I didn't stand a chance against him on my own.'

'I suspect he isn't best pleased, then?' Richard pondered.

'No,' she confirmed, 'he has promised revenge.'

'So you were unjustly beaten?'

'Yes, uncle.'

'And now you are to be justly spanked.'

She shook her head in denial. 'I don't think so, uncle,' she said. 'You have no right. I'm not a child. I don't even live here any more.'

'On the contrary, I do have the right, Alice,' he argued. 'The right as your legal guardian. The right as your moral guide. All the time you are under my jurisdiction I shall take that responsibility seriously. And whether you are still a child is a matter of conduct, not the curves you choose to flaunt.'

Alice shook her head in defiance. 'No, Richard, you're not going to spank me. I'll fight back, I warn you.'

'You have one last chance, Alice,' he went on, ignoring her insubordination. 'Either you lay over my lap voluntarily, or it will ultimately be the worse for you.'

Alice trembled with fear, rage and frustration. Her pride would not permit submission. That was the decisive point.

184

If she complied willingly then she lost the battle for all time. She had come to confront the beast, to vilify, to demonstrate her newfound strength. Deference was beyond her. 'No,' she whispered rebelliously.

Richard glared, his eyes chips of ice. 'So be it, Alice,' he said ominously, and from where he sat he opened a drawer and removed a rectangular wooden clothes brush. 'I am certain you will regret that decision.'

The man rose slowly, menacingly. Alice dashed into the scullery and tried to open the backdoor. 'I'll scream the house down!' she warned, the exit route refusing any movement.

'Scream all you want, girl,' he said casually. 'If you manage to arouse sympathy I will simply explain the circumstances. The brat cannot take her medicine. Spanking a mischievous teenager is not illegal.'

Richard closed the distance between them. 'I have reached a decision, Alice,' he went on, watching her wrenching futilely on the backdoor handle. 'You will remain with me during holiday periods. You have demonstrated that you are out of control and require a firm hand. It was remiss of me to allow you to stay with the Howells. I can see that now, in hindsight.'

'I am not staying with you!' she shouted. 'I am not being punished at your every whim. And there is no way you can make me.'

'We'll see…' he mused, 'we'll see.'

He moved surprisingly quickly, grabbed a defending hand and twisted, using it as a lever, forcing the girl back into the kitchen and over the table, her feet scraping the floor for some kind of a purchase. Richard held her there, looking down on that skirt-covered rump, vulnerable before him.

'You know the seven deadly sins, don't you, girl?' he quizzed rhetorically.

'Of course I do,' she gasped, his weight on her back, her breasts squeezed to the tabletop, its edge pressing painfully into her hips.

'Pride, Alice: a trait that will see *you* repeatedly in trouble. There is no room for pride in the God-fearing mortal.' He gazed at the roundness of her bottom, youthful, firm and replete. 'Pride begets arrogance, conceit. Mirrors are forbidden in the halls of the devout, to remove temptation. What reason can woman have for gazing at her reflection? Other than vanity.' His arm rose. The hand flashed and struck material-covered flank, the quiver of a provocative cheek engrossing.

Alice grimaced, her face contorted as the smart penetrated, burning fiercely. It began. Pain. Humiliation. The despot's response to her attempt at independence.

A sidelong glance at a window offered his own image, except Richard had no interest in that. It was the picture of domination, of him restraining the beautiful girl, the alternative view of those tempting buttocks, the girl's torso pressed to the scrubbed surface, the shapely legs straining to support her, and the look of fear on the brat's face. That's what intrigued him so.

'Anger: a manifestation of inadequacy,' he went on, as though preaching from a pulpit. 'You have neither the words nor the wit to discuss equally, so you resort to rage. Too much time spent on licentious preparation and not enough on modestly studying the gospel.'

Her other buttock reeled to a withering detonation. Teeth clenched, she wished she had listened to Kate and Jay.

Richard inhaled sharply. Energy consumed his groin. Trousers gave to the lurch of excitement, the development disturbing, the pious man delirious. Sexual commotion crept insidious, stirred where cold fortitude should reside, gripped the organ as if estranged from the rationale of righteousness.

Trying to ignore the presumption he persevered. 'Lust: you are no stranger to concupiscence, are you, girl?' That illicit erection gathered strength. Disconcerting, it sought an exit from shabby Y-fronts. It hardened, pulsed free of the greying cotton and drove a relentless tent into the trousers.

'Every stitch of this flagrant clothing is designed to enamour, to goad the temptation that resides in every earthly being.'

The stiffening distraction pressed to soft flank, the sensation bewildering, the contact inflaming long suppressed passions. He struck in frustration, the palm slapping haunch in close proximity to that enraged stalk. The toned jostle and vibrations of such feminine corpulence assaulted the excited phallus, the message sent unequivocally to susceptible intellect.

In desperation, refusing to accept the truth of such excitation, Richard resorted to his religion. 'Temptress!' he almost screamed, hitting that entrapped rump with all his strength. 'You seek to undermine years of devotion.' Her bottom shuddered. 'You come here in clothes that render every inch of that damnable body discernible.' Fire swathed her burning dunes. 'You flaunt your thighs!' Alice gripped the table's edge tenaciously, desperately, the man's hand unbelievably severe. 'Your backside!' The thunder of hand slaps matched the gravity of suffering Alice endured. 'Everything!'

She fought down the urge to squeal, not wishing to give Richard the satisfaction. But his hand rained unadulterated purgatory, a knot forming in her gullet.

He failed to mention her breasts, his mouth refusing that word. 'And then, you harlot, you parade that disgusting cleavage, display it as if it was something precious.'

Her bottom approached the intolerable and he still hadn't used that brush.

'Precious to you, maybe,' he hissed scornfully. 'Impressive to a fornicator who scours the lamp-lit streets in search of the promiscuous. But your chest hanging out only incenses the principled.'

Alice kicked, the inferno flaring insufferably. Each swinging blow sickening, she thrashed in a limited fashion, Richard's arm pinning her down.

That frenzied reaction seemed only to ferment, the man drooling, spittle spraying, teeth bared. 'And then you had the temerity to expose yourself! What effect did you think that would have? Did you hope to enamour me with your nudity? Enslave me with your curves?' Each detonation proved untenable. Alice surrendered to vocal relief. Her mind capitulated to subservience. She couldn't take any more.

His erection throbbed. It annoyed him with an insatiable irritation. Constantly lurching it thrust against his trousers, the action arousing, inducing further unrest.

'Does this pain please?' he demanded. 'Did you display your behind to invoke such a retaliation?' He gasped, the punishing hand held aloft. Sticky wetness soaked into the flannel where his penis pressed. Richard gazed down in disbelief at the seeping stain, still light-headed from the effects of his orgasm. The realisation dawned. Lips tightened and curled in exasperation. Eyebrows knitted. Facial muscles drew tight.

'You are damnation!' he bellowed, hitting that tightly packed rump with all his might. 'You emphasise this lewd physique to attract, beguile and ensnare the unwary. To confound and seduce the gullible. To lead them into temptation. You walk in the shadow of perdition. Your soul hangs in the balance. The devil may well soon have you!

'Is that what you want, girl? To spend eternity in the fires of hell? To embrace Satan rather than God?'

Unbelievably, without him realising it, his cruel treatment of Alice and his assertion proved poignant to an ingenuous girl who seriously doubted her current approach to life. He awoke the dedicated, reverential Alice, bludgeoned the

188

divided psyche. He resurrected the persuasion of the Catholic Church, a doctrine Alice had taken very seriously not so long before. Principles ingrained since childhood, a godliness that would forever torment in the recesses of her conscience-stricken mind. Her greatest fear was eternal damnation.

Richard removed his hand from her back, keeping the stain from her view. He let himself out of the kitchen, locking the door behind him. She remained on the table, all energy spent, listening to his footfalls on the stairs and in the bedroom, dread slicing her gut.

She dare not move, nothing but contempt in her heart. Place a knife in her hand and she would have gladly plunged it into the bastard's chest. Why didn't she listen to Kate? Why did she come alone? She might have guessed what would happen. And to deliberately antagonise the man was an act of sheer lunacy.

Her poor bottom smouldered. The skin felt raw, flayed. She had the protection of her skirt and panties, but his hand penetrated as if she had none. What further horrors had he in store for her? What else would the deranged Richard do? She didn't dare to contemplate.

The devil in question returned, fresh trousers and underwear in place. Alice had no idea of what had occurred and would have been appalled had she realised.

He settled on a chair, content for the moment to observe. Alice, thankful for the respite, turned her face away, not wishing to behold the tyrant.

'Showing your bottom off like you did could give a man the wrong message, Alice,' he warned. 'A red-blooded male might see it as an invitation.'

'It was no invitation,' she whispered, her cheek, moistened by tears, still pressed to the tabletop. 'It was a stupid, irresponsible mistake.'

'It's a shame you only realise that after the insult. Yes, insult, Alice. The Maoris used that to outrage their adversaries. In fact, certain barbaric tribes have down the centuries. I'm astounded to see a so-called educated girl do it. Appalled that my niece would resort to such a primitive show.'

He reached out and stroked the nearest cheek, his intrusive hand soothing the discomfort. 'It doesn't have to be like this, Alice,' he said, his tone surprisingly comforting. 'It *shouldn't* be like this. I can be tender and considerate. I am very fond of you. It galls me to have to resort to physical punishment. If only we could reach an agreeable arrangement. If you please me, Alice, I would offer certain benefits…'

He ran his hand down over her bottom to the top of her nearest thigh, his fingers curling around it, the feel of her satisfying one aspect, irritating another.

'What… what are you doing, uncle?' Alice asked, confused by the touch, but he offered no answer. The soothing proved preferable to the sting of his hand, so she accepted it as a tentative attempt at an apology and offered no objection.

The hem of the skirt rose a few inches, and then refused further inducement. Tight against her thighs and hips and impeded by her position over the table, the garment proved obstinate.

Richard told himself he only intended to examine the damage, to see how her bottom had faired against the unremitting onslaught. But his libido urged a different path. Deep in the recesses of his troubled mind demons coaxed, veiled the pious conscience, pressured to conquer moral resistance.

Interpreting the stubborn skirt as the source of his recent depravity and not the obstruction to her naked bottom, he took the hem in clenched fists and wrenched, the seam splitting, naked thigh instantly revealed. Before Alice could react in any way Richard tore the skirt to her waist and peeled the flap back over panty-clad buttocks, their scarlet hue clearly discernable through the diaphanous white.

'You've torn it!' Alice complained all too late, struggling to rise. 'You've ruined my skirt! How am I going to get home in that?'

'You haven't been listening, have you?' he said, easily pushing her back down onto the scrubbed worktop. 'This is your home. Forget the Howells. You're not going back.' His eyes didn't move from that entrancing revelation. Smooth, shapely legs slightly parted, supporting her crimson bottom, only partially covered by stretched white panties. Richard licked dry lips.

'But my clothes,' she protested. 'My possessions, my uniform; they're all at the Howells' house.'

'I will ring Mr Howell later and explain,' he declared. 'I dare say he can drop them off at *Heptonstall* for you.' Alice peered wide-eyed and anxiously back over her shoulder at Richard, his stare fixed to the vision of her bottom, a leer on his lips as he placed a clammy hand on those tortured cheeks, the panties concealing little. Enrapt, he stroked the punished flesh.

'I'd rather you didn't do that, uncle,' Alice whispered carefully, befuddled by the uninvited petting.

'If your bottom was properly covered I wouldn't be able to,' he countered. 'What would you sooner have, Alice, kindness or chastisement?'

'But this isn't right, feeling my bottom like you are,' she argued. 'Can't you see that?'

Richard smirked triumphantly, scornfully, recognising the rebuke as lacking conviction, from a girl who was flustered, from a girl who was angered by her own participation.

'Oh, you are so quick to preach morals to me, aren't you?' she went on. 'But when it boils down to the basics, you are just a sordid old pervert.' She no longer gave a damn about his reaction. Anything would be better than him pawing her – and her indulgent, shameful toleration of it. Where would his hand dare wander next if she didn't bring a halt to his excesses? And what would her reprehensible response be if he did venture further?

'You will be sorry you said that, Alice,' he assured her in a manner that left her in no doubt that she would, indeed, be sorry. His tone was controlled but menacing. 'When will you ever learn? You live in a dream world, dear girl. And it's about time someone brought you back to reality.' He straightened up. 'I think you need cooling off,' he decided, grabbed a fistful of lustrous auburn hair and hauled her to her feet, the girl crying out in pain. He marched her into the scullery, and there he forced her head under the cold tap and turned it on full.

Disdainfully he held her struggling body, again savouring the feel of her wrestling against him as water engulfed her face, driving into her nostrils and gasping mouth alike, smothering, threatening to choke. Alice gripped the sink, her head thrashing, rearing against the pressure that kept her there.

His slight but determined weight pinned her, held her firm to the unit, groin pushed against bottom, renewed erection hard between the divide of clenched buttocks.

Water cascaded, saturating hair, a constant stream stemming her breath. She had to fill her lungs and gasped for air, chilled fluid filling her mouth, encroaching on throat and stinging her windpipe. She choked, she coughed, she fought to escape, clutching hands blindly seeking the tap, Richard seizing it first to prevent her interfering. She clamped hands to the sink instead, pushing back, hoping to escape the torment, but he held her firm, wet auburn locks wound about a white-knuckled fist.

She feared she would drown, that his brutality would end her there. But he released her and she pushed back from the spout, water streaming down her face, soaking her blouse and raining to the floor. She stood shaking, spluttering, terrified, hands wiping surplus water from her eyes, appalled by his savagery.

'I suspect that has cooled your arrogance somewhat,' he decided, drinking of the clinging blouse, its partial transparency, the explicitness of her breasts, the outline of her cleavage and bra clearly discernible.

'You... you... you could have killed me!' she stammered.

'Now, now, that's an exaggeration,' he mocked flippantly. 'Accept your place, Alice, and life will become so much easier for you.'

She dropped her hands from wiping her face, her hair plastered to her forehead and cheeks and throat. Her eyes glared, red-rimmed. Water still dripped from her, the transparency and darkening of her blouse increasing. 'I would sooner die than submit to your vile principles,' she said vehemently.

'You think yourself so clever, don't you?'

'No,' she denied, shaking her head and creating another flurry of droplets. 'If I was clever I wouldn't have come here to be abused.'

'I will crush your defiance, Alice,' he said with conviction. 'You will succeed in life. You will become a responsible young woman. One that Mr Al-Awadi may rely upon.'

'I'm not going to work for him,' Alice blurted in defiance. 'Jay has offered me a job, and I am going to accept.'

'No, you won't,' he told her.

'Yes, I will.' Alice thought she detected fear in the man's eyes.

'He has paid for your schooling.'

'You said you had.'

'No, Mr Al-Awadi has. You must work for him.'

'I can do exactly what I want when I leave *Heptonstall*, uncle,' Alice insisted. 'And there isn't a thing you can do about it.'

'He is not a man to upset, Alice, and you would regret such a petulant decision.'

'So let him sue me,' she challenged, her chin raised boldly.

Richard snorted. 'He won't sue you, Alice. That's not his style.'

'What are you suggesting?' she asked, alarmed by the insinuation.

'I'm just pointing out that if you know what's good for you, you won't renege on this arrangement.'

'Jay will see no harm comes to me,' she said hopefully.

'Jay? Ha! Al-Awadi would snap him like a dry twig. He may seem the big I am to you, Alice, but believe me, compared to your benefactor he is nothing more than a worm.'

'So what, exactly, will I be doing in my new job?' she questioned suspiciously.

'I've told you already,' Richard said, somewhat evasively, 'you will work for him.'

'Yes, but doing what?'

'Whatever he deems fit. And if you don't learn some manners, I have no doubt he will have you scrubbing floors or some such menial task. So you see, it is up to you.'

'And how do you know him?' Alice probed for more information.

'Who do you think you are, questioning me?' Richard suddenly snapped.

'The girl, I suspect, that you've sold down the river,' Alice accused stubbornly.

'You impertinent brat!' he cursed, his patience snapping again. 'How dare you speak to me like that, after all I've done for you? It is the chance of a lifetime, provided you apply yourself appropriately. But I suspect even that is too much to ask, isn't it? Alice Hussey making the most of such an opportunity. You want it dropped in your lap,

I suppose. Honest hard work is beyond you.'

'Then tell me about him,' she insisted. 'And the job. Or have you something to hide?'

'Where is your trust, Alice?' he asked, with mock indignation.

'Trust?' she laughed. 'You? What have you ever done to earn my trust?'

Richard could see the argument pursuing the same repetitive course. Alice would not concede and he didn't see why he should explain himself. And he wasn't even sure he could, not to her satisfaction. She rebelled no matter what he did. She wouldn't back down. She possessed a pride and courage he had not foreseen. Pride he would have to subdue. Courage he would have to break.

'You seem impervious and disrespectful to whatever I do or say, Alice,' he observed. 'What does it take to penetrate that thick skull of yours? How many times do I have to remind you that I am in charge here in my own home and you do what I tell you.'

Alice leaned against the sink, arms protectively concealing the translucent outline of her bra and breasts. 'And how many times do I have to tell you,' she stated slowly, determinedly, 'that I am beyond your control now? That whatever transpires here today is no more than common assault.'

She witnessed the anger rising, his face colouring, the veins protruding from neck and forehead. His eyes narrowed and glared. He opened his mouth, spittle dotting his lips.

'Fractious...' His finger jabbed the accusation, accentuating it.

'Pretentious...' He advanced, his breathing laboured.

'Profane...' The finger emphasised the aggression.

'Wanton...'

Alice scrambled to the backdoor again, desperately wrenching on the handle as before, silently begging it to open whilst knowing it was hopeless.

'Wilful…' Richard grabbed the neckline of the blouse and dragged her back through to the kitchen table.

'Obstreperous…' He threw her down on the surface.

'Trollop…!' he bellowed, utterly relentless.

Alice gasped and recoiled from the impact of hitting the table, knowing what would follow. Fearfully she watched from the corner of her eye as Richard picked up the clothes brush. She hung her head between her elbows and closed her eyes, her hands clutching her wet hair she braced herself. Why did she provoke him so? Why repeatedly incur his wrath? Did her perversion extend subconsciously to Richard's volatile maltreatment? Did she unwittingly bring about his retaliation, to feed from his dominating hand? Was that her bias, plain and sweet? A manic desire to be ill-treated?

The first swat of the clothes brush ignited her yielding buttock and she flinched, rocking against the table. He reserved nothing. Pain drove into her flesh, a blast of heat. He struck again, the opposite buttock, barely two seconds between.

An intangible energy thrummed, the atmosphere charged. Katy's hypothesis rang true. '*So, Ali, sex hangs in the air. Electricity buzzes between you both.*' But how could that be? Not only was he so much older than her; not only did she find him about as attractive as a weasel; not only did she loath him; but it would be a cardinal sin. Simply thinking about it was a cardinal sin and one that made her feel sick!

Her bottom blazed, the rectangular wood pounding without mercy. Alice grimaced, the torment approaching the unacceptable. It would be ironic if she could transform the hurt, indulge in the hiding, turn the scald to that phenomenal glow that she and Katy joked about so often. But with Richard the perpetrator of her punishment, that was not going to happen.

The man in question ceased the trouncing, her bottom raw, burning intensely. Had he tired? Had she fully paid the price of impertinence? He again peeled away the torn skirt and exposed those scarlet, panty-encased dunes. Alice clenched her teeth apprehensively, realising he'd cleared the target of any obstruction, her brief panties providing none.

Sweating profusely, Richard ogled those near-naked cheeks, the imprint of hand and brush boldly and satisfyingly illustrated. Her legs pressed together, her bent position straining the tendons in thigh and calf. He took his time, savoured the moment, gloated in silence, watching Alice anticipate and flex heated buttocks, the indentation of haunches and tightening of flesh having their effect on him.

He lashed out, the brush slapping naked flesh, the sound explicit, more pronounced. Alice rocked and gasped as the consequence sickened. She laboured to keep the silence, to refuse him the satisfaction of her howls.

Transfixed by the shudder of buttock flesh, Richard pursued that grisly revenge. Constantly aroused his penis lurched, ached with the unremitting pressure and restricted confinement. He clamped a hand to the bulge, rubbing, squeezing the length, the other actively punishing that vulnerable, rosy bottom.

Acceptance provided a turning point. Alice ceased to fret, reconciled to a long and torturous spanking. The flesh numbed, those potent blasts of fire receding in gravity. Admission of guilt and submission to discipline assisted that deliverance. She lay hypnotised by the report of wood on flesh. She relaxed to the continuous detonations. She placed herself in Richard's shoes, the vision of her own near-naked bottom, beaten and mauled, consuming.

The fire burned deep, accosted her sexual hub, teased between her thighs and began the process of sensual promotion. Alice frowned and squeezed the edge of the tabletop in frustration, the occurrence beyond her comprehension. She presumed it as divine intervention, an injustice righted. She was content to let the sensations simmer, not to attain a climax. Should that develop then pain would return in unacceptable force.

Her clenched cheeks Richard took to be suffering, her bottom marked, crimson and inflamed. He puzzled at the lack of protest, at the absence of tormented cries. Perhaps the brush wasn't the disciple of despair he had assumed. Perhaps the girl was tougher than he thought.

Richard placed the brush back in its drawer. Then he rested against a work surface, looking down on the girl, and asked expectantly, 'Well, Alice, have you anything you want to say to me?'

'Yes...' she said softly, her voice barely audible to his ear, despite the quietness of the room. 'Can I get up now?'

'You may,' he acquiesced. 'You may stand by all means. Stand and face me.'

Alice lifted herself stiffly from the table and settled watery green eyes on her uncle. With her face flushed she posed, the chastened schoolgirl, hands clasped before her, head bowed.

Richard tried to conceal that traitorous swelling of excitation, hands draped over the offensive part. Still attempting to deny the primitive influence he settled his gaze on the girl's wet chest, the heaving bosom enthralling. The effect of transparency unsettled. The adherence of cloth outlining teasing breasts closed him on an unbearable and unthinkable ambition.

'Well, girl?' he said ambiguously. 'Cat got your tongue?'

'You want me to say I'm sorry?' Her bottom throbbed. It stung continuously.

'I would like an apology, yes,' he confirmed. 'But it has to come from you. Can't you see that?'

'I'm sorry, uncle,' she said bravely. 'I'm sorry for teasing by flaunting my bottom. I'm sorry for teasing you with my breasts. I'm sorry for calling you a pitiful excuse for manhood, and a pathetic frustrated lecher who has gone too long without a woman. I'm sorry for being born. I'm sorry for being considered attractive. I'm sorry for arousing you. I'm sorry for…'

The man's face fell, an act of traumatised slow motion. Her impertinence struck like hammer blows, his ego severely dented. 'You… you… you…' he stammered, words refusing to flow.

'Harlot?' Alice prompted. 'Tart? Slut? Obscenity? Filth? I suspect you've run out of adjectives to describe me, uncle. How about obstinate floozy? You haven't called me a floozy yet.'

Richard straightened, mien enraged. He unbuckled his belt, the action intended to unsettle, to instil fear.

'Oh, you're not taking your trousers off, are you, uncle?' she taunted. 'It's not bath time already, is it?'

'You push your luck too far, my girl,' he seethed. 'I am going to take my belt to you. This will not end until you demonstrate true contrition once and for all.'

'I said I'm sorry and mind your trousers don't fall down,' she cheeked. 'I'd hate to see you embarrassed or *humiliated*.'

'Face the wall!'

'Which one, uncle?' She smiled disquietingly.

'I wish I owned a horsewhip,' he said. 'I'd wipe that arrogant grin off your misbegotten face.'

Alice turned and leant, feet apart, hands pressed to the kitchen wall, her sore bottom proffered. Richard moved in on her and unfastened the two buttons securing her skirt waistband, and let it fall, descending to her knees and then to her ankles.

Hot knives delved Alice's stomach and butterflies swarmed. She found the act of her uncle removing her clothing disturbing, frightening – yet it kindled a sordid thrill.

Her aggressor faired no better. Hell-bent on making her regret her flippant outbursts he succumbed briefly to the presentation of a flawless bottom encased in neat white panties. Although seen before, it still captivated more than ever.

He wiped his mouth with the back of a hand, raised the belt, the length doubled in his fist, and savouring those tensed cheeks he dished out a stroke of devastating proportion. Leather cracked on presented buttocks. Flesh quivered beneath the broad band, a two-inch path of scalded hide left in its wake. Alice grimaced, face contorted, the smart gripping, protracted, a taste of hell.

She glanced down to witness the skin near her groin rapidly change colour. The belt had navigated hip and whipped with rigour that susceptible region. She sucked in air, the implication rocking her libido.

'He wants you all right. The trouble is he can't. So he beats you instead. So, Ali, sex hangs in the air. Electricity buzzes between you both.'

Madness veiled all sane logic. Richard overwhelmed by natural and unnatural urges whipped Alice, and she, having cast aside the terror, was afflicted by a frenzied desire, a lust that no mortal physique could quench. She welcomed his belt, fell for its swingeing embrace, devoured each blast of fire and dined on the crippling smart.

She perceived Jay, his cock, that Goliath of straining phallus, that shaft of hot meat. She manufactured his presence. That stem parting the gates, intruding, forcing a passage, opening her burrow, fucking her.

Unforgiving leather carved attendance on erogenous corpulence. Left its brand on that and fragile groin, Alice groaning, the inferno furthering the furore, compounding the sexual insanity.

Trousers tented in lewd praise, the stiffness endeavouring to penetrate the flies. Richard commanded visions of his own. His hands slipping around her as she stood bracing herself against the wall, filling with her youthful breasts. The rapturous descent, over flat belly to her tussle of silky curls. Fingers delving, nestling, probing the valley between firm buttocks and vaginal valley.

Pious principles in disarray he strapped her bottom with blows left and right, the haunches decimated, fine welts smothering that once fair seat. He didn't want to end the flagellation. Alice didn't want a cessation either, but he had to call a halt and the girl had to abide.

Richard threaded the belt back through his trouser loops, Alice still braced against the wall, her head hanging, her eyes shut, the only movement from her slow breathing and the minute quiver of her haunches.

He had nothing to say, no words of condemnation, only a guilty conscience to deal with and an analysis of his lurid impulses.

He retired; took an armchair in the parlour, mind on those disturbing compulsions; penance a prospect.

Alice, also embarrassed by the outcome, collected her skirt and examined the damage. Where would it all end? She had been aroused to the point of no return. Hardly a divine intervention; she had come oh so close to a revolting conclusion. Had the proposal arisen, she didn't know what she would have done.

She sought Richard, shameful, not able to look him in the eye. She stood in the doorway of the parlour waiting for him to notice her.

Eventually he glanced her way and cocked an eyebrow in question.

'I was wondering if you had a needle and thread, uncle,' she whispered, as if he read her thoughts.

'Upstairs, in my bedroom,' he informed her. 'In the bedside cupboard drawer.'

She turned to leave, her scarlet rump presented to him. 'Alice,' he called after her.

She paused and looked over her shoulder at him. 'Yes,

uncle?'

'I'm sorry about the skirt,' he said.

She smiled wearily and nodded.

It was the calm after the storm, both parties coming to terms with impossible feelings. Alice felt no urge to hurry home now. She needed time. Time to dissect that intangible thirst.

Chapter Eleven

Richard breathed deep, trying to suppress the turmoil. Those dreadful undercurrents made a mockery of his sanctimonious preaching. Never before had he been so tempted, so pressed by latent forces. The girl threw him into a spin, twisted the hot knife of lust; enticed him from entrenched convictions.

Richard couldn't comprehend the situation. He worked hard. He didn't blaspheme or swear. He regularly attended Mass and prayed every day. He viewed himself as a righteous man. A man devoted to the Almighty and resolved to spread the good word. So why? Why was this happening to him?

Temptation, his intolerance would accept. Alice the Jezebel sent to draw him from that path of righteousness. She exploited the unwary, ensnared and led them to purgatory. Once seduced they would be blinded and used for the corruption of others. Much like the vampire myth, a slow spread of evil, each victim helpless, the fires of hell awaiting.

He had tried to help, but she always rebelled. She resisted all attempts at reparation. Discipline had little effect. Oh yes, she would behave until the discomfort eased, became a distant memory, then she would revert to that self-indulgent, brazen tramp, quick with the offensive language and recalcitrant in behaviour.

Hadn't she returned with seduction in mind? Why wear such immodest clothing? Why show off her chest? Why flaunt her bottom? *That bottom. Oh, that bottom.* Why ask if he would like to stripe it? She sought to undermine a devout disciple. A major coup for Satan.

Richard rose determinedly from the chair. He pulled the sideboard open and removed one of those rattans. Flexing the gleaming rod his mouth tightened. He had lovingly nourished the cane, regularly wiped it with oiled cloth, the porous vine absorbing linseed, adding to its weight and flexibility.

Would she respond positively? Richard doubted that. He swapped it for the thickest. She seemed subdued. Had the thrashing with hand, brush and belt brought her to her senses? For she had to help herself. He could awaken the innocent, but Alice had to persevere.

She had slept with that Howell scum. That arrogant, self-important bourgeoisie. She wouldn't admit it, but her refusal to deny the fact incriminated. He was a married man with a daughter of the same age as her. What sort of liaison was that? Out of wedlock, the man more than twice her age. She didn't possess one scruple. She ran amok.

Perhaps he should adopt the same cunning and teach her a lesson she would never forget; flaunt that indecency in the face of evil; demonstrate that sex isn't something to be taken lightly.

Richard felt relieved. He only had to analyse the situation, see it was Alice and not he at fault.

Noticing the bankbook perched on the mantelpiece might have been an act of God. His mouth suddenly dry he couldn't resist glancing at the recent entries. The payment from Jonathan and earlier the substantial sum from Al-Awadi. Richard didn't see it as selling her, not with his maladjusted conception. He believed he did her a great service, securing her future. Had the Arab not assured he would provide for her needs, ensure her future and cater for the necessities in life? What more could the ungrateful wretch want? It was better than the life she procured for herself, bedding everything in trousers and falling to corruption.

Richard straightened his tie, the old Southport grammar school one that he treasured so much. Five maximum grades. Not many had managed such a fine result. It was just a shame that prospective employers didn't view his achievement with the same gravity he did. He picked up the cane and advanced to the stairs, reconciled. There the bolero caught his eye, hanging on the newel post; the cherry-red gingerbread; a façade; Alice's treasure. He picked it up and carried it into the kitchen.

Alice had located the needle and thread, carefully stitched the seam and laid the skirt aside. Curiously she investigated the damage, offering her bottom to the mirror and examining the plethora of crimson blotches. She didn't understand why she reacted the way she did. Masochism had roots, so one only had to determine what fed them. Certain ingredients, she concluded. An overbearing tyrant? She smiled. Or a loving guardian? Austerity. Severity. Adrenaline. Fear. Perhaps not fear – anticipation of the unknown?

Alice couldn't ignore the nettlesome effects of that confrontation, nor the colour and feel of her poor rear. She had attained a delirious high and still had yet to settle. The flagellation had soothed one desire but she needed a prod for the other. No matter how she tried to blank that erogenous hectoring the stimulus wouldn't desist.

Closing the door she lay on the bed – Richard's bed. There was something cruelly improper about abusing oneself there; an added thrill. Alice placed a hand on the silk-covered mound between her slightly parted thighs and gently toyed. She concentrated on Jay and what might have been if the damned telephone hadn't rung. She quickly succumbed, fingers slipping inside the panties and locating the moist lips hiding there. She dipped a finger, the feel erotic, illicit. Not the pride of a full erection, simply a mere taste of what she might expect.

Alice fucked herself, energetically poking with one digit, and then two, and then three. She rapidly closed on a needed climax, concentrating on an image of Jay and the unrestrained manner in which she appeased herself.

She didn't hear her uncle climbing the stairs.

She failed to notice the bedroom door opening.

The first she knew of Richard's presence was when he hissed, incredulous. 'What the devil do you think you are doing?!'

Alice scrambled from the bed, her indecent hand rapidly withdrawn. She caught sight of the cane and backed to the window.

Richard pointed the threatening implement at her. 'You just can't help yourself, can you?' he hissed. 'Your whole damnable world revolves around smut. You know it's a sin! You know the Catholic tenet. What the hell is the matter with you?'

Alice shook her head, tears falling down her cheeks. 'I don't know, uncle,' she pleaded. 'I don't know. I just don't know!'

'I've said it before and I will say it again,' he went on without compassion. 'You, young lady, are out of control. You have no shame. You have no morals. How many times do I have to discipline you? You obviously have no self-restraint. You are without moral fibre and incapable of self-denial. Have you anything to say for yourself before I cane you?'

Again she shook her head, missing the fact that he had the rod with him, and the implication that held.

'Nothing at all?' he demanded.

'I'm sorry, uncle,' she offered feebly. 'What else can I say?'

'I'm afraid that doesn't right the wrong,' he said dourly. 'Regret doesn't countenance the crime.'

'I'm confused,' she uttered. 'I feel so lonely. I have no one. I need to be loved. Everyone needs that. I had a loving family, but they were taken from me so suddenly. I just feel so hollow inside. So empty.'

'Nothing you have done, no crime you have committed, can be blamed on loneliness, only on depravity. Kneel on the bed, Alice, then place your head on the blanket.'

Eyeing the cane with trepidation she assumed the required position, her ill-treated bottom thrust up, wanton commotion flustering.

Richard placed the length against those coloured cheeks, satisfied at the stretch of skin, the vulnerability of the target. 'Before I commence, Alice,' he stated, 'I want to know if you have slept with Mr Howell.'

'No, uncle,' she whispered, 'I haven't.'

'I'll put it another way, then,' he persisted. 'Have you had intimate relations with him?'

'No,' was the only answer Alice could offer. To admit to any amour with Jay would be akin to placing the noose around her own neck – and Jay's too.

Lips twisted in bitter response, Richard levied the rod on her upper thighs, the result excruciating, her concupiscence doused.

'I'll ask you that question again, Alice. Have you had intimate relations with Mr Howell?'

'He's not interested in me,' she sobbed. 'He's married. He loves his wife.'

The cane sliced an inch lower, the hurt piercing. 'I don't believe you. I think there is something going on and I will find out, eventually.'

'Please, uncle, cane me for what you caught me doing, but not for something I am innocent of.'

Certain of his suspicions, he struck again.

'Why won't you listen to me?' Alice whined.

'I hear you. I just don't believe you. And I will thrash you until you admit to those relations.'

Alice held out until the eighth stroke, her thighs tortured, the smart agonising. 'All right!' she near screamed. 'All right, we have kissed, I admit it.'

'Kissed?' he derided. 'I think you have done more than kissed.' He slashed her striped limbs. 'The truth, Alice; I will have the truth.'

'Honestly, uncle, we haven't had sex. I'm still a virgin.'

'But you've done more than kiss, haven't you?' He added another stroke to emphasise his determination to get to the truth.

'Petting, that's all,' she wailed.

'Slowly I drag the truth from your disreputable body. Slowly we unearth the filth. He's old enough to be your father. In fact, he has taken up that station. I knew I couldn't trust him, or you come to that. This only justifies my fears.'

He whipped her rump, the cut severe. 'So what do you see in him? I can guess what the lecher sees in you.'

'He's handsome, kind, generous and thoughtful,' Alice wailed.

'Everything I'm not, you mean?'

'I didn't say that.'

'But you are thinking it.'

'No, all I ever wanted from you was an uncle's affection.'

Richard sneered. 'You want my affection?'

'Yes, I need it.'

Richard studied her for a few moments, and then laying the cane on the bed he gently stroked her beaten spheres, his hand wandering, caressing the cheeks.

'What are you doing, uncle?' she asked timorously.

'I'm being affectionate, Alice,' he stated. 'It's what

you want, isn't it?'

'I meant an uncle's love,' she mumbled, her thoughts in a spin.

'You find Jonathan attractive but not I?' he asked, his tone heavy with mock hurt. 'Is that it, my dear?'

'You keep putting words in my mouth, uncle,' she protested, the mention of her mouth and putting something in it making the flesh pulse again in the secrecy of his trousers.

'I simply seek the truth, Alice,' he told her. 'No more than that.'

'I can't be attracted to a relation, can I?' she reasoned. 'It wouldn't be right.'

'You could try to understand me,' he said. 'Understand my needs instead of always your own.'

'What are you suggesting?' She rolled onto her back and snatched at the blankets, covering her lower half, wincing as her beaten bottom made contact with the sheet.

Richard climbed onto the bed beside her, his hand possessively seeking and then feeling her nearest breast through the still damp material of her blouse. 'I'm as much of a man as that Howell,' he growled. 'Admittedly I don't have his money, but that isn't everything.'

'It's not his money, uncle, it's him,' she said, his comment momentarily distracting her attentions from the uninvited hand that cupped and pawed her breast.

'And does Jennifer know about this dalliance?' he asked, observing and gauging her reactions carefully.

'What do you think?' she said sulkily, her pout confirming that the woman did indeed know, the thought of that seeming to distract her even further and allow him to trace the outline of her nipple with the ball of his thumb.

'Oh dear, Alice,' he said, shaking his head and tutting, 'you certainly know how to live dangerously…' Not prepared to wait any longer, and assessing the battle already won, Richard unfastened those same top three buttons of the blouse, paused, ready to quash any last rebellion, and seeing none in her eyes, slid his hand inside, the feel of her supple warm breast exquisite against his searching fingers.

'I don't think you should be doing that, uncle,' she whispered, lying inert on the bed as he knelt beside her, as though pinned there by his intimidating presence. 'I'd rather you didn't, uncle.'

'And I'd rather you didn't *fuck* with *Mr* Howell,' he said viciously, his use of that offensive verb astounding them both in equal measure. Alice had never heard him swear, Richard normally incapable of forming such a word.

'This is sick,' she said and rolled her head to the side, unable to look at him, nauseated by his clammy groping.

'Oh, I don't think so, my dear,' he replied smugly. 'You are being taught an important lesson of life. A girl such as you, attractive and shapely, will invite unwanted attention by emphasising her body. I could be that stranger who asked you out. I could be that butler who thrashed you. In fact, I could be just about anyone. Be thankful it is me here with you, teaching you, someone you can trust, someone with nothing but your best interests at heart...'

'If you say so,' she mumbled, unconvinced, feeling her treacherous nipples responding to his loathsome touch, rolling her head to look back up at him, her damp auburn hair spread out on his pillow. 'I think I'm getting to understand your message.'

Gaining in the confidence of attaining certain victory his fingers probed further, his hand tilting to facilitate their early exploration just inside her lacy bra cup, finding an erect nipple waiting there for them. 'No, Alice, I don't think you do,' he differed, his voice heavy. 'But you will. That I can assure you.'

His hand withdrew and Alice dared relax for a moment, thinking his staunch beliefs had re-established reason in his mind, but then she squealed as he gripped her blouse and aggressively tugged it apart, the last of the buttons yielding without resistance. Before she could respond he yanked the blouse off her shoulders to her elbows, utilising it as an effective piece of bondage, pinning her arms to her sides. Alice squirmed and tried to recoil, but without her hands to protect herself he grinned down triumphantly, then swooped and pressed his face to her cleavage, burying his nose between her soft, fragrant breasts, his vile tongue licking and slobbering as he muttered incoherently against her flesh.

She tried to roll to the side, to dislodge the frenzied man, but he easily pinned her, refused her escape. Never did she anticipate such a blatant sexual advance, not from her uncle, not from the pious Richard. She protested again. 'This is wrong, *uncle*,' she pleaded. 'For whatever reasons you may have for doing what you're doing, this is still against God's laws.'

He rose from those succulent breasts, saliva wetting the upper slopes of the fleshy orbs and his chin. He rebuked her, his face a snarl. 'Don't you dare lecture me on God's laws!' he growled threateningly. 'You little hypocrite. I know exactly what I do and I can assure you I will be rewarded in the hereafter, not vilified.'

Frozen to the bed, completely unable to move, Alice gazed up at him with wide, disbelieving eyes. He was punishing her for her own sake. Is that what he was doing? He was demonstrating the consequence of what he saw as her folly; what she might expect by attracting the wrong sort. But what was the alternative for her? To wear a sackcloth and a veil? She would escape his vile clutches. She would never return. Perhaps she should take her revenge, do what she came for. Inflame him. Drive the twisted little bastard mad, knowing he couldn't take that final satisfaction, for that would be incest, and even the demented Richard wouldn't chance incurring the wrath of the authorities or God by doing that.

Deciding it was her only chance of finally getting away from the creep, she took a deep breath, managed to release one of her hands without him intervening, and reached up to gently stroke his thinning hair, the feel of the lank strands repulsive. 'It's okay, uncle,' she whispered gently. 'I do understand. You're doing all this for me…'

For the moment he seemed pacified, kneeling without touching her, merely gazing down at her perfection, her breasts still encased snugly in her bra, one arm still pinned to her side by her blouse, her lustrous hair spread like silk on his pillow. She continued to soothe his temple, his tongue licking slack lips. He was a shabby, pathetic worm, and she could see why he had never married. No woman in her right mind would have him. He was a selfish, arrogant egotist. His unkempt clothes screamed miser; that threadbare grey shirt, the collar and cuffs worn through; those baggy trousers, oh neatly pressed but discoloured at the knees and, she wrinkled her nose, the flies.

'Uncle,' she whispered, wanting to conclude the nightmare as quickly as possible. 'Uncle, let me sit up. I want to do something for you. It'll be nice, I promise…'

Richard watched the girl carefully, considering any possible deceptions, and deciding she posed no threat allowed her to sit and remove the remnants of her tattered blouse, devouring her every movement with beady eyes, every quiver of youthful flesh.

She sat beside him in the centre of his bed, stared deeply into his eyes, then slowly reached behind her back with both hands, the movement pushing her bra-encased breasts towards him, her cleavage tight and inviting as one just brushed tantalisingly against his shirt-sleeved arm. Alice paused, her sweet breath drifting over moist, slightly parted lips. The man waited, an urgency in his mien, and then a nerve twitched in his cheek as she moved slightly and he knew she had unclasped her bra.

Alice adroitly moved her hands forward and clasped the cups without letting them fall, then offering her most seductive pout, her fingers spread over her breasts, holding the bra to them, she asked, 'Do you want to see them, uncle? Would you like to see my breasts?'

His eyes transfixed to those delicate hands, his lips moved but no words came.

'Uncle,' she pressed, 'perhaps you might even like to touch them. It would be very naughty of us, but perhaps just a little feel wouldn't be sinful, would it?'

Again his lips moved, and this time he managed a croak.

'I'd like you to look at me, and perhaps touch me, uncle,' she whispered. 'I want to do this for you. Wouldn't you like that?'

'Yes, Alice,' he finally sighed. 'Yes, I would like that, very much.'

'Good,' she whispered, 'because I want to please you,' and taking another very deep breath to summon her resolve, she moved her hands and dropped the lacy cups from those exquisite breasts, Richard groaning audibly as he feasted his eyes on the delectable spheres of soft flesh. They thrust towards him, trim and perfectly shaped, uplifted and firm. Richard groaned again, shaking hands reaching out, encompassing, grasping those juicy morsels as Alice tried not to recoil from the clammy touch.

So he had done all that had gone before to teach her a lesson for her own good, to help her? The weasel was beside himself with lust, she knew that. What would he do later, sin whilst alone? Masturbate himself stupid? Alice had little doubt that he would, and the thought made her cringe inwardly.

Wanting to convince him of her gratitude and acceptance, Alice placed one hand over one of his, guiding its slow movements on her breast as she whispered words of encouragement, and with the other she lifted his chin, almost faltered as she saw his wet, loose lips, but closed

213

her eyes and leant forward, pressing her lips to his, kissing him.

The incendiary planted, Richard rocked to the explosion. No one had ever kissed him in such a disturbing fashion. His guts took on wings and flew. His heart held the promise of a cardiac arrest. His legs weakened, despite the fact he was not standing, that projectile rigid between scrawny thighs close to bursting point. If Alice truly intended to arouse him, then she had succeeded beyond his wildest dreams.

Alice withdrew, leaned back, the man staring wildly, mouth agape. She said nothing, but still held his hand to her breast, moving it slowly. Words could only rankle. She knew not, nor cared not what he thought.

Gathering wits he savoured the feel of her, squeezing and mauling. Wanting to regain the initiative he leaned forward and engaged teeth, biting the sleek orbs. Alice gasped, and experienced a pang that shouldn't be. Nefarious activity tingled tight between her thighs. Treacherous bursts of energy fired her body. Her mind screamed no, she was losing the control she'd only so recently gained, but despicable lust stood firm, impervious.

Richard laboured on her, slobbered and fed from her, fevered by her pliant flesh, his continuous manipulation of spheroids, areola and extended nipples intensifying licentious emotions within her. She had to detach herself from them; it was her only chance of finding another avenue of retreat.

The man disengaged from all virtuous doubts, committed himself wholeheartedly to animal instincts. He descended her smooth torso, licking and nibbling her flat belly, his hands constantly roaming, possessing, feeling, pinching, despairing of fulfilment.

He tugged away the blanket she'd previously used for cover, Alice knowing she should cling to it, but unable to. His nose and lips burrowed between her thighs, prising them apart.

'Uncle,' she whispered, fingers entwining in his thinning strands of greasy hair, her strength to push him away failing her, 'you shouldn't... you can't...'

Her feeble protests encouraged him, their lack of conviction speaking volumes. Her hands on his head clearly urged him on, giving her agreement to venture further, marking her as a collaborator in his avaricious act. Not that he had any intention of being denied now. So he pressed her flat to the mattress, enjoying her hiss as her welted bottom sank more firmly against abrasive material, positioning her perfectly for him to feast upon. He forced her thighs even wider with his chin, then peeled the narrow 'V' of her white panties aside, savoured her sweet fragrance for one conquering moment, and then buried his face into her silky pubic curls, his lips seeking, his teeth nipping. Alice arched, her hips lifting from the bed as the enormity of what he was doing swamped her. And he was clumsy, hurting her a little with his teeth. Jay had always been considerate, but inexperienced Richard vent all frustration, his animal approach having an unexpected effect on the uninitiated girl.

He slavered hungrily for long minutes, his grunting and wet suckling filling the room, Alice's fingers clawing the sheets as she lay there, her eyes closed, her legs lolling on either side of his pasty shoulders, her breasts rising and falling as she breathed heavily, trying to deny what he was doing to her, but gradually accepting the pleasure too.

Then he rose from that sweetly scented divide and began undoing the buttons of his shirt. Alice watched curiously, emotionally and physically drained, believing the ordeal must be over. What they had done together was already way beyond the realms of decency, but to go any further was unthinkable, surely?

Meticulous about everything, he slipped the shirt from

bony shoulders and neatly folded it. Alice noted the limp vest, hanging baggy on his feeble torso, but she was too drained to consider how pathetic he was.

He then got up and stood beside the bed, and Alice inwardly sighed with relief. But instead of apologising for his shameful excesses and ending the evening, he started to unbutton his trousers and let them fall, revealing time-worn Y-fronts, the bulge from within alarmingly conspicuous. Too tired to think straight, and pretty certain that he would be equally tired, she assumed they were going to share his bed for the one night, occupying opposite sides, of course. After all, he probably hadn't made a bed up for her in the other room, not expecting her to be staying the night, and it was too late to worry about such things now. She didn't much care for the idea, but supposed it wouldn't hurt for one night.

He kicked off his shoes and pulled off his socks, then removed the trousers completely. Seeming content to remain in his underwear he then urged Alice to roll over, confirming her suspicions for their sleeping arrangements for the night. Laying on her front she felt the mattress shift under his weight as he got back on the bed, felt him settling himself and the blankets, but then she was shocked to feel him ease her flimsy panties down over her smarting cheeks.

'Uncle…?' she whispered, but his hands continued to wander, roaming with impunity, fondling, drinking of her sleek flesh, the heat and the welts. Alice knew her reaction to be wrong, but she began to secretly enjoy the soothing attention. He was only being kind for once, so what harm could it do? Besides, they'd both be asleep in no time…

Alice sensed him kneel and wondered what he was doing, then his hands delved between her hips and the mattress and lifted. 'Uncle…?' she whispered again as he guided her onto her knees and forearms, and then shuffled a knee between her calves. 'Uncle, what are you doing…?

His other knee nudged its way between her calves too, forcing them wider apart so he could kneel behind her, stretching her panties into a thin white strip between her thighs, just below the under-swell of her ravaged buttocks… and then Alice froze in horror. Something bulbous and pulsing touched one buttock, leaving a drop of slimy residue there.

'Oh no,' she gasped, barely able to believe it, and desperately managed to roll to one side, onto her back, seeing the man with his underpants around his knees, his erection deployed, foreskin drawn back. 'What are you doing?' she shrieked, trying to back away from him but finding nowhere to go.

With an icy stare his lips disclosed, seemingly remote and devoid of all feeling. 'You parade yourself,' he accused. 'You explicitly emphasise every salacious feature of your body. You tempt and tease with exposure and now you act the innocent. Innocent? You? You, Alice Hussey, are filth. The devil's disciple.

'Well, disciple, this God-fearing man is going to educate you, once and for all. He is going to make you rue the day you dared to try and humiliate him. He is going to show you what sort of respect decency holds for the likes of you.'

'No, uncle, we can't,' she babbled desperately. 'And I'm a virgin. How can I be a slut if I'm a virgin?'

He absorbed this information for a few moments. 'Are you indeed?' he mused.

'Yes, I am,' she asserted, hoping she was seeing a chink of hope.

'And you expect me to simply take your word for it?'

'I've been with no man,' she insisted. 'It's all in your mind, uncle.'

Richard laughed. 'So that kiss?' he demanded. 'Was that the embrace of the virtuous? I think not.' He moved rapidly, a hand seizing her nearest breast. 'And this!' He

217

squeezed until Alice grimaced with pain. '"Would you like to feel my breasts?"' He mimicked her sultry tone.

'I did that to frustrate you,' she said defensively. 'Can't you see that? I've had it up to here with you.' Her hand indicated her forehead. 'Your pretences. Your lies. Your cruelty.' Alice pushed him away and scrambled from the bed. 'I'm going, and this time you won't stop me.'

'Alice?' His tone held an implication, halting her. 'What will Jennifer do when she finds out you've been fucking her husband?'

'Don't threaten me, uncle,' she said determinedly 'There are matters you know nothing about.'

'It's not a threat, Alice. It's a promise. I will go to the papers. I will tell them that Mr Howell, a married man and owner of *Witness Publications*, is screwing a girl less than half his age. Taking advantage of a poor naïve orphan. A girl he has turned against her own uncle, the man who tried desperately to save her from that fate. It will highlight his interests in scandalous magazines and torrid books. A concern I'm sure he wishes to remain isolated from. Think what the neighbours will say. Then the authorities could become involved. A pornographer. What might happen to a pornographer, Alice?'

She stood frozen, her back to him.

'One might conclude he seduced you for business interests. The sweet little innocent. Fancy your picture in the papers, do you, Alice? "Girl drawn into vice". And Jonathan's, "Unscrupulous decadent exploits naïve girl". I can see the headlines now. And let's not forget the shame that will be heaped upon poor Katy.'

'So,' Alice said, understanding exactly where this was all leading, 'if I have… if I have sex with you, you won't say anything to anyone. Is that it?'

'Not quite, Alice, no. Understand, it is not a matter of satisfying a lust. It will be a crucial lesson in life.'

'A punishment, for your own gratification.'

'No, Alice, a lesson.'

'We'll burn in the fires of hell, uncle. What you propose is wrong.'

'No, Alice, it isn't in the least bit wrong,' he countered. 'It will be fitting. You act the whore, and I treat you as one.'

Alice remained silent, knowing she was defeated, that the slimy weasel had won again, that he'd secured his ultimate prize.

'Were you aware of what your lover did for a living?' he went on, making her loath him even more.

'I knew he was in publishing,' she said noncommittally.

'Perhaps you've had a narrow escape.'

'He wouldn't do anything untoward.'

'You see, you're in his thrall already.' He patted the mattress, a sound she was dreading. 'Now, Alice, come here…'

Alice turned slowly. Richard sat on the edge of the bed, his expression benevolent, his underpants back in place. With her lower lip trembling, unsure what else she could do, she complied.

'So, Alice, you're a virgin, are you?' he asked with sickening normality, as though what they were about to do together was no more out of the ordinary than taking a picnic to the park.

She nodded, and as she sat beside him a cold hand settled on the top of her nearest thigh, his fingers sinking into the tight 'V' between them. With his eyes locked to hers, challenging her to revolt, those disgusting fingers searched and quickly found her vaginal lips. One burrowed and parted her fragile labia, and demanded an entry. Richard smiled, triumphant, his breath stale.

'Well, dear Alice,' he crooned, goading her, 'do I detect a sign of indulgence? Can it be that you are not as reluctant as you make out?'

She couldn't dodge the evidence. The snake's earlier

219

oral attentions and fumbling had aroused her. She didn't understand why, only that it had and she'd succumbed to it. 'It doesn't make it right,' she offered in weak defence.

'So, what are you saying?' he pressed, savouring his moment, enjoying her mental squirming, looking forward to witnessing her physical squirming even more. 'I know females are purported to be capricious, but either you enjoyed my attention or you didn't.'

'The body did…' she whispered shamefully, 'but the soul certainly didn't.'

'So it is the body that is possessed?' he gloated. 'Now we are getting somewhere. That would indeed affect the character. Its intention is to entice and corrupt. But together we will offer a show of strength, prove that not all are easily taken.'

Richard removed his vest, ribs pressured pallid skin. The belly folded, bloated and sagging, a deep crease between that and his thighs, the underpants barely visible.

He ushered Alice onto her back, silencing her attempted futile complaint by placing a bony finger to her lips, then rolled partly over her, managing to get his groin between her thighs. She could clearly feel his presence distending his underwear and pressing into her pubic mound, and it made her cringe.

'I can't let you do this,' she gasped, trying to reason with him one last time. 'This is utterly wrong, and you know it is. I'd sooner suffer purgatory in life than eternal damnation.'

'Suddenly religious are we, Alice?' he mocked. 'When it suits, I suppose. But I'm not fooled and God certainly won't be.' As his diatribe went on he wriggled his underpants down, his released stiffness nudging between her thighs as he moved. 'You'll suffer unless you repent. Pride is a sin. Vanity is a sin. So repent, Alice. Suffer your punishment, your humiliation, and cast out the devil.'

'If you weren't my uncle, Richard,' she whispered

desperately, feeling him pulsing, there, against her pubic lips, so close to his goal. 'If the Almighty hadn't been so adamant in his scriptures, then I would. I would listen to you. I would accept your reasoning. But I can't, uncle.' She attempted to appease the insanity. 'I just can't.'

He paused for a moment, and then shocked her, filled her with hope, only to dash it again almost instantly. 'Very well, Alice,' he said, and lifted his body from hers, shuffled around in ungainly fashion until he knelt astride her, his buttocks resting on the luxurious cushion of her breasts, the sensation intensely appealing to him. A fist gripped his erection and aimed it at her face, her expression frozen, aghast. 'Then take me orally,' he demanded. 'That is not forbidden. There is no danger of our seed meeting.'

As Alice grimaced and tried to turn her head away there was no more cajolery, no more debate. Richard gripped her hair and lifted her head until her lips met with his moist helmet. 'Take it…' he grunted. 'Take it in your mouth. You *will* learn your place. You *will* learn subservience. Come on, Alice, I'm doing this for you…'

With one hand keeping her there he waited, and gradually her full lips parted and Richard lowered his hips, his cock sinking into cocooning, wet warmth. He suppressed a shudder, not wanting her to know how utterly exquisite her mouth felt. 'Now suck me,' he ordered heavily. 'Humility, Alice. Degrading, isn't it?'

The man not being particularly well endowed she managed his girth without gagging, half the nominal six inches immersed.

Richard settled both hands in her hair, curled around each fist. 'Now lick me, you teasing harlot. Taste defeat. Sample obedience.'

He lifted his face to the ceiling as those first sensuous caresses of tongue and lips urged him to Nirvana. That tongue lapped innocently against his veined underside, and those lips tightened around gnarled length and sucked as

221

she breathed through her nose.

'As I thought, you learn quickly,' he grunted, relishing the nature of the sex; his stiff cock intruding into her mouth, withdrawing with her wetness coating it, her lips like a rubber seal around it. The power. The domination. The eventual smile on Mr Al-Awadi's face. All augmented the elation he experienced.

He relaxed back onto her breasts, pulling her head with him, keeping his erection engaged deep in her mouth. He let her lick and suckle instinctively, learning her vocation on him, explicit bursts of galvanising energy assaulting his crotch. Then suddenly sneering he jerked her even closer between his thighs, utilising her hair, his stem filling her mouth, the tip nudging the back of her throat, savouring the vibrations of her hummed and muted squeal.

'Preferable to a thrashing, don't you think, Alice? Better than having your buttocks flogged?'

He moved her face back and forth, controlling his thrusts, wanting to prolong his pleasure, basking in her confusion, savouring her compliance.

'I might make this a standard punishment,' he mused aloud. 'See how you conduct yourself then.'

Alice felt numb, mainly due to who he was and what she was doing for him. She loathed him with every ounce of her body. He knew how to cajole, to goad and hurt, and exactly how to make her feel guilty.

'Come on, my dear, put some effort into it,' he coaxed.

She struggled to meet the impetus of his moving groin.

'Do you feel so high and mighty now? Would you like to see yourself in the mirror, humbly serving your better with your mouth? Do you still want to defy me? Insult me? Eh, do you?' He pulled her with force, sinking his stiffness between her lips again and again, her shame and ignominy crucifying.

Alice felt worthless. He had reduced her to a chattel, a lackey fit only for pleasure.

She dreaded the spurt, the flow of warm seed, for she guessed he would make her drink it. But Richard had more planned for her and abruptly withdrew, climbed off and pushed her away, withholding his ejaculation, the phallus still rampant, glistening with saliva.

She rested against the iron frame, exhausted, naked shoulders to cold metal. Richard sneered, took hold of her ankles and pulled her down to where he knelt. Before she could retaliate he lay on top of her, bony chest compressing comfortable, arousing, prominent breasts. Slack paunch to toned belly. Rampant erection pressed against forbidden fruits. Puny, hirsute legs between shapely, youthful thighs.

His mouth nestled close to her ear and he whispered. 'And now, my dear Alice, I shall have what you so freely surrender. I shall give you the affection you crave. The attention you demand. The recognition you deserve.'

'Uncle,' she whispered, totally drained, 'what do you mean? You can't,' she went on, knowing exactly what he meant. 'Your faith forbids it. The law forbids it. You'll end up in prison and then in hell.'

'No I won't, Alice,' he crooned. 'I appreciate your loyal and touching concern for my welfare, but there'll be no hell for me. No eternal damnation. No prison. Trust me, my dear…'

He stared into her eyes, wanting to gauge and remember forever her expression as she absorbed his next words…

'We are not related by blood…' he whispered exultantly, 'only circumstance.'

Words failed Alice as the import of his words sank in, and as she lay there he parted her succulent pussy lips and settled the head of that rearing stem just within, Alice tensing, knowing again that he'd won, that he'd beaten her, and that he would forever have a hold over her.

'My father killed my mother,' he went on in a perverse conversational manner as his penis pulsed at the entrance to her sex. 'He strangled her with his bare hands. They hanged him for it. Your grandparents took me in, gave me a home. They fostered me, but never took up an adoption. So when I reached maturity I changed my name by deed poll. It was the least I could do. Honour thy mother. Honour thy father.'

Alice experienced a chill. Ice travelled down her spine, a vacuum plaguing her stomach. 'No, you're lying,' she responded weakly.

'No, Alice, I'm not,' he gloated. 'You know me. I never lie. We are uncle and niece in name only. Intercourse is quite legal, by man and God's law.'

She said nothing. Shock enveloped her. In her wildest nightmare she would have never guessed the truth. Her ultimate defence had been brushed aside. She had only a short time before, in a misguided attempt to escape his clutches, insisted she would have sex with him if they were not related, and now he had called her bluff.

So as Alice experienced the bitter taste of final defeat he pressed home the indignity, his cock sinking triumphantly inside her, her unsullied walls gripping, tending blissful comfort.

'And the profit?' he hissed, his mouth close to her ear as she stared up at the ceiling, barely daring to breathe, barely able to believe what was happening. 'All whores should profit, Alice, so for giving yourself to me I won't punish your licentious behaviour.'

He only penetrated a little way, but he withdrew, wanting to extract the maximum mental and physical pleasure from his victory as he could. He paused, his helmet once again at her tight entrance, and then his hips began to sink again, Alice arching her back, her fingers digging into his shoulders. 'I won't flog you for illicit sex, Alice,' he sighed.

Again his penis receded, having bored a little deeper on its second incursion than on its first. Again he paused, lifting his torso so he could stare down into her flushed face, and he watched her as his hips began their descent again, the girl's body tensing deliciously beneath him, those heavenly breasts lifting to his chest.

'I won't cane your naked bottom.'

The conqueror taunted, teased, revelled in her torment and the uncomprehending look etched on that utterly beautiful countenance.

'You've a lovely body, Alice. Something a man of my age would never expect to enjoy. So I thank you for the gift, dear girl. It will be the first of many such gifts and experiences, believe me.'

Alice's heart sank, not only at his treacherous disclosure or his evident desire to enjoy repeat performances, but also because of the stirrings she felt in the pit of her stomach and in her invaded sex. How could she respond to him? He had deceived her, spouted religious rhetoric, done all he could to get what he wanted. And what he wanted was her. Not because he adored her, or even because he liked her. It was primitive animal instinct. Frustration. Too long without his nuptials. Perhaps more. Vindictive domination. Assertion of power. The belittling of her rights.

He began to thrust with increasing energy, the bed creaking, the titillation of her clitoris purely incidental.

'I suppose you're wondering why I never told you before?' he said, his voice getting more laboured. 'I suspect you can't understand why your mother never did.'

Tears trickled down Alice's cheeks. She had reached the lowest ebb.

'I didn't want to tell you,' he panted. 'I wanted you to feel you had someone left in this harsh world. A relative. Someone to look after you, to care for you. Someone to talk to in the darkest hour. But I didn't foresee the depths of depravity you would sink into. I couldn't foresee how I would have to ultimately punish you in such a drastic manner. For this is a penance, Alice. You offer it to all and sundry and eventually you will be taken.'

She listened, that damnable bubble of pleasure expanding with every lunge of the despicable man's hips and every accompanying creak of the bed. The words echoed in the vaults of her guilt. Reap what you sow. His seed. Richard's seed. His cock. Not Jay's cock. Richard's hateful cock. Not her beloved Jay's. His hands mauling her breasts. Not Jay's tender petting. His voice, Richard's, whispering vile insincerities. Not Jay whispering words of love and adoration.

The impetus increased. He sank home with increasing vigour, plunging deep, the effort more profound and contorting his ugly face. 'Your mother was sworn to secrecy,' he said, his voice increasingly strained. 'Your grandfather thought it best. How does a man's affection feel, Alice? Is this what you wanted? Is that why you flaunted your body in front of me? How is your bottom, Alice? Does it still smart? Does my contact aggravate that sting? Your bottom is quite red. Perhaps I should rub some cream into it. Would you like that, Alice? My attention? My affection?'

She wiped the tears away, sparkling emeralds staring into space.

'Affection is earned. It is not an automatic right.' He studied her face. Her expression. His hungry eyes wandered to her breasts, jostling firmly beneath the increasingly frenetic rhythm of intercourse.

'We meet Satan on his own terms. We demonstrate our contempt for his machinations. Offer yourself to meekness, for the meek will inherit the earth. Cast off the chains of immorality. See misuse of the body for what it is.'

Alice barely listened to his ranting. She observed his rise and full. The withdrawal and thrust of his distended cock. She could barely remember her drunken seduction at the hands of that other snake, Guilio, so this was her first real act of sexual intercourse. Her first real poke. Her first real fuck. An iniquitous deed. A disgusting perverted complication. It stirred. It pleased in an animal way. Was that due to her instability? Was it because of who he was? Because of his dominance? Or due to the immorality of the situation?

'Forgiveness, Alice,' he grunted through clenched teeth. 'Seek forgiveness. Absolution. Repent, and I will love you. I will embrace you as a kindred spirit. I will protect and comfort...'

The impossible, the unimaginable occurred. Alice clutched the sheets and climaxed. With virtually no warning the bubble exploded, her belly filled with iced fire. She gasped, tensed, disbelieving. Richard smirked, watching, taking it as a testament to his virility and increasing the momentum. Alice's body shuddered to the increased force, the man's groin slapping down against hers, a rampant column of flesh ravaging her sex, sliding without resistance in that vaginal lubricant.

'The devil flees,' he whispered hoarsely. 'This maiden is liberated.'

'*The whore is consummated*,' penetrated her skull, a red-hot nail.

Richard rapidly attained his own orgasm, pulling his glistening cock clear at the last moment, ejaculating slimy seed over her quivering belly, filling her tummy button with the first spurt, anointing her breasts with the second, her cleavage with the third, his fist squeezing and pumping to extract every last drop onto the shapely altar of warm flesh laying exhausted beneath him.

He breathed heavily, his body covered in sweat, and sneered disdainfully. 'When you are worthy of it, then I shall fully commit. Then I shall ejaculate inside you. But for now the slut doesn't warrant the pleasure.' He settled on her, bony chest supported by fleshy breasts – breasts

227

baptised with his seed.

He nuzzled into her neck, whispering. 'You are a worthless piece of trash, Alice. See how easily you succumbed? See how quickly and readily you availed yourself. For all your protestation and loathing you reached the pinnacle. Tell me, was it agreeable? Did your conscience not trouble you at all? Perhaps you have sunk beyond salvage in the mire of turpitude.

'Can you leave here with your head held high? Can you? Knowing the shameful thing you have just done? How can I love a wastrel like you? You are only fit to serve. To lead, to be somebody worthy you have to have morals, Alice. You obviously retain none.

'In the shed. You remember the shed? I have installed a chain and collar. I shall tether you there later. You can spend the night there. A bitch in the kennel. Naked like an animal. You are nothing, Alice Hussey. You are nothing.'

Alice waited. She bided her time. The swine eventually lapsed into sleep, his snores a declaration of that loss of conscious thought. Alice climbed silently from the bed. She dressed, her clothes still damp and now in tatters. She sought the key to the bedroom door and let herself out. She would flee, but where to? She had no idea. The Howells' house was the obvious place, but Richard could cause too much trouble for them. She recalled the young solicitor on the train; his business card she had tucked in the pocket of her bolero. Maybe he might help. Desperation clouded clear thought.

Downstairs she soon found the garment, thrown carelessly into the corner of the kitchen. She picked it up and held it to her face – a comforter. In her mind it was the finest thing she had ever owned. Then still in shock, spirit crushed, Alice slipped the jacket on and checked the pockets. The card was still there. Alexander Bradley. She counted her money – nine pounds, seven shillings and sixpence.

Cautiously she made her way to the front door, and passing a mirror recently acquired she stopped and scowled, studying her reflection. 'Bastard!' she spat. 'You vindictive bastard!'

Alice went back to the kitchen. There she opened a drawer and removed a carving knife, and holding it in a clenched fist she ascended the stairs again. Silently she drifted back into the bedroom, the slumbering Richard lying naked on his back.

She pressed the point of the knife to his belly and slowly drew it over the loose skin. Richard abruptly awoke, immediately startled. 'What the hell do you think you're doing?' he demanded.

Alice offered no reply, but with her eyes glazed she held the knife to his vitals, and seeing the girl's manic stare Richard paled. Sweat beaded his gaunt face. A chill delved his spine and gut. His genitals squirmed.

'Please, Alice,' he said carefully, not wanting to startle her or upset her further. 'Don't do anything rash. You'll end up in Holloway. You don't want that, now do you?'

'Why did you do it?' she asked, the voice haunting.

'W-what?' he stammered, petrified. 'I told you. To drive the devil from you. To?'

'Not that!' she barked. 'I know why you did that. My jacket. Why did you ruin it?'

Partial relief flowed through his puny frame. 'I'll buy you another,' he promised, but cringed as he felt cold sharp steel prod his testicles.

'Why, Richard? Why? Why did you paint "tramp" on the back? I love this jacket, and you've ruined it.'

'The heat of the moment,' he gabbled, wincing as Alice applied pressure. 'I'm sorry. Really I am. Please Alice, don't do anything foolish. Please.'

'I already have,' she said flatly, her voice and presence lacking any spark. 'I came here against others' advice.

Why did you do it, Richard? Why?'

'Because…' he tried desperately to find something to say to her, something that would not trigger a violent reaction, 'because…'

'An answer,' she said dully. 'I want an answer.'

'To teach you a lesson,' he blurted. 'Ostentation is a sin. Can't you see that?'

'Ostentation?' she echoed. 'I'll give you ostentation.' Her arm ascended, her eyes riveted on his privates.

'No, Alice, for God's sake no!' Richard raised a hand in futile defence.

The arm descended. The knife flashed. Richard came close to fainting. He heard the sound of ripping cloth, for a sickening moment believing it to be his flesh, then the unmistakable grind of steel hitting mattress spring.

Alice turned and strode to the door, the knife sunk to the hilt in the bed between the terrified man's legs.

'You're mad!' he screamed. 'Do you hear me? Mad! Mad, just like your mother!'

She spun and pointed a shaking finger at him. 'It's not me who's mad, it's you,' she hissed.

'Mad!' he shouted. 'Insane like your mother was. Do you hear me, Alice? Just like your mother!'

'My mother wasn't mad. How dare you say such a thing? How dare you speak ill of the dead?'

'Not Edith, Alice,' he giggled, as though losing his mind. 'No, Edith wasn't your mother. You were named after your mother. Your lunatic mother. Rose Hussey was your mother.'

'Liar!' she screamed, not wanting to hear any more. 'There's no such person.'

'You've not seen your birth certificate, have you? There again, why should you have? It's a very informative piece of paper, Alice. A significant revelation. Oh, I knew about Rose. That was a secret impossible to keep. But she your mother? What a bombshell.

'Like all, I thought Edith was your mother and Reggie your father. But on examining the contents of your old home I came across that revealing paperwork. Birth certificate, Alice. Mother, Rose Hussey. Father unknown. Born, nineteen twenty-two. Oh, she was young when she had you. Adoption papers. No need to change the surname, was there? All legal and above board. Committal papers. Sectioned as feeble-minded and a risk to society.' He grinned spiteful.

'You filthy bastard liar!' she screamed again. 'You're making it all up!'

'Am I? I think you'll find it is you that's the bastard, Alice.' Richard remained smug. 'Check the papers for yourself. They're all downstairs in the bureau. Who knows, she might be still alive. You might have a relative after all. A lunatic admittedly, but still kin.

'Oh, there's a photograph of her as well. And do you know, girl, you are the dead spit of her. You could be peas in a pod. Both mad.'

'I want to see them.'

'Help yourself, Alice. The bureau's not locked.' Richard lay back, laughing.

Downstairs Alice found the envelope, apprehensively withdrawing the contents. Richard told the truth. She read the birth certificate, her mother being Rose Hussey, the father a blank. Papers confirmed the adoption. She read the committal papers sick to the pit of her stomach. Then finally there was the old sepia photograph. A picture of the young Rose, the unmistakable outline of the Golden Mile behind. She could have been looking at a picture of herself, irrefutable evidence.

Tears cantered, beads of confusion, sadness, partial relief. A hotchpotch of emotions.

Alice replaced the documents and tucked them inside her ruined jacket. She spotted the bankbook on the mantelpiece and curiously examined the entries that had so thrilled Richard. Mouth tightening, eyes angry, she tucked the book into a pocket too.

Alice made her way to the front door, Richard halfway down the stairs. 'Where do you think you are going, young lady?' he demanded to know.

Alice settled a defiant gaze on him. 'I'll be in touch,' she said.

'No, Alice, you stay here. You know what I will do if you don't.'

'Do what you like. I'm not going back to the Howells. I'm not going to *Heptonstall*. I've a few matters to sort out and then, like I said, I will be in touch.'

Richard watched impotently as the hostile Alice left, in no mind to try and stop her.

Epilogue

Alice returned to the Howells' house, not to stay, merely to pack. A few useful clothes, underwear and necessities she crammed into a small overnight bag. With it slung over a shoulder and the attire ruined by Richard left on her bed, she proceeded downstairs to Jonathan's study.

She sat at his desk, the scent of the man arousing sentiment. She wrote a short letter of partial explanation, which she slipped into an envelope and sealed. She opened the bottom drawer, took out his cashbox and helped herself to fifty pounds. As an afterthought she quickly scribbled an IOU and placed it beneath the cash tray.

Her expression fraught she sought Odette, and handed her the letter asking where everybody was.

'Gone looking for you I think, miss,' the maid disclosed. 'Mr and Mrs Howell and Kate left about an hour ago.'

'Perhaps that's just as well. Look, Odette, make sure Jonathan gets that letter, will you?'

'Are you leaving, miss?'

'Yes, Odette, I have to. Hopefully only for a short while. Now, that letter is extremely important.'

'Don't worry, miss, I'll see he gets it.'

Alice turned and walked to the front door, Odette calling after her. 'Good luck, miss. I hope we see you again… soon.'

Without another word Alice left, and as Odette opened her apron pocket and was about to slip the letter in it, Harris appeared and took it from her.

'Give it back,' she snapped.

'Go and play, Odette.'

'Look,' she tried again, 'give it back.'

'Diamonds, Odette,' Harris warned, a snarl on his pug features as Odette's face coloured.

'Run along now, girl,' he ordered patronisingly. 'Oh, and you haven't seen this, either.' He waved the letter. 'You understand me?'

With the maid scurrying out of sight, Harris tore open the envelope. Intrigued, he read, the contents spilled from whispering lips.

'Sorry, Jay, I have to go away for a while. I will be in touch. Please don't try to find me. Thank you for everything. And I mean everything. I have to sort some problems out. I have borrowed fifty pounds from your cashbox. I will repay you, I promise. I wouldn't have taken it unless I really needed it. I know you will understand. I love you, Jay. Alice.

'So,' the elderly butler mused, 'the bird flies the cage. Ungrateful reprobate. Well, young lady, maybe your obedient servant can ensure you a rough ride.' Smiling slyly, plans already formulating, Harris tore the letter up.

Jonathan knocked on the front door, and a few seconds later Richard opened it. Jonathan didn't bother with niceties, but seized the wretch by the throat, lifting him onto tiptoes and bundling him back into the hall, Richard gasping for breath, eyes protruding, fingers wrestling futilely with the hand that threatened to choke him. Jonathan slammed him against the hall wall, knocking the remaining breath from him.

'Now, you fucking little weasel,' he snarled, his face an inch from Richard's. 'Where is she? Where is Alice?'

'She left here hours ago,' the terrified man rasped.

'What kept her?' Jonathan demanded.

'I don't know! She didn't stop more than an hour.'

'Listen to me, cunt,' Richard growled, 'she hasn't

234

returned home. That's unlike Alice. If I find out you've hurt or upset her in any way, I will come back here and personally break both your fucking legs. Do you hear me?'

Richard nodded. 'I swear, Mr Howell,' he whined, 'I didn't harm a hair of her head. Why would I? She doesn't live here any more.'

'Then you won't mind if I check the house.'

'I don't think that is necessary.'

'I do.' Jonathan let him go, Richard sinking to the floor, reaching for his assaulted throat.

Jonathan stormed from room to room, searching. He noted the cane lying on the bed. He stomped down the stairs, roughly pushed Richard out of his way and checked the back garden and shed.

Satisfied Alice wasn't there he pointed a finger at the obsequious man. 'She had better be at home, Barker, or I swear I'll do time for you!'

To be continued...

More exciting titles available from **Chimera**

***

The full range of our wonderfully erotic titles are now available as downloadable e-books at our great new website:

www.chimerabooks.co.uk

All **Chimera** titles are available from your local bookshop or newsagent, or direct from our mail order department. Please send your order with your credit card details, a cheque or postal order (made payable to *Chimera Publishing Ltd*) to: **Chimera Publishing Ltd., Readers' Services, PO Box 152, Waterlooville, Hants, PO8 9FS**. Or call our **24 hour telephone/fax credit card hotline: +44 (0)23 92 646062** (Visa, Mastercard, Switch, JCB and Solo only).

To order, send: Title, author, ISBN number and price for each book ordered, your full name and address, cheque or postal order for the total amount, and include the following for postage and packing:
UK and BFPO: £1.00 for the first book, and 50p for each additional book to a maximum of £3.50.
Overseas and Eire: £2.00 for the first book, £1.00 for the second and 50p for each additional book.

*Titles £5.99. **All others (latest releases) £6.99**

For a copy of our free catalogue please write to:

Chimera Publishing Ltd
Readers' Services
PO Box 152
Waterlooville
Hants
PO8 9FS

or email us at:
chimera@chimerabooks.co.uk

or purchase from our range of superb titles at:
www.chimerabooks.co.uk

Alice - Promise of Heaven. Promise of Hell

This is the first in a biographical series, in 1950's Lancashire. Her parents killed in a freak accident, naïve Alice falls to the custody of the austere Richard Barker, the girl's only relative. Tyrannical and scheming, the pious Barker ensures the innocent girl's stay is not a happy one.

Kate Howell, precocious schoolmate and intimate, offers the exquisite Alice the means of escape. But life is never that simple.

Embracing opposing ideals the pair begin the journey of life – a trek that takes the vulnerable Alice directly into the arms of an older man.

The trials of Alice is a story of harsh discipline, lust and infatuation – of sexual confusion, carnal exploration, and the coming to terms with curious cravings.

1-903931-27-4 ● £6.99